On the summit of La Esperanza

Pastor Castillo

Editorial Lunetra

To my grandchildren, Ivón, Carlos Andres, Jr., and Victoria

Chapter 1

Mystery envelops La Esperanza. From its highest hill in this farm of near circular shape, peered my house, painted all white with its doors and windows of a green not so rich anymore. A worn Bible belied the lack of books and forks. Its most welcoming feature, a fresh breeze from the northeast that blessed us year-round, and with it the aromas of basil and jasmine. The small guava orchards, the mango groves, and the royal palms enlivened this landscape bordering a modest mountain range.

The cradle into which I was deposited at the moment of my birth, and in which I stood up as soon as I could, was rather square, and it hung from a ceiling trestle in the bedroom with two strong ropes. Its frame was made of marabú [1], lined with flour sacks printed with large red letters that spelled Made in USA.

Just delivered, and once deflated the huge pouch that held me captive for nine months, my Aunt Iluminada, who was clairvoyant, surveying me from top to bottom and stopping only at the head and the hands, said, "This one is going to like coloring and he will be

---

[1] *Dichrostachys cinereal:* Commonly reaches maximum heights of 4 to 5 m. Invasive pest in Cuba; its wood is hard, durable, immune to attack by fungi and insects, combustible, produces long-lasting embers with little smoke and ash. *(Editor's notes unless otherwise indicated.)*

our savior." Those around the cradle were perplexed. Everyone knew that when Iluminada spoke, you could bet on her being right. Cirilo was there. And since he too was convinced that when she spoke, there was no turning back because she knew about good writing and when words should have a capital letter and when they just needed a small and simple lower-case letter, even if he didn't understand such things, he couldn't help but tell Anastasia, his wife.

And given that Anastasia was not inclined to exaggeration, she subjected the information to public scrutiny in the neighborhood, presenting it as clearly as she was able. But as often happens in gossip circles, Anastasia's tale became popular, and soon the words began to darken. Some substituted coloring for painting and gambled on that possibility since Ñata, one of my sisters, was always drawing with a piece of coal on the trunks of palm trees or anything else she could find, and made dolls and vases with clay. Still, it was no less doubtful that the spirit of a living sibling could travel to another still in the mother's womb. How, if he still couldn't open his eyes, would he know that his sister liked making charcoal messes and figurines?

The most daring doubted that I would become the Savior. I looked nothing like the Christ the priest pointed out in the holy cards, except maybe a little like the Christ of El Guayabo. This would be unfortunate. Besides being extremely flamboyant and quite ugly, his scant fame was ruined. The things of this world incited him to commit scandalous sins, the last one, still fresh, traveled from mouth to mouth: "Those Gonzalez fell into the trap. Adolfina, the eldest daughter will not wed dressed in white: It's the Christ's fault."

I think nothing of some additional comments as they have little to do with the future reality. I will only say what remarks they made about my head. They said that it didn't match my small body, that I would come into the world as a cheater and a cock fight gambler. And the least moderate spoke against God's will, about my cojones and some things I did as a newborn.

Aunt Iluminada, bristling with anger when she heard of such wickedness, lashed out against the malicious gossips. The interpretation she gave of the message left to her by her spirit, Gregorio, had nothing to do with the disproportionate rumors. Also, savior was not spelled with a capital letter, but I could end up becoming a little of everything.

Surely, Gregorio told her important things the boy would do, and that were oh so prodigious, with such entanglements nearly impossible to unravel, but they would have to gather patience and wait a long time to know the entire truth.

Iluminada knew what avid gossips her neighbors were and how prone to misunderstanding despite great, yet futile, efforts by the priest, the protestants, and Bienvenido, the medicine man, to reform the argumentative, the cowards, and the bastards. They even lacked faith enough to believe what they were told and to patiently await better times as had all previous generations. He repeatedly warned, "If such talk spreads again, I will communicate in writing with Mr. Willey, with the priest, and Bienvenido, the medicine man, and I will provide the names of the followers implicated in sowing discord, so the three of them can take matters into their hands. I will not notify the Christ of El Guayabo because it isn't worth it. I will not inform the mayor either, poor man, always in Babia, always daydreaming." Thus, his last words forced the beginning of a new predicament.

Taking into consideration recent events, Aunt Iluminada swiftly pointed out the urgent need for my baptism. The difficulty of the situation could be a bad omen. It was quite probable, or better said, she was certain, that I had been cursed. In the evenings, I suffered from low-grade fevers, and prayers and offerings to the saints that dealt with these things counted for nothing. I was getting worse.

My parents were faithful followers of the protestants, who baptized by immersion but only to those of majority age. Both paternal and maternal grandparents insisted on complying with Aunt Iluminada's instructions from the dearly departed. They believed in God, but they didn't dismiss the judgment of the dead. And so, she proposed herself as godmother and El Cubano as godfather.

The dispute began to fade as days passed. Those who were to be my godparents appeared at the village church on a cold early morning in February to baptize the newborn. And it so happened that in spite of all the gentle entreaties to the priest through his bedroom window, and the improprieties they later screamed at him, he didn't even get up. My fever was high, my eyes rolled back in my head, and to make matters worse, they say I started to produce greenish diarrhea with the foulest odor. Meanwhile, the bad-tempered priest ranted, "Never, such business is not conducted at this ungodly hour, and besides, I've been out of holy water for days."

There was nothing else those poor people could do for me. The sun was already breaking up the night when they took me to La Esperanza. A bit of good luck, a few visits to Aunt Iluminada from dead Gregorio, prayers, hard resin broth and herbs, and little by little, they helped me recover. But, scrawny as I was through no fault of mine, I was nicknamed "jew" for a long time.

The growth of my belly and the nightly teeth grinding were finally cured by Antoñica Izquierdo. Gaunt but strong was Antoñica. One Sunday, when she hadn't been able to break her small son's fever, she sat him astride over her shoulders and off she went. No one wanted to follow her. She crossed rivers, climbed mountains, garnered energy, and buried her exhaustion. The sun was in its apogee, and their heads burned when they passed by The Valley, the great valley everyone wants to see, beautiful like no other. Not mountains but hills resembling enormous, misleading elephants surround it, pretending to sleep while guarding it and keeping anything or anyone from snatching its charm.

From far away came the stone elephants. Some say it happened during one of Earth's ups or downs, or perhaps from the very bowels of Earth they were pushed out by intraterrestrials, or they simply ordered them out. No one can help gazing at them, unyielding and faithful protectors of that landscape.

Antoñica didn't look, she didn't think about it, but she felt joy as she passed. She felt joy because she had arrived at the highest point, the lookout, and the distance left to enter the small village hidden within a smaller valley was downhill, almost always in a slippery curve, but downhill.

Upon arriving, she found silence, deliberate silence. A lifeless old wood hamlet with red roof tiles, grimy with time. The whole village was just two long lanes. She thought she was living a dream from the inside out. A dream about things that were true yet unbelievable. Neither doctors, nor the pharmacist, not even the hospice opened the doors for them. Antoñica shouted, roared, bellowed. No one answered. The asphyxiating August sun didn't daunt her, she walked uphill and downhill. A large dog, howling ominously, followed them from the moment they made their entrance, but she didn't hear it. She had no strength to hear. She couldn't scare him away.

"All because of the damn money I don't have! They know even what they dream is no good. They dream of money. They know it well. That's why they left me alone. In the difficult hours of battle against death, they wouldn't come with me."

The bright sun made her see black spots as she walked the village, a village in deep slumber. On the sidewalk, covered by the shade of a tree, men played dominoes. She approached them. She spoke, she begged… The pharmacist went out with the double nine and hollered in victory. He felt vindicated after the *"pollona"* ass-kicking he got the previous day, but now he'd won with an advantage

A group of hooligans joined in with the dog's barks and screamed at the top of their lungs:

"Go! Go! Scram!"

No one had ever told her about the dogs, the thugs, how nobody in the village listens, about the horrible indifference, the senseless death. Although fatigued, Antoñica had no alternative but to return to the mountain, over there, in Cayos de San Felipe, where she lived.

The highway behind her, she had been on the dirt road for some time when she began to feel afraid. Afraid of the withered leaves that fell from the trees and crumbled from the intense heat. Afraid of the singing birds. Of the silence. Afraid to fall asleep while walking.

"Sit up so you won't feel so heavy on me, son. Don't sleep, it's not good to sleep when you're feverish. Wake up. Don't be suspicious of the oxen's bellows. They say that sound is a bad sign, but no, nothing will happen. We're not alone. There's three of us… They say

God punishes, but not you. This is no punishment. You're but a babe, and you can't have done anything he might not like. Are you tired? Move, move, even if just to know that you're not... "Son! We're almost at the clean river! I won't rest, I have no strength to pick you up and start again. I have none. I can't. Touch my head with your hands, do it hard so I can feel you.

"You will live. You will live to tell this tale. And you must tell it right. All of it. Don't sleep now. Take heart, your mother is talking to you. Listen, don't leave anything out. You can't leave out anything that happened in the village. You'll do it. You'll be able to tell it. Me, in my astrakhan coat right at noon, in the stifling sun, and I didn't even feel it. Now I don't need to take it off, not that I could, I'm too weak. If I fall apart on the way, take my strength. Take it so your voice will be heard. Tell about the silence, about the doors that wouldn't open, about the double nine and how they threw us out. Come to think of it, maybe it's best if you don't tell about the kids and the dog, it makes us seem undignified. But you can tell it all to the river and the mountain. Shout it out to them who know us well, who know that we are honorable, and we don't ask for or take more than we need. Let the smallest stone on this road know what happened to us."

To the fighting race, the tough race, belonged Antoñica. That's how she lived. The hair that once swirled into shells to cover her ears, the black tresses that reached her waist, now tousled and aimless, moved at the mercy of any gust of wind. She was breathless, faint from so many hours climbing and descending hills.

The path, thick with trees, and the humidity made her sense again the proximity of a river, the big one, the one near her house, the one that announced strong rains over its mouth with a roar. She used to go with her children to pick wild fruit and bathe in that river, as had the entire Izquierdo generation. The *biajacas*[2] her husband caught there didn't smell of mud, not those. You could even eat them in soup with a little salt, and they were good for clearing your mind and avoid perturbations.

With reeds and vines, a small hanging bridge had been made for the waters didn't always allow passage. The rose apple trees that watched over the bridge intertwined to create a roof that kept the sun out. It was dark and humid. Mystery surrounded this tiny place; yes, mystery. Some were amused by it and others feared the tall tales and other things seen or said by possible yellow bellies. But there was no alternative. It was the only lifeline.

When she believed everything lost and approached the left margin to pray for consolation, she almost couldn't. Then, her hands began to look for rest

---

[2] *Nandopsis tetracanthus:* Fish endemic to Cuba that can reach 20 cm; it was quite common in rivers and creeks, and therefore, used often by farmers as food.

and her numb body for relief. She felt fear. She placed the boy over a great rock of unpolished gray marble, and in that silence of river, mountain, and hill, a pygmy owl began to sing. It's an ugly bird. Its white legs hold the body with its red-stained back, and the eyes are yellow and bulging. Its head is large and round and incongruous. The pygmy owl is unpleasant. No one wants to hear it. It horrified, but she didn't even notice the bird's death song nor that her feet would not awaken, and her neck couldn't withstand the slightest movement.

Stretched on the ground with no knowledge of how long, the farmer woman lied in her torpid state. An echo descended from the mountain, bounced off the rocks, and faded into the tree branches until it collided with the hills. Far away it went and returned over and over, but Antoñica couldn't break from her paralysis.
"Dip him in the water, so he can receive the pure water from the spring, dip him in the water. Do it three times. Do it three times. Do it three times."
Antoñica began to hear the echo's muffled message. With supreme effort, she pushed herself to overcome her weakness. She felt urgency to comply with the mandate. She had no misgivings. She followed the order given as best she could. She touched the boy's small body when she noticed that he struggled to move; she was shaking. He didn't seem as warm, but she couldn't feel hopeful. She couldn't wait, she fell unconscious next to him, dying.

How much time had passed? No one knows.

"Mamma, Mamma, the echo, it's the echo! Wake up, wake up! The echo is coming, it's speaking to you and saying your name, it's saying it nice and clear, listen Mamma!"

"Antoñiiica, from now on you will heal all who come to you. You will heal with the water from this spring. Three times you will pour it over the head of the ill, and three times you will repeat: damn demon, go to hell! Like you did with your son."

The boy listened. The echo circled, time and time again.

With great effort, Antoñica began to recover. She touched her son many times to make certain he was healed. She labored to get on her feet, to take off the astrakhan coat now dry. She raised her arms in the air, and with her voice almost extinct, she devoted a profusion of praises to the river and the mountain. It was they, since always, that had not abandoned her. Grateful, she vowed to dedicate herself to obeying the order given: to heal the sick.

She was home. Taking no time for rest from the tiresome journey nearly all the way to death's door, she gathered her husband, children, grandchildren, in-laws, which were many, and from her lips only these words came:

"I will heal. I will heal anyone who comes to me with water from the river. Take all your junk out of this house and find some other place to go. Nothing and no one can get in my way. Disappear immediately. All of you, disappear. And may this spigot never want for water, pure water from the spring."

She was unrecognizable. The hardness in her expression and her protuberant eyes gave a fright. That woman, who without opening her mouth, with just a gesture, commanded her offspring, didn't talk unless necessary, and much less boast, now gave orders, precise orders. No one understood her new boldness, but all obeyed her instructions readily.

Her name and surname, Antoñica Izquierdo, began to gain unstoppable force. In less time than was comprehensible, roads populated with those in search of the woman who healed with water.

Chapter 2

My belly had been growing for a long time. I spent my nights grinding my teeth, and sometimes I still had fevers. Suddenly, my mother decided that it was time to deal with these problems and some others of my siblings and relatives. But not Ñata. Already Juana La Grifa had cured her from the dirt-eating habit that kept her pale and small. For nine days, before the sun began to heat up, she made nine little piles of dirt in the garden. From the top of each one, with her fingers she took a bit, stirred it, and boiled it in water. La Grifa said you had to let it settle, like you did with *café carretero* (wagoner's coffee), and when it was tepid, she should drink it. That is how Ñata lost her craving for dirt. That's why she didn't go with us.

The cart in which they took us to Antoñica wasn't big. They had to make two trips, and that wasn't enough. Antoñica cured everything, charged nothing, and didn't accept donations. A sea of people had taken over those mountains. Gas lamps, oil lamps, flashlights, small bonfires, and even a little electric plant illuminated the place. Strange, all of it. I was in the presence of both heavenly star's earthly stars. I don't remember ever before seeing a village at night. It's beautiful if you see it from above.

All types of convalescents, of people, of social groups, of religious beliefs, appeared in a short time. Skilled prostitutes, procurers, and self-seekers abounded and explored the environment for the opportunity to set up some business or other. You could find anything there. It was an improvised town, unique, something no one understood, but necessity and novelty became magnetic. I was happy to find myself in the middle of this adventure and enjoyed every moment. The landscape was beautiful, unbelievably beautiful. No greater river had I ever seen, not to mention stone elephants. I tried not to stare at the sick or deformed, to not dwell on the unpleasant and sometimes horrible. I was just another boy in that odd, entertaining chaos.

Three days had gone by when Prieta and Tesoro were able to stick my head, not a small one, through a window while they squeezed my waist like a corn tamale and I, frightened, kicked my legs. I watched in detail the face of that woman who sprayed my head with water and three times repeated "damn demon, go to hell." She left a mark within me, a bitter taste, I left soaking wet, as they all did, saying that my belly was smaller and that I felt better. Upon hearing such words, those who awaited their turn burned with hope. No one could stop that human horde unwilling to surrender.

Altagracia, mistress of the village judge, was up in arms. She had arrived with her bedroom set, including dresser and mirror. To protect it from the covetous and the gossips, she had it covered with canvas held by four stakes facing the four compass points, under the shade of a leafy carob tree. Although there were hundred-year-old guásimas[3] with abundant foliage, she didn't want to be under them because they were popular for suicidal hangings. The beautiful woman was willing to stay there until she had an answer to her situation, strangely rumored not to be a physical illness. People said that her problem was localized from the waist down. It was a whoring problem. Anyway, in dark glasses, denim suit, and red tie, the judge walked through the thickets, suffocating, intense, not caring what anyone thought. He stalked her. He wouldn't leave the makeshift village, the water village, as they began to call it.

Owing to the lack of hygiene, the cockroaches, the rats, the mosquitos, all insects imaginable, and to the uncontainable social problems that were arising, the Rural Guard made an appearance. They removed Antoñica thinking it would be enough to end the bedlam. Doctors and pharmacists complained about the lack of patients and the slow sale of medicines. So, she was driven to the capital of the province, a trial was held, and she was forbidden to continue her healing practices.

When news of her return spread, the mountain populated once again, and she continued the fulfillment of the task assigned by the echo. Her preaching took on new force. From even farther away, from other

---

[3] *Guazuma ulmifolia:* Tree native to tropical America, heavily branched, it can reach 20 m. in height.

provinces, they came in search of the woman that healed with water. The healer was becoming a national problem.

Again, the Rural Guard came to her house. Without any consideration, they took her away. And into the neglected and disgraced loony bin they unloaded her. Some say that the President of the Republic discreetly came in search of her assistance, but Antoñica wouldn't speak. She never spoke again. She was sad. Only going out to the yard gave her joy, looking at the pigeons and listening to the birds in the great hog plum tree. She couldn't learn to live without the river and the mountain. One early morning, she couldn't go on. The echo, in a struggle with death, took her. It took her there, to the place from where she came.

Neither time nor science have been able to steal the custom of healing by water. Water worshippers remain faithful to Antoñica's legacy. She continues to resonate. She cured my belly and my teeth-grinding. It's not the first time I tell the story. In the intimacy of a stupendous landscape, near the road, sitting on a rock on the banks of the creek, watching how the pebbles that we tossed made bubbles in the murky water, I told it to my pretty Margarita. Not about my big belly, that was embarrassing.

Rompetambor (Drumbuster) was the first great treasure I owned. No one would have thought he was my pet, and he wasn't, really. He was given to me from the womb of the mother nanny goat. And right in front of my vivacious young eyes, the newborn came to the world in a brown color I didn't like. I would've preferred him like the orange blossom, with socks and a star on his forehead, an evening star, because in his mischief, disoriented in the dry grass, I could lose him. But since that didn't depend on me, soon I began to love him.

I applied all my farming knowledge to the instruction and education of the little goat, always reminding him, just as Aunt Iluminada told me, of the relationship between his name and the expression, "A goat that breaks a drum, pays with its hide," and how that sentence could be imposed at any time if he didn't follow the rules.

I also spoke to him about the need to accept that name not for its beauty, because perhaps another might be more pleasant to the ear, but for the strength it carried. The word drum had been used since the time of the Spanish colonization to name a musical instrument common in the Antilles, and in ceremonies and rituals of African origin. This last fact I couldn't explain to him since I learned it much later. I preached to him about how things should be and about the expectations I had of turning him into a Great Billy Goat. Together we began our journey, first to the boundary that marked the circle of La Esperanza. With the passing of time, we expanded our walks from my maternal grandparents' big house to the American farm. Day by day we lengthened our travels to far corners. No one could picture me without the company of my goat.

It happened one Holy Saturday. I'd just arrived home when my mother gave me a list and two pesetas (forty cents): supper and some leftover for the next day. I liked the idea because the bodega was far. Rompetambor could be confirmed as my mode of transportation, and I could enjoy riding him. The trip would be fun.

I took the opportunity, as it was relevant, to explain why he shouldn't pay attention to the nanny goats that would flirt with him. That could bring big problems and he had a good reputation in addition to being known as the best domesticated goat ever seen. I would find him his perfect nanny.

The journey was animated. Both of us had reason to feel happy. I won't deny his bewilderment when he saw that grayish road, wide and shiny, which I called highway. There was no way he would put his hooves over it. I wasn't upset. I had already learned that everything takes its own time.

We walked the trail close to the ditch without the vaguest idea that the worst was yet to come. In front of José Miguel, the grocer, and all his customers, which were many, my right hand went into my pants' pocket, and I searched for the money and the list of items I had to buy not knowing how or when they had disappeared. I cannot even describe my reaction or that of the curious, who up to now had been distracted looking at Rompetambor with envy. Nine people were waiting to eat that evening, not including coffee and the tobacco leaves for Grandfather Rafael to chew.

That great embarrassment is directly related to my first life project, asking Heaven for a deluge of pesetas that would cover the entire farm. My conviction in the possibility of success was such, and my hope so overwhelming, considering it was the only realistic solution to all we lacked, that the next morning I had already forgotten the bitter taste of the previous day, and I concentrated all my energy into getting on with it. I would do it all with the greatest discretion. My success depended on keeping the secret. Nothing would impede the raining of pesetas right where I needed them to fall. The boundary markers would be set soon.

With morning dew still on my feet, and while Rompetambor enjoyed the fresh grass near me, I began to inspect the *piña de ratón*[4] that separated us from Pancho the alderman. He was the biggest gossip of all the neighbors. When he paid visits and they asked him what had been on the news, the answer was always the same:

"It was good, but to my misfortune, the kids interrupted, and I couldn't understand…"

---

[4] *Bromelia penguin lindl.* Common plant in Cuba used to create fences and live hedges in farms and rural yards.

To say nothing of his three children, chubby and white as milk. At lunch time in school we were always bickering. They would never trade the sweet potato I offered them for their bread and butter or strawberry popsicles.

I grew up hearing that sweet potato is good for your sight and that pumpkin plumps the calves. Not even an abundance of sweet potatoes and pumpkins solved those problems. But I am convinced that sweet potato makes you want to fight; those fatties fell at the first strike. Once I threw a right hook at the middle one. He fell on his back, and he just wouldn't wake up. We had to pee on his head. He gave us a blurry stare and after much struggle, we got him up. Meanwhile, Rompetambor, sheltered under the shade of a mamoncillo[5] plant, waited to take me back home on his back. He lived difficult moments; the poor animal always suspected that the worst would happen to me in such situations. His desperate bleating told me so.

Little by little, I cut out the *piña de ratón* that would keep pesetas from falling where I wanted. I watched the sky. I couldn't let it surprise me. After a short rest, I moved on to the marker with León, Aunt Modesta's husband. I liked crossing his farm on my way to school. I always wished for a repeat of that day. A bee, looking for male mangos as I was, stung me on the sole

---

[5] *Meliococcus bijugatus*. Tree from America's intertropical zone appreciated for its edible fruit.

of my foot, exactly where my sneaker had a huge hole. Consequently, I had, once again, a good excuse to return home and not go to school.

A barbed wire fence separated us from León and from Antonio Cañon. I think it was this day when Cañon, Aunt Valentina's husband, was returning from playing cards. The woods slept the deep sleep of midnight. It did what all of us peasants do when the moon retires and won't come out. Sometimes we whistle and sometimes we sing to drive off the fear of the darkness upon us. But since the devil's the devil for a reason, Prieta, the smartest of all the girls, had learned that well and placed a scarecrow with a candle lighting its face on the path thick with rose apple trees. This was the only path for many. Cañon couldn't react in time and lost control. No one ever knew where his horse went, and no one could explain how it was possible that after going into unknown trails in the darkness of night, that wretched man arrived alive to Aunt Valentina, rosary in hand and ready to eat him alive, surrounded by her sad and sickly children.

Antonio never provided an explanation of the event, he never spoke of it, but those who knew were perfectly aware that after that scandalous incident, whenever he saw Prieta, his face became disfigured, jets of steam came out of his nostrils, and his hairy ears took on the appearance of fully open hand fans.

During that entire journey, I straightened four or five posts and tied together a few pieces of barbed wire as best I could. Everything seemed to indicate that soon the longed-for rain would fall.

Every day Rompetambor felt more unrestricted. That morning he jumped high to reach the appetizing leaves of pine nut trees. A long row of old cashew trees isolated us from the tract of land belonging to Rufino, whom we called El Cubano, although he didn't look it. He was at peace with his lot in life. Deeply in love with Aunt Iluminada from a young age, whenever someone asked why they weren't affianced, he answered: "I asked her. It wasn't meant to be, it wasn't meant to be." Aunt Iluminada didn't like that man at all, possibly because of his long sideburns and the yellowish color of his mustache which covered a great portion of his shriveled-up face.

The bark on those cashew trees told that they had been planted by our ancestors. It amused me that nature had thought to create a fruit in the shape of a small pear with the seed on the outside. I ate them despite their rough and spicy flavor. Perhaps their reddish color enticed me, and they were good for easing hunger. I was chewing on a cashew when the memory of the previous night began to trouble me. Rungo said that on moonless Fridays a small green light left the top of the avocado plant between the piñon botija[6] and the Santo Domingo

---

[6] *Jatropa curcas L*. Popular bush in all of Cuba used to create hedges in fences for farms and yards.

mamey[7], went over the trestle in my house, and landed on the *quiebrahacha*[8] near the little blind well. It was a spirit settling some outstanding business from a big or small person. In those parts, nearly no one had any debts. There weren't many people from whom to borrow. But since Rungo also spoke of a small person, I was on alert. I thought I might be included in the sanction to be settled by the nocturnal spirit that haunted us. I was doing things that were related to the heavens. No question about it, the dead had carried the pesetas up there.

I was comforted by the memory of what Catulo had said. Measured in his speech and always negotiating, he denied everything Rungo said. He declared that the presence of the light only happened on nights when the earth was wet, and that it landed anywhere. It was the product of earth gases, or maybe, shooting stars. According to him, only the dead who had been evil in life should be feared. Even men were afraid of that light. I was suspicious. Not one voice was heard in the noon stillness. Meanwhile, Palomo, from the thickest part of the woods howled in fear to let me know I had to hurry up. My determination was to cut only the branches that could divert some of my coins and leave that place as

---

[7] *Mammea Americana*. Tree similar in appearance to the magnolia; it can reach more than 20 m. in height in tropical zones; its fruit is of firm pulp, aromatic and sweet, of orange and reddish color.
[8] *Guibourtia hymenaeifolia*: Cuban tree of valuable wood, hard, resistant, and incorruptible; it can reach 50 feet high and 16 inches in diameter. On the eastern region of the country, it is known as "caguairán."

quickly as possible. The sky began to hide behind storm clouds that, to my thinking, contained my treasure.

A discreet façade appeared as I came upon the American farm. A few meters away was the church where I was taught to believe in God, not to steal the oranges they planted, to give my tithes. Then I thought, "If Mom has to give one peseta for every four boxes of guava, how much will the pastor want as a result of the ones sent from Heaven?" I couldn't imagine. Scriptures came to mind: "Give to Caesar that which is Caesar's and to God that which is God's" and "It is easier for a camel to go through the eye of a needle than for a rich man to enter the kingdom of God." I emerged from those perplexing thoughts when I heard the only tractor I'd ever seen in my life. It came from deep in the woods. Maybe the cattleman turned tractor driver was picking up palmiche[9].

That noise and the smell released by the tractor took me to the marker by Cirilo. There I didn't have to think too hard. Not a tree, not a fence, nothing separated us: You there. Me here.

The seminarians called Cirilo a philosopher, because one day, while they boasted of their knowledge to break the silence in which the poor man had fallen, they asked him: "Cirilo, what is life?" To which he, buttoning the top of his mended shirt and raising his belt

---

[9] Small, round fruit bunches produced by the royal palm in its highest section; popular among farmers as feed for pigs.

almost to the nipples, which accentuated his thinness, fixed his blue gaze on the palm frond ceiling and with solemnity answered: "Life… night, day, lunch, supper." His answer became famous. And after a time, I realized that he answered so because that was his dilemma, the reason for his constant battle, his horizon.

Cirilo had the patience of a teacher. He turned our corn husks and bottles into yokes for oxen; with small cans he made us wheels for carts. He enlivened our nights with tales of Bertoldo, everyone's favorite, a canary that appeared to be clumsy, but always found a way to get out of tight spots.

According to Cirilo, one unfortunate day, Bertoldo was walking through the forest and had a stomachache so strong, it twisted his insides. Before squatting, he took off his brand-new watch and hung it from the branch of a young tree. He forgot it. No matter how much he tried to remember where he had left it, he couldn't. Every day he went in search of his watch.

One Sunday, when all the animals of the forest were quiet, and the feeble air wouldn't make the slightest attempt to move a leaf, Bertoldo heard a tic-toc coming from the sky. He put his ear to the tree trunk from where he thought the sound was coming. From there, from that tree, came the tic-toc. It was his watch. The tree was fifteen meters, and twenty years had passed.

While I was cutting vines, I had to reprimand Rompetambor because he wanted to eat them. I tied them and put them where the marker with Cirilo was to be, although I would've preferred to keep it as it was: You there. Me here. A fresh aroma of wet earth gave me joy as I felt the proximity of my fulfilment.

My project was almost finished. Grandfather Rafael's pasture reached the piña de ratón. Grandfather was like a dry coconut: skin and bones. But how strong he was! With the same leather strap, he used to frighten the animals, he frightened us kids. Always quiet. He spoke the most to the priest when he came to call. In truth, it was the priest who spoke. Grandfather only named things, he spoke in phrases and precise words.

My gut still has not forgiven me for that noontime when just arrived, and of course after having asked for their blessings, Grandmother offered me lunch. Out of mere shyness I said no, but I was starving; I would wait for her to ask again. As she began to insist, Grandfather, at the speed of thunder, short and grumpy, rebuked her: "Diantre, the boy said no. Things should be said only once!" And he whipped his strap in the air barely missing my nose. Grandmother had an expression of contempt, but she didn't speak, she wouldn't dare. I don't even remember saying goodbye.

I crossed the fence. The air brought me a waft of the coal oven we were burning, probably with marabú firewood, because the smoke was nice and blue. I was in a hurry and was near a small house built on the banks of the creek. Tesoro lived there with a little parrot and Battle, her half-wit dog. Perhaps hunger and the recent embarrassment made me remember a décima poem I'd heard her sing:

With eagerness I pray to God
     That when another cloud I see,
     Of roast pork please let it be
     Of guava jam and bread, so nice.
     Lots of saffroned rice,
     Empanadas and blood sausage,
     Several eggs will suffice
     Let us see them fall,
     And down the creek a crawl
     Of soup with yellow rice.

I reached the highest point of the pasture. I set Rompetambor loose to play and graze to his heart's content. From there, with his amorous bleating, he called the young nanny goats to indulge in his delights, and I would pretend not to see him so he wouldn't be self-conscious. I sat on the back of a dried royal palm frond. Had anyone been looking, they would've thought I was about to roll down like so many other times with the goat jumping by my side. That little hill was so inviting. Not this time. I could see the entire La Esperanza farm right before me.

I day-dreamed:

I had purchased a pick-up truck so Cuca wouldn't have to walk to town carrying those heavy sacks. I saw her nursing a foal with a white birth mark on its forehead so he would never forget the mother that birthed him, and his entire body chestnut, like his father Nelson, Mr. Willey's horse, given that name in honor of George Washington's horse. He rejected her for her tired gait and for being ugly and bony. I also contributed a whitish tractor, so Maravilla and Cubana wouldn't have to plow but only birth calves and give plenty of good milk. Palomo would fatten up, his coat would change, and he would guard the house well. His fangs, just like mine, would be feasting all the time. He wouldn't want chocolates and mint candy, but surely bread and butter and strawberry popsicles. Surely.

A question came to mind: Would I have to stop being a guajiro[10] when the moment came? I answered quickly. No, no. First, because I like it, then because it's something that gets into your body, and you can't stop it from pouring out through your clothes. I will continue to be a guajiro, a purebred guajiro.

The sun punished my face, and I didn't realize that more time had passed than I had intended, focused as I was on how to settle our luminous future, bright as a ray of light. Rompetambor approached jumping, skipping in an elegant trot. He appeared with such beautiful demeanor, that no one would've recognized him. He was resplendent. Saddened by my passivity, he lowered his head. We walked next to each other, like we did when on a stroll or on our way to a Sunday party. I'm certain that

---

[10] Coloquialism referring to someone originally from the country.

he observed how the other goats and nanny goats turned away when he passed. They appeared to be eating grass or busy drinking water, but they didn't want to look at him. They didn't want to see him gilded and with a certain air of superiority. They didn't understand that we were dreamers. Then, we both looked to the sky shrouded under a great dark cape intent on covering us, the boiling blackish clouds moving in a hurry toward the south.

To see Rompetambor's relatives turn their backsides to him, gave me a bad feeling. It was a concerning sign that they began to reject him because he tried to appear better when he was an equal. I felt uncomfortable. I would have time to think about him as well as myself later. It was late and there was much work to do if the sky didn't release what I needed.

That night I sat on the floor like Buddha. I was all ears. León said that Aunt Iluminada had another apparition, Gregorio, the spirit that always came to her. Gregorio was handsome, respected by everyone. A slave to my great-grandmother Micaela, he told Iluminada nice and clear to go to the kapok tree where the money was buried for her and the nephew she had "baptized," but she had to go alone. León also said that Matungo the slave had not gone to sleep the night of the money interment, and through the slits in his hut he heard and saw everything. Gregorio and Mrs. Micaela walked in a hurry, and the mule carrying the load kept falling behind. It was old, and the load was heavy. León said that

Matungo didn't open his mouth to tell the secret until after Gregorio died. He was scared, more of Gregorio than of Mrs. Micaela.

Catulo, as usual, made an even bigger mess of it. He claimed that Anacleto, Micaela's little black son, had come out black as coal because Gregorio was not only her husband but also her slave. When he spoke of Gregorio he seemed to exaggerate sharp, nobody knew his secrets, mobilized slaves whenever he pleased. In those parts, the fugitives were his main followers, they listened to him. He had his tricks to keep them dispersed around the hills, his connections to do what he wanted. One cleanup was enough, and a person's wish would be all but granted. They put the death of Herrera, the owner of the sugar mill, on his account. A rooster of a breeder he was too. Not one Mrs. or Miss escaped when he wanted to take them to the woods. He was God and devil. The white men feared him.

Catulo said that Matungo was an ingrate and a cheater, but I don't think anyone believed him. Come to think of it, something was going on because no one contradicted him. They knew him well, that he was well versed in the stories of those unhappy slaves. His grandfather and Herrera were in-laws.

I couldn't understand all the grown-up scuttlebutt. Besides, I felt sorry for Mamma, making coffee in the kitchen, and listening to the conversation. Surely, she didn't like hearing such things about her family. I went to bed. I needed to dream, dream about my rain. Dream my dreams, dream about me.

As soon as I laid down, a rain shower began in no hurry to end. I was so happy that I waited awake for dawn.

Chapter 3

Walking on a narrow path in a cold sweat, I searched for a way out onto King's Road. In my shirt pocket I carried a small paper my mother was sending to old Bienvenido. This time I made sure to put it in a safe place. I didn't read it.

The arrival!

What would I say?

Would he remember whose son I am?

Would I have to mention my grandmother? I'd heard that he was Gregorio's grandson.

Many questions and their answers appeared in my mind while still quite young.

I reckoned I could see Bienvenido ahead. He was dark brown, with a deep voice and fine features. He was large and elegant. Always in a Panama hat, cream guayabera, and low-cut shoes. A medicine man by trade, he was a master. I'd seen him many times, but I was still impressed.

Along the way I saw Rungo. He was returning from trouble and I was on my way to it. I hid behind a majagua[11]. Everyone, for one reason or another, went that way, but no one wanted it known. That's why I didn't want to show my face, so he wouldn't see me.

---

[11] Talipariti elatum. Timber tree, tall and leafy, common in the Cuban countryside.

From my hiding place, I watched Bienvenido's house and hoped to find him alone.

I took off my hat and asked permission to come in, but I forgot to greet him. He was surprised to see me.

"What are you doing here? Who sent you?" I hesitated. The situation was difficult. I stretched my hand and with misty eyes and a broken voice, I said:

"Mamma sent me, I brought you a note."

He read it calmly and in astonishment. He leaned back and furrowed his brow.

"She wants me to go to her house? They waited too long, very little can be done."

"Can't you do anything?" I asked.

I had come from the shade, and yet cold sweat blinded me. Bienvenido took his time, lit a cigar, sucked on it a few times, and took a shot of cold coffee. While he arranged the herbs he could reach, he swiped his right hand across his face several times, released two mouthfuls of smelly smoke, and finally said:

"I'll go tonight. Don't expect me early. I'll work on it now."

"Write it all on the back of the note. I get many messages and I get them mixed up."

While he wrote, he said in his thick voice:

"You're growing up troubled and hurried. Easy, boy, go easy, things happen when they have to happen."

Bienvenido kept his promise. Late at night and delayed, he arrived, but his presence was needed in those difficult moments. Neither the priest nor the American church would like that visit, which they would know about soon, but he understood that we were caught between two fires, forced to grab on to any branch we could reach, and that's why he went.

He had tossed all kinds of herbs in a sack. He gave instructions on how to divide them in small portions and boil them in enough water to make soaking baths. And the snake oil to massage the joints was vital. He gave no words of encouragement. He didn't like to lie.

Point by point, every day, what Bienvenido instructed was done, but as he had said: Things happen when they have to happen. The hen and the seven chicks soon lost our father rooster.

Not quite in full mourning attire thanks to the use of dyes, just into their teenage years, my sisters Prieta and Nene began to frequent a group of more than one hundred women who were greeted daily by a board filled with tobacco leaves. A grand colonial house was the compound where tobacco leaves were stripped and sorted. There, the women welcomed each new day and there they said goodbye.

A small room had been turned into a confessional, a place to open the curtain of their sins so the priest could see them. Having to confess their sins to the priest, the same one that called on my grandparents, was a possibility the workers faced each week. The Padre walked discreetly along each of the seats telling the women in what order they should come.

It must have been a Friday. Prieta, fully concentrated on her task, began to worry about the lack of moisture in the tobacco which made it difficult for her to stretch each leaf. The slippery priest, barely allowing his presence to be noticed, whispered in her ear: "It's a shame that you can't take confession! Your deceased father is in hell because not even at the end of his life would he accept my religion: the catholic, apostolic, roman church. The true faith."

I had gone to take their lunch, and from a long window that nearly reached the floor, and positioned behind the balustrades, I saw how Prieta, as bold as brass and with board in hand, sprinkled the tobacco on the floor while the air took care of spreading it all around the room. She flew over tables and fell face down hanging from the Padre's neck who was trying to escape and fought back as much as he could. The great chorus of desperate women surrounded them and screamed: "Let go of the Padre, Prieta, let go of the priest! Dear God, have mercy, the devil has possessed this girl! Run, Celestino, run, we'll lose our priest!"

That's when the chaos began. The priest freed his head trying not to fall down the stairs, but now he was a prisoner of his disheveled black cassock.

Celestino came bounding up the stairs two at a time and repeating in despair:

"Prieeeta, Prieeeta, you'll destroy me, you goddamned bitch, you'll destroy me! Prieta, fuck, holy shit, goddamn motherfucker!"

After much struggle, Celestino picked up the battered body he thought was dead carrying him between chest and back.

Silence took ownership of the room. The women were frightened, but also with a healthy dose of curiosity, continued to stare and wouldn't return to work until they were out of sight.

"You got your wish, you've ruined me, you've ruined me, Prieta, fuck, damn bitch," said Celestino in a murmur while he disappeared with the priest on his shoulder like a sack of potatoes, knowing his income was in peril.

Still irate, Prieta didn't seem to hear his words or notice the grave expression on the manager's face. She continued to screech at the Padre at the top of her lungs:

"I'm your hell! Hell will be waiting for you! Come, you can't escape me!

I returned home with the food in my canteen untouched.

"There's little tobacco, they're coming home early," I decided to tell Mamma. That day, I got to school late, and I couldn't write.

The American church prospered quickly. It became a backwoods seminary and gained followers even with their strict rules: women couldn't cut their hair, wear makeup or nail polish, show their calves, wear sandals or tight clothes, or dance or participate in secular parties. Men, among other things, had to abandon vices

40

such as smoking, betting in cock fights, and drinking alcoholic beverages, and they endeavored to avoid looking at any woman who wasn't their own. Very rigorous. However, under different circumstances, it was quite probable that parents wouldn't send their sons and daughters to become missionaries.

From Mister's house, you could see where his farm ended, if you could call that little piece of land a farm. Soon, what was believed impossible, surprised everyone. A windmill appeared, and water sprang from a well that had been dry until that moment. The difficult land became productive and pleasant as it lost all the brush to be surrounded by modest buildings, orange groves, and orchards.

With a Bible under his arm, Negrobueno was the first to take the trip. As many others did, every Sunday the long line of Filomenos, their Christian name, would attend the worship in the American church. They only had to cross the Canalta woods and there was the church where their daughter Caridad had found work.

On the edge of the Canalta woods, he had raised his shack. He was old. His siblings, born in slavery, did not survive. No one knows when he showed up with his woman Candita and a bunch of kids. The nickname Negrobueno was given by one of the Misters because soon they understood the integrity with which this man lived his life and the effort he made to believe in God, the only Savior. On Wednesdays, his son Yayo and I tried to pass the time as best we could during prayers while the kneeling parishioners, with eyes closed tight, thanked God for all the blessings received, and unloaded a list of petitions for Him to resolve. Their talent for improvisation during prayers was incredible.

They seemed to me to be better composed than the stories about Christopher Columbus's four voyages to America that our teacher dictated and that I would repeat flawlessly days later. Such a fascinating feat must've been planned with extreme care. I could see the defiant and argumentative men that traveled with their risk-taking chief Christoper in the vessels with thoughtfully chosen names: La Niña and La Pinta (the prostitutes) followed the largest, the Santa Maria. I found those unbelievable episodes fascinating. It was the only thing that captivated me in school where I went almost by force.

With no malicious intent, I once pointed out to Yayo how attentive his father was toward a young blond girl, the accordion player at the church. He answered that he probably did it because he liked the color crimson, and she always wore clothes in that color.

Alert, concerned about our positioning, Yayo and I would find a way to sit in strategic locations. Most of the time we dedicated ourselves to examine the funny messages and exchanges between the amorous youths and others, not so youthful or amorous. Perhaps that is why we became exceptional witnesses, anonymous still today, to some of the happenings at the church.

The audacious farmer Pantaleón Respetancia was not a parishioner. He attended the worship that night to please his family, especially his wife, Crudencia. I can't confirm that Respetancia was Pantaleón's real last name, but perhaps what follows can shed some light on the uncertainty.

He didn't waste a second and took advantage of the first few moments of contemplation to signal Fortuna with the intention of communicating to her that the next day, when Prío Diez blew his horn at eleven, they would meet in the woods at the foot of the palm that was stripped by lightning. Then, he changed his mind and signaled that it wouldn't be there but near another palm, one more hidden from view, the one split in the middle by the last deluge which lasted a week. Amazingly, his sign language was perfect, but Yayo and I were able to decipher it to the last detail.

He asked her, among other naughty things, to take Fortunito with her so he could hold him and play with him. The sad boy had no resemblance to any of Fortuna's other four children, but his profile, eye color, hair, the birthmark on his neck, and the navel in the shape of a bottle cap, were identical to those of Respetancia's youngest son, Crudencito, and to top it off, he had been born a day after the other little one. That matter didn't produce much controversy perhaps because Respetancia did not have the reputation of doing wicked deeds in the woods.

Frequently, the neighbors' children would look like each other and have birth marks in the same places: village folk almost always resemble each other. Or that's what I heard the late María say. She didn't say it meaning to defame. María was like few women, and I'm not the only one who says it, everyone agreed. From the moment of her death, they were sure she'd gone to Heaven, and if she's not in Heaven, she must at least be waiting at the entrance.

Back to the issue of "the daring ones," that night of meditation things were going swimmingly for them, so enthusiastic about their fairy tale, they didn't notice the final words of the sermon. So, from behind the pulpit, under a cloak of silence, the preacher cleared his throat, coughed, but nothing would break their enchantment. Faced with that situation, we watched and said nothing until all eyes were on them, except the one who we accepted as Fortunito's father. We'll call him Manuel, since we had no written proof of what was being whispered, and such a good man deserved respect. Amid such an event, he appeared to have all five senses firmly planted on the last book of the Bible. "He who testifies to these things says, "Yes, I am coming soon. Amen. Come, Lord Jesus." Revelation 22:20

From the back pew in the women's wing, a voice was heard that resonated like thunder:

"Respetancia! What's going on? Disappear immediately, disappear!" It was Crudencia, his wife, direct and precise. The entire brood followed the loud,

44

snorting, breathless woman as she searched for the church's false door.

Gripped by the proceedings, Yayo and I pricked up our ears to catch every action.

Pantaleón, not noticing that he had been disowned of his last name forever, forgot his hat and was reduced to complying with his wife's orders. Tesoro, Fortuna's brother in-law, discreetly told her to return home immediately with her children. Those of us who stayed behind, perhaps the most curious, began to drip out of the church in small groups toward the courtyard until the church was empty,

With great difficulty, the reverend got through the worship and assumed it finished when Respetancia and Fortuna starred in the scandalous episode. He displayed his grief; his disappointment was visible. He had no strength to react to the new reality that was unfolding. He remained inside the temple relocating objects he thought were in the wrong place.

Apolinar Gato was there that night. From far away, from Río Sequito, he came on his Moorish horse with its gleaming plated harness. He tied him to a holm oak near the temple like all peasants who lived far and had horses.

Apolinar's presence at church was intermittent. When he received warnings about his behavior, Gato only answered that he admitted he was an engine Christian, and engines, he said, needed a rest every once in a while. He thought that argument was extremely convincing.

Apolinar, bitter and ill-disposed to an extreme, was furious when he arrived at the place where he had left his beast. He felt a strong jab in his heart; his horse was not among the ones waiting for their riders. It wasn't where he had left it just an hour before, and the horse there was not his. Without compunction, forgetting where he was, befuddled, he began to gripe at all the saints in Heaven and God for all the dirty tricks they allowed while he was there, confined in church, thanking them for all the prosperity he still expected. He kicked up dust with his big boots and moved his hat from his head to his left hand and then to his right, over and over. Simeón, one of the best parishioners, worried and nervous, made fruitless attempts to control Apolinar.

It so happened that selfish Pantaleón, ashamed and in the darkness of a moonless night, jumped on the first beast that crossed his path. An American watching the action understood that it wasn't a case of carelessness or ill-intention, simply confusion. But he couldn't find the right words to quickly translate into Spanish and pacify the unyielding man. Instead of saying calm, he said calf, instead of angry he pronounced animal... Then, he decided to put his hand on Apolinar's shoulder to call him into prudence and reflection, but he slipped again and called him Apolonia. Those present broke into laughter and boisterous guffawing. That was the last straw for the incensed farmer. Like so many times before, he took his knife out of its scabbard and looked for someone to attack. The "assholes" and "fucks" blurted entered and exited de doors and windows of the church, the air twisted them and tried to make them flee into the woods and spread throughout the lowlands.

Crestfallen, as always, and heartbroken over the hoaxes and atrocities committed by his crazy brother, who kept the whole family in constant uncertainty, he couldn't fathom that if he had come on good faith to refresh his mind, he would have to leave without his Moorish horse.

Someone recalled how once, that tough, evasive man, thought himself unable to continue carrying his misery and showed up at the cemetery. He argued with the undertaker to get himself into one of the coffins. He maintained there was benefit in resting in peace as soon as possible so no one could bother him. He took the opportunity to purge all the misery and anxiety he carried because the only slice of fortune he ever received, and at great cost, was the horse and its harness. He stoked his own fire: his ever-lasting battle without reward.

Finally exhausted, Apolinar sat on the entrance steps to the church and roared a challenge, a warning: "I will not move from here until my animal is returned." Filomeno and Simeón were willing to stay with him as long as necessary. Mister himself asked me to be his guide to Pantaleón's house. We both walked. I held the horse by the bridle and wore the forgotten hat on my head.

The narrow dirt paths were invisible. Only the hooting of an owl interrupted our silence several times until the light from the filthy, tarnished lantern that had accompanied them that night to the church shone translucent through the empty spaces in the planking of the house.

We heard fake snoring. Pantaleón and his offspring pretended to be in a deep sleep, to be ignorant of the neighing of two horses as they smelled each other. Dogs barking, the flutter of hens and guinea fowl, all birds protesting that ill-timed visit contributed in breaking the stillness and making the moment more dramatic. Crudencia, as always, as if the animals had eaten her tongue, had no alternative or support while presiding over the trade.

Gato's eyes lit up like those of a child with a new toy when he saw us coming with his Moorish horse. The night had begun to whiten from the light of the moon when, dejected and with hardly a goodbye, he pressed the spurs against the flanks of the beast without compassion and took off through a pathway surrounded by undergrowth. It took a long time for Apolinar's engine to revv up again.

Chapter 4

The following Saturday, I was glad to visit Negrobueno's house. I was charged with buying one of his good and reasonably priced cauliflowers. His neighbor, Simeón, was there with his yoke of oxen since early that morning to plow a parcel of land where they would plant corn. He was one of those people that fully enjoyed doing something right. His skinny body was simple and freckled, his small blue eyes sparkled in the noontime sun when we finished. Joy was reflected even in his walk. The labor had been quite fruitful. The Christian was happy. Yayo and I dedicated ourselves to plowing the field and weren't bothered by our exertion.

To celebrate, Filomeno decided to open a bottle of home-made liquor. Nothing better than to share it with such a helpful friend. He'd learned to make it with his mother when he was still small. He said it was an African beverage. He made it with vinegar, sour orange, and sugar. He poured, and they drank for a long time. Yayo and I were in charge of removing the baked sweet potatoes from the cinders and put them in their hands, warm still. The two men enjoyed the coolness of the new evening sitting on the roots of a great holm oak.

The fatigue of age wasn't as pronounced in Filomeno as other times, even if you couldn't tell whetherhe was sad or happy. He, who always bit his tongue as if not wanting to let the words come out, spoke that day with the greatest ease from the moment he began his toast with a tiny, worn mug of white pewter with blue stripes. He sounded as tender as a child.

"I like this drink, it reminds me of my mother, that's why I always have some around. Petrona was her name, a pretty Congolese born in the village of Loango. A group of men assaulted her when she was bathing in the river with her family, and she tried to fight back. It was useless. They dragged her to the slave ship by the arm, and pulled it so hard, it was always a little loose after that. When the weather changed, she would complain of a miserable pain. Many times, she wore a big kerchief as a sling and worked with only one hand. It was criminal what they did to my mother. Her sister, who came on the voyage, never made it. She plunged into the middle of the ocean when she learned that she would be a slave and said she would return to "her nationals". They say because us black folk like crimson so much, they would decorate the ships with cloth of that color so we would fall into the trap. But not Petrona, my mother. She was refined. She died a long time ago. I don't know if her spirit is in Africa or here. She knew how to communicate with the other world through the gourd with the plaster cross and the sparrow hawk feathers. You must respect the sparrow hawk. She also communicated through a small, round pumpkin. That's when she started to get old, when the moon dried her up.

"Before, when she arrived on the island, she was the slave of a man who called himself Laffite. He didn't take her to the coffee plantation. He kept her in his house, got her pregnant, and made the children disappear. Her mother's milk had to be for his own, the legitimate ones. Never again did my mother hear about hers. Many mosquitoes and flies did she swat away from the master for as long as he said, balancing a heavy flyswatter custom made for him. She also had to guess what dish he wanted and when she made a mistake, he punished her himself where no one could see. She told her friend that once, Mr. Laffite took a cigar from his pocket, she ran to find the coal ember, she tried to get there before the master bit off the tip. Begging in fear, she inched the ember toward him, but he didn't want to light it. That mistake cost Petrona dearly. That's why, when they set her free, she wanted to live in the backwoods near the river, ten leagues away at least she wanted to put between her and them, to never see or hear from those people again. That's where I was born. She never left me until her death."

With tears in his eyes, old Filomeno continued his story:

"I don't remember the place, I have no idea where exactly I was born. I started to work… I've been working since I got me a little height, but I can't complain, work is good, it gets rid of bad thoughts and you find things to eat."

"And Candita, where was she born?" asked Simeón.

He didn't answer. He didn't know, or he didn't want to say.

"Candita doesn't understand what they say at the worship. She just goes to get out and to take the kids somewhere, and for the singing. Yes, she goes for the singing too. How Candita likes the singing! But bless her, she can't sing, she's off key and people notice. She doesn't understand about African gods either. Every time we're alone in the woods, I tell her the story about Ochún and Changó, the one everyone knows, but she has no malice, she doesn't even smile. It's like she's in another world, maybe thinking of all the sad things she's been through, because she's lived very bad moments, but she doesn't talk. She looks off in the distance without a word. I like when they say that Ochún likes the woods. She sings and dances with the animals, tames beasts, scorpions won't sting her. I like Ochún, what they say about her is nice.

"Because it turns out that Ochún was poor, and her dress was worn from washing it in the river, but she loved revelry, she was a charmer and a lot of fun. That damn goddess is a tease. Yellow is her color. That was the color of the dress and necklace she wore to the feast of the Saint. And she began playing a drum and drinking beer and rum. And Changó wouldn't notice her, until, after much flattery, she left an impression while she danced. Changó couldn't resist, tasted her honey, he

52

liked it, and asked her why her juices were so nice and sweet. She didn't tell him; they danced, romanced, and he put red beads on her yellow necklace.

"Candita is odd, I find small red and yellow seeds for her and she won't even make herself a little bracelet. Ochún was like my mother, but she was blue like me, and Ochún was mulatta, with long, wavy hair."

The alcohol had spilled all of Filomeno's feelings. Simeón was not much of a talker and didn't understand anything about saints, but he took advantage of the momentary silence from the speaker to express the delight he felt after accepting God as his only savior.

Meanwhile, Yayo and I ate baked sweet potato and listened to Filomeno.

"I like the American religion," continued the old man. "I have to deal with only one god, and with the son. I want to. That's a good thing. The Congo gods are strong and each has his domain, but Candita doesn't know them well, and she doesn't know how to ask them, she often asks what they can't give. I think that's why we haven't moved up in life. My mother knew how to ask. She knew them, and the herbs too, the ones that bring life and the ones that bring death. The woods have everything. That's why you must treat them with respect. Even black flowers are said to grow there. Now I'm better and in better company. I have the woods and the American church. They're good people and they treat us well. Thanks to them, my children have clothes and shoes, and they couldn't be nicer to Caridad. True, she's skinny as a beanpole, but she's the salt of the Earth. That's why they love her."

A vulture flew over the woods, it appeared and disappeared from time to time.

"Do you see the vulture when it breaks away from the woods and peeks at that clearing? It's wise and strange, that fucking bird. When it spreads its wings and flies sideways, it means that you have an enemy that wants to settle a problem, and you must listen because it never fails. It's as if it protects you. I respect butterflies too, much more the yellow ones with the little black ovals. When they close their wings and feed, I don't like to look at them. It brings evil. I tell the kids and they don't listen, but it's gospel truth."

Between gods and drinks we bid farewell to the day. Simeón looked a bit dizzy, but he was happy because Filomeno accepted his god, even if only half way.

With all those tales buzzing around in my head, through nearly impassable pathways, Cuca and I returned home. In the middle of the Canalta woods, already dark as tall trees refused to let through the agonizing light of day, we saw something strange. It had to be an apparition, no less. It blocked our way. I wanted to run, but from the moment Cuca felt its presence, she stopped dead. On his knees, with his hands and eyes pointing to heaven, the spirit seemed to stand on clouds.

I coughed twice, and he didn't even move. The third time, he turned his head and stared at us. It took me a moment to grasp the reality of what I was facing. Strange and all, after looking at him for a long time, I was convinced that it was a man, a living man. I stopped to inspect him from top to bottom. He wasn't just any Joe Blow. Blond, with yellowish hair and beard, he didn't seem to have endured the seven stages of hell like the rest of us that lived around. From head to toe he was dressed in white, pants to mid-calf, low-cut tennis shoes, and by the way, so skinny he seemed brittle. And I still had my nice big cauliflower, the one I was entrusted to buy for supper. I thought about what awaited at home.

My hair stood on end when I pinched the mare to flee, because that's what I wanted, to bolt, and she, once again, didn't respond. Had she been able to talk, she would've remained silent. She was paralyzed. My trance was even worse as that blond began to speak in a language I didn't know, as if he were waking from a stupor. Finally, I understood that he was trying to ask me to get him out and to take him to the other blonds. Cuca and I were not the only ones having a rough time. He had no idea what time it was and much less how to get out of there.

I had no choice but to put the apparition on the mare and walk her to the Americans' home. John, worried about the visitor's delay, smiled happily when he welcomed us. His father was out evangelizing around Los Remates. It's the first time I tell this story, and Mister Tom, on Earth or in heaven, knows it's the truth. He had chosen that place for a spiritual retreat. That's what the lanky little American told me when he thanked me after I delivered him late that night. I never made fun of Antonio Cañon again: anyone can be spooked by a scarecrow.

The sea nearby and flying spirits began to dominate my interest. "Search and you shall find, ask and you shall receive." That scripture from the Bible was firmly set in my head. I didn't like to ask for anything, but when it came to searching, I was among the best. Perhaps that was why I was confident in the good fortune that would come with such a promising trip. It's not that I had given up on the possible deluge of pesetas, but the idea of hidden treasures was a passion for me. Being included in the journey to carry wood made me happy. I was sure it would be worth it and a nice break.

That early morning no one at home slept. Between reminiscences, good wishes, and güiros[12] of hot coffee, we were given our sendoff.

"If you think you're lost, remember you're going west. Always follow the west. El Matagañán —the morning star— will soon appear in the south. Look for it at night to guide you."

"Remember to let the animals rest," said Grandfather Rafael.

---

[12] Container for drinking, also known in Cuba as jicara, made from the hard rind of the Crescentia cujete fruit, a tall tree from Cuba and Central America.

They said all those things. It was a way for them to feel they were part of every detail.

León owned the cart and the two yokes of oxen. The other yoke belonged to Antonio Cañón. I didn't like the idea of having León as my boss. I thought he was grotesque and too old for his jokes. He made bets with Paco, his cousin, to see who could fart more after eating avocados. He almost always won, but it was still in bad taste, and the laughter it produced didn't last long. Luckily for him, he was a hard worker and that kept him from being rejected by most of the farmers. Many times, he fought with my grandfather to take his land from him. Perhaps he wasn't comfortable with my presence either. He would've preferred to take his twin boys, but he didn't mention it.

At that age, I thought I knew nearly every plant, its flower, and its seeds, the animals that walk or slither, the ones that fly and… their shit. Yes, "you can tell a lot about birds and people from their shit." That's what Catulo said and I proved it.

You can find out, if you really try, when the blackbird ate rice or ateje[13]. And I just had to hang around Rufino's house where there was no latrine to verify if the day before they had eaten cornmeal and pumpkin, or rice and black beans. You can tell easily,

---

[13] *Cordia coloccok*. Wild tree that yields bunches of small red fruit often consumed by birds.

without complication. If you study nature a bit, she shows you the way.

The sun had warmed our backs, but now it blazed directly over us. The straw hats made a nest of moist fire in the middle of our heads that made the sweat flow. From the high mountains we could see, deep below, small splendid valleys where men planted their crops and in humble shacks started families, almost wild but honest, as begets country life.

I remembered Margarita, my blossoming Margarita. I imagined her there, a few hours later, in the evening, leaning against a huge pine, and strong breezes wanting to steal her long hair, and she trying to keep her red and blue checkered skirt from lifting higher than prudence and modesty allow, and unable to braid her hair or simply tie a ponytail. I saw her running around, place her shiny black gaze on the grassquits, and butterflies surrounding her because she smelled like nectar. I followed her at a full run thinking I would reach her, and we would play together in the grass with no one watching. We smiled with happy abandon. And then, when the insolent wind lifted her skirt to her waist, I scolded my eyes for wanting to take what they shouldn't. I looked crossly at the wagoners thinking they too had captured her image with their leers.

The oxen drooled from exhaustion, thirst, and heat. At the end of a dangerous cliff we were surprised by the sweet, cool water that awaited in the depths of a creek. Batallón y Forastero, the walking team, were the first to drink, then followed the first third, and finally, the guiding team, the one closest to the road. We rested and cooled off.

Drowsy with fatigue and hunger we arrived at the Cuatro Caminos oak grove at six in the evening. At that time, the trees already cast their sparse shadows. Huge bonfires, hanging hammocks, starving dogs trying to steal from us, and men who greeted us as if they had always known us alleviated our loneliness. Wagoners are one even if we haven't met.

I went into the woods looking for branches to stoke the fire. I discovered the guayabitas del pinar[14] used to make the rum identified with the region. The small plants where heavy with bunches of fruit, almost all yellowish, a good sign of ripeness and sweetness. I ate as many as I could and brought some back for my travel companions. The evening darkened as we devoured yucca and cod. I was not interested in the yucca, but I relished the cod. They served me big chunks without skin; it was glorious. Amid décimas recited in chest voice, for lack of a guitar, and tall tales, we ended the night. From our group, Tomás was the most seasoned at speaking and stood for us. Anacleto, a man of poise, in khaki shirt and pants, wide belt, and a watch, said he had come in his cart from Peña Blanca and was going

---

[14] *Psidium salutare*. Small bush, exclusive to western Cuba, yielding small fruit.

our way. Good decimista[15] and improvisor, he was the one to close:

> I invited Trabuco the dog
> He hunts hutia a lot,
> He told me he could not
> Run between the vines.
> I told him: I'll find you
> Clear and thick woods,
> He said: Would if I could,
> But later, at home,
> You eat the meat
> And leave me the bones.

Again, the Matagañán. The sound of bells hanging from the necks of the oxen, and the squeaking of the wagons in need of grease became lost in the silence of dawn, verbal commands were rare. No one spoke. A path through the prairie opened in the morning. The day seemed dreary. The voyage was slow, and the silences lasted for hours. Finally, a gate: the entrance to a pasture. Someone had drawn a cat wearing a bell with a stick of coal. That was the name of the place: "The Cat's Bell." We were greeted by Tulio and his son Tulopío. They had watched us from far away. We continued on foot toward his house.

---

[15] Person with ability to improvise decima poems orally.

Tulio introduced his wife as La Vieja, and that's what we called her. Toothless and dry, she reminded me of my paternal grandfather, frozen in time, worn from the sun and a hard life. Her eyes were brown like his. She welcomed us with honey, beans, yucca, and baked hutia.

I'd heard that the hutia, like women, were made to bleed between the legs by the moon. I tried to forget about that while I ate. Tulopío said that they also ate macao[16] and that hutia broth was very good.

"You shouldn't eat too much of it because it's your first time. You could get hutia sickness, although like this, baked, it's not harmful," said La Vieja.

In Cuba there used to be more than ten types of hutia. Now only three remain. They look like rats, live on tree branches, and are herbivores. Sometimes they eat lizards.

"No one's ever died of it; besides, there's no change in the moon," explained Tulio. "But, during a certain time of the year, dogs go crazy when they eat it, they start running in desperation: that's hutia sickness. That's what it's called. Once, there was a lot of hutia eating here, I think it was December 17 to celebrate San Lázaro, and a dog ate some, it made him sick, it went up to the frond roof up there in the tobacco house and didn't stop until he got to the trestle. It fell off, drooled a bucketful, and then, poor wretch, had no life left. But eat

---

[16] *Paguroidea malacostraca*. Crustacean that lives in other's shells and yields a savory meat although scant.

without fear. The bones are the ones that are harmful, that's why we throw them up to the roof or bury them. We've never seen a Christian die from eating hutia. People make up things." explained Tulopío.

I stopped eating it. My stomach was already upset, and this just finished me. Apparently, La Vieja found me a bit unstable and to help me snap out of it, she offered me caramelized turtle egg. I lowered my head and stayed silent. Tomás saved me from the predicament by saying that he was told it was delicious, that he wanted to try some.

The after-supper talk not yet concluded, the locals began to arrive. It was the custom to narrate events in the evenings, or sing, if the occasion warranted. Tulopío brought out several bottles of alcohol from the bedroom, and said they were made from garañon[17] and sugar cane moonshine. He served everyone. While they drank, Tulio and the man with the watch exchanged malicious smiles. Antonio Cañón and I didn't drink.

"It's called Garañé," Tulopío said. A Frenchman named it and now he comes all the time and takes it by the jug. It's good for giving men urges."

During the conversation, Tulopío left no doubt that he was the best treasure hunter in Cabo de San Antonio. And that's the point I wanted to get to: the treasures of Vigía Antigua, of Tetas de Maria La Gorda,

---

[17] *Morinda royoc*. Herbaceous species, lively, sometimes it winds over bushes or trees. Its use is popular in the treatment of anorexia, diminished energy or libido.

or simply, Maria La Gorda. Everyone called that place whatever they pleased.

Tulopío stood up and walked a certain distance from the stool he had been sitting on a few seconds before as if to occupy more space, for greater breadth to make his words more credible.

"I go into dark caves, naked and in tattered rope sandals. The fish is in the water, saints don't lie, and be assured, the Mexican Cross is buried there. I'll find it in time."

Everyone looked around and signaled each other under their hats. I did not.

León said we'd see about that with a narrow look. He appeared to give no credence to what was being said, to avoid the subject. It hadn't been that long since Hernández, the pharmacist, for several nights, had made holes in tree trunks in his mango grove with a little machine. He was looking for money. They say he found coins and other things, but León didn't want to talk about that, it wasn't prudent.

We were exhausted. It was late, and the Garañé wouldn't stop running. Talentino Toledano, quiet up to now, uncorked and ended the night. That one sure knew how to tell tales, good ones and well narrated. No one ever dared doubt the least bit of what he said, according to Tulio.

"Valdemar owned some land near here. He built a vacation home in Playita Baja. His son Publio, who had nothing to do but swim in the ocean and hunt animals for the pleasure of watching them die, went and fell in love with Anita, daughter of the late Primitivo, who by the way, turned up hanged a while back now.

"Mrs. Leonor, mother after all, became her son's accomplice and would keep his secret for as long as necessary, but Valdemar was always against that union. No less than thirty meters from the house, someone took vengeance and made the son pay. They say an evil soul intervened, although no one knows for sure.

"Early morning on Ash Wednesday, two shots were fired toward the sea, the bullets entered Publio's chest, and came out the lower rib cage. Those who saw it said that when they turned him over, his face and arms were shredded from the briar thorns. It was a creepy sight.

"Valdemar, who until then hadn't believed in spirits, still carries his revolver on his waist. He declared that Primitivo, always doing as he pleased and in love with Leonor all his life, had something to do with his son's death. He'll take him out of the ground, he has to own up, he'll have to answer to him.

"It's also rumored that Mrs. Leonor, scared, closed every door in the house, and won't even come out for fresh air, always miserably tearful in her bedroom not wanting to hear any news. Tiburcio, the house boy, began to suffer from severe headaches since that fatal day. He mourns the deceased as his own. No herb or wood branch can cure him. And poor Anita, no matter how much they try to console her, she refuses to see the

64

sun. She's but a bundle of pure suffering for the lost boyfriend, and her dead father is in danger, a disconcerting living hell. So serious is the situation, that even the most daring around here, the ones who claim to have the hairiest chests, aren't willing to show up in Playita Baja."

Chapter 5

The moon was like glass. It reminded me of January moons, clear and dazzling. I thought about Palomo, I missed him. He wasn't just another dog, he was my dog, and right now, he was probably barking at the moon. I went to the hammock with thoughts of the Mexican Cross and the gunshots. Not surprisingly, I didn't sleep well. I had nightmares about Margarita. I thought the dawn was late as ever.

While drinking coffee, I asked Tulopío if we could herd the oxen together. I wanted to befriend him, and I asked if I could stay with him a few days. I wanted to hang out at the caves and the beach.

And so it was. We talked for the entire twenty kilometers of the trip. At times, the path was rocky, sparks flew from the wagon wheels making deafening noise. I extended my stay. Tomás took care to tell León that I would remain until they came back for the new load.

That afternoon we filled the wagon with raw wood and bat fertilizer to repair and insulate our homes. I said goodbye the next day without regret, although I thought Mamma would find it strange when I didn't arrive. I had told her about the deluge of pesetas, and I believe she didn't think it right, although she lived with the conviction that God is in heaven, and whatever comes from above must be good, except lightning because it destroys whatever it finds in its path. From that moment, when I least expected it, she'd be watching me. This would also concern her. It had to do with the dead, but it's not that she was fearful. When the chips were down, nothing got in her way. She believed in God. She went to church, read the Bible, and said pretty prayers. She was famous for that. I think she was the most intelligent of the Christian women. I imagined her in the early evening watching a couple of hummingbirds feeding and making their nest on the redbird flower shrub by the front porch. Many times, I would surprise her looking at them, dazed as she always was. Perhaps at that moment she was remembering me and thinking who knows what. She would miss me.

The sea in Vigía Antigua, Maria La Gorda, greeted us. Waves crashing into the cliffs could be seen from the beach. My eyes were lost in the horizon. A massive sun fell into the pearly blue water. Now reddish and golden, it blended with the sky. No gift could be greater. My adventures and misadventures with Tulopío began the next day. I spent the night in restless battle with gnats. I couldn't concentrate on how to convince my friend not to go into the caves naked, and to at least take a wick.

Even before the day appeared, we were already in the Vigía Antigua palm forest, where corsairs, or pirates, during Spanish colonial times, built a little lighthouse to trick ships into entering. There, they would be captured and pillaged. The pirates would leave clues in caves, trees, and even rocks to return for the loot when it was safe, that being the reason for so much leftover money and treasure all over, as Tulopío told me.

"Look, there, behind those rocks, is the big cave. Everyone says there's treasure hidden inside. We're not going in, I'll never go in again. What's in there is not for me. Once, I was about to grab the treasure at the mouth, by the entrance. Everything was ready, but a man came and beat me to it. He had good equipment, he found it easy and he covered it. He ran to the parish of Los Remates so they would bless him with holy water, afraid to do such things without the priest knowing. Poor man! No one ever saw him again. He died in the woods on the way back. Not even the vultures helped in the search. He didn't get to touch the money, he left it intact. There you go! The woods take what they give. They swallow you if you're not careful."

"Yeah, sometimes the woods are merciful, sometimes vengeful. Don't you think we've done enough for today? Let's go." Tulopío didn't show any signs of having heard me and continued ahead.

"Come 'ere, come close, boy. You see that other cave?" Tulopío signaled after much walking.

"Yes, I'm watching everything," I answered.

He stopped to call me to reflection with one of his experiences.

"You have to go in, maybe luck will follow you. You go in by yourself, I'll wait for you out here. Not long ago, I was deep inside and a fireball fell from above, it burned everything, not even moisture would douse it. I got out by rolling and jumping like a goat. It took a long time for me to heal. I still have the burn marks. It looks like they hid coins. When money is in coins, it has a lot to do with the dead, and almost always, they become eviler than they were when alive, but I'm sure that this is for you. Go on, take a wick if you want, go, don't be afraid."

Tulopío reassured me that it was to me that they would give the treasure, and I would be the true owner. He wasn't envious or putting conditions on me, but he also didn't seem to have any idea what to do with so much wealth. His ambition was no more than a desire to go against the dead, to win the battle and discover the treasure.

I went in. I can't deny I was worried. The possibility that the fireball that had put my friend's life in jeopardy might reappear besieged me. I searched as best I could, always thinking of the risk of being trapped or of some sorcery. Tulopío's previous attempt was fresh on my mind when a strange brightness emerged before my eyes and an icy shiver ran up from the tips of my big toes to my knees. I wasted no time and ran out like a bat out of the fires of hell. I didn't say anything, yet Tulopío, feigning ignorance, knew that something strange had happened to me too.

No two days were the same, although no matter how much I searched, I only saw one sign on a rock that looked real. I wondered why coalmen did such hard work instead of looking for what was hidden in the woods. Not all of them can be fools. I had my doubts, and the path seemed uncertain, though Tulopío had spoken a great truth: "The fish is in the water."

Food was scarce, and the coalmen invited me to hang out at the beach. It was turtle nesting time. We promised to meet at the place and time proposed by Fausto, the fisherman. There would be nights of guard shifts ahead in unbearable heat. It doesn't rain much in those parts. What do come to that area often are hurricanes looking for the Gulf, as if they had a familiar pathway in the sea, but in those days, there was a mighty drought. We spread out at forty to fifty meters from each other. I was left alone and there was no moon. I couldn't even see my hands!

We were deep into the night, the possibility of seeing a turtle ever further from my thoughts. I'd been standing in the same spot for more than an hour attentive to any strange movement, when a clear light over the sea made me shake. It went into the shore and out until finally, it rested over a tall bush about nine or ten feet from me. I figured, based on what I knew, no more no less, that it guided a spirit. I was terrified. If a turtle passed by me then, I didn't see it, my attention on what I was seeing and not what I might see. It was not a mirage. I found out later that for hundreds of years, every night, the pirate repeated this action, punishment for not knowing where the treasure was when they came for it; they had left him guarding it and he couldn't give a reason why he didn't know.

At three in the morning, a turtle appeared with a light step and soft movements, barely heard. My instructions were to pretend to ignore it, and we let her dig in the sand and lay her eggs. When she turned back, we were ready to catch her. Gradually, we surrounded her and pounced on her with all our strength. No one can explain how she escaped. Maybe we were too eager. While some of us pulled on one side, trying to make her turn on her back, others pulled on the other side, and in that struggle, we were left empty-handed. I was disconsolate, my lousy luck seemed endless.

When the moon rose, we followed the trail left on the sand by the animal. She had made a huge hole to lay eggs. Fausto said that if we were really interested in capturing her, we had to try again the following Wednesday when she would return to the same place to lay more eggs, because when the number of eggs was odd, it meant she wasn't done laying. And so it was. The following Wednesday night at eleven o'clock, she came and calmly laid her eggs. This time we captured her. No one could find out. It was forbidden to take turtles and their eggs, but we had good food for many days.

Tulopío and I returned to our adventures, and as almost always, it was he who began the dialogue.

"All types of ships and people came here, and the majority ended up sinking in the depths. Maybe you'll

71

get lucky and they'll give you one of those treasures they hid, because you're the latest to show an interest in these things. The dead are like that, they don't think like the living. A long time ago, a troublesome foreigner came. He was long and as skinny as tobacco thread, with shiny green eyes and brand-new sandals. The swindler gave black Anselmo fifty American pesos to show him where the treasure was buried. He knew it was under a lonely bush near the ocean, a few steps from the sand. Anselmo showed him a big mangrove and ran into the woods to hide from him so he wouldn't lose his fifty greens. They treat us natives as if we're worthless, they think us fools."

"Does Anselmo want the money for himself?"

"No, no. He knows they won't give it to him, or anybody of his generation, none of them are worth a rusty peso. But you need to understand that dealing with the woods and the dead is not easy."

"I see that."

"Go, don't be afraid, I'll wait for you here. If anything, scream and I'll come help you."
"I'm not afraid, if I went in once, I can go in twice, but not today."

"Let me know when you're ready."
I never went. That afternoon I had supper with the coalmen. They ate dwarf palm seeds instead of rice; according to them, they had the same flavor. As soon as I tasted that extremely bitter stew, I didn't like it. Hunger

made me drink a broth made with peje, their name for fish, and some sweet potatoes.

Tobías was there, his gaze lost over the sea, sitting on his legs. He was an old coalman of dark skin with deep traces of time, worn out by life. He unsheathed his tongue, spoke slowly as everyone did there, chunked his words and gave them an accent unfamiliar to me. No joke made him laugh. He says that when he was young he could chop wood, he could chop a lot, and now he couldn't. Now he just planted and burned ovens.

"We need lumberjacks," he said staring at me. "I've seen you walking, you're light on your feet. You'd be good at this. Stay. With us you can do something, and when you grow some, you might end up okay."

"Not yet. I have other ideas. If they don't work out, I'll find a way to let you know."

"That's good, think over things so that later, when the years fall on you, you have no regrets."

The man's enthusiasm became contagious. He was polite and quite the talker. Perhaps my presence brought back memories in him.

Tobías told me that a nice, purebred little Chinese man worked with him, but one day, a Galician came and said he was an oven technician and the Chinese man wanted to try him out, because according to the Galician, no one could beat him. The Chinese man wanted to try his luck and work with the newcomer to improve his situation.

"We liked the Galician's company," Tobías said. He spoke in a nice way and we were tired of hearing each other, but from the beginning, things started to go wrong. They couldn't agree. The Galician would tell him that he too was Spanish, and the Chinese man would tell him that in that case he too was Asian. There was always some controversy between them, but in the end, the Chinese man was the one working and the Galician gave orders. When he had a huge oven burning, and a little blue smoke came out, a sign that everything was on point, tragedy struck. From above, it began to make openings like mouths that spit out fireballs; one expanded since they had poured little dirt and hay on that side. It was the highest point and the Chinese man, Tumualdo said, scratched the ground with his fingers. He said things we couldn't understand, I suppose in Chinese. Yes, yes, it had to be Chinese."

"Galician, let's cover the fire pits with dirt and hay so they'll hold and the oven won't blow."

"Chino, not yet, I know when to do it."

"Galician, that big opening has to be covered, the oven is gonna blow."

"I'm the technician, and you can't know more than a technician."

The little Chinese man's head was clear as water and knew the misfortune about to come. A great flame came out of the biggest opening and smaller ones formed. The Galician calmly decided to go up only then. Meanwhile, the little Chinese man handed him a bucket of dirt and bunches of hay. With nothing more to do, the Chinese man sat down serenely to watch the technician work.

"I was just arriving," said Tobías. "I started to holler at the Chinese man to help the Galician who was roasting alive, but the Chinese man, with his head held high, either didn't know, didn't give a damn, or thought everything was lost, and said:

"He's the technician, the technician knows, the technician knows."

"I could only fan my hat in every direction and scream in desperation, but I could do nothing to help the poor Galician. The first thing that went into the opening was the bucket, then his hands trying to recover it, and his head followed; the feet were the last to exit, his feet in rope sandals with brand new white laces. They served to abate the smell of charred flesh, and mixing with the rubber and burnt rags, they seemed to be saying goodbye as they followed the man. The saddest sight was how the Galician went upside down on his way to Heaven.

"The little Chinese man had his reward. When the technician went up for his last trip, he left him in charge of the relatively new black hat he always wore. But he lost the oven and the partner in which he had placed his hopes. Perhaps that's why he never tired of saying:

"Even those who know get swallowed by the earth. You get swallowed when you least expect it."

"The technician got swallowed with his rope sandals and his brand-new laces. And the Galician must be remembering that he died for being a fool," Tobías said, "because the little Chinese man warned him ahead of time and he must be sorry. Maybe not. Maybe he's resting, but who knows. You hear that in Heaven everything is good, if the devil doesn't take you first. I tell folks, on the tenth anniversary of my death, say: Today Tobías began his rest. That's the time I need to start resting because I've worked so much. They say there's lots of nice things to see out there. I've never left this place, so I haven't seen them. Those who are doing bad things want to try good things, and those who are doing good things want to try bad things; no one can understand people. Tulopío knows it well because the Frenchman that comes around looking for alcohol says I'm an expert at making coal, and that here it's nice and pretty. He goes goofy with the parrots, the deer, the hutias, and any animal in the woods, and we don't look at them unless we want to eat them. It's not that I want to leave the woods, but damn, my friend, you get bored with living your entire life only on what they give you, always the same thing, and sometimes not so good things, 'cause some die before their time because of some trifle."

What happened to the Chinese man and the Galician left me thinking, but I wanted to take advantage of how much that man liked talking to find out what he might know about the Mexican Cross, the one from the cathedral of Mérida.

He told me it was true, that they carried it in a ship to Havana, and from there to who knows where. From there all ships left together in convoys toward Spain. They did so to avoid attacks from pirates meant to take them to different destinations. But the ship from Mérida was being followed and the pirates forced it toward land. They left it in María la Gorda. The entire treasure consists of six hundred gold bars, twenty múcuras[18] filled with gold coins, many candelabra, and the Virgin's crown of gold and precious stones. Christians of all types have shown interest in the case, but no one has found the burial place.

The coalman ended the subject with these words: "And you can be sure that people here shorten or lengthen, but few speak lies. I'm just saying, boy."

We had clear iced coffee that Tobías had stashed away, and I offered him cigarettes since he said he hadn't smoked in days. It was late, and the hammock called. I went convinced that it was easier to think pesetas would rain from the sky than to find treasure here on earth. I would have to leave no frond unturned in who knows how many acres of forest, swamp, and dog's tooth grass… I thought it impossible. I watched the glass-like moon for quite a while. If I'd had the means, I would've left at dawn.

---

[18] Earthenware jug of medium size, larger than the botija (*pitcher*), round and with a narrow opening.

I had to wait for someone to take me when they came for more fertilizer. The sea, the nesting parrots, and the sunsets began to lose their charm, but I kept hanging out at the caves and the beach until the last day.

I hopped on the cart and the bells on the oxen livened the countryside. Tulopío followed us on foot for a long stretch, and nearly screaming, he said goodbye with these words:

"Come back, boy, come back soon, a good spirit told me last night that great treasure awaits you."

Chapter 6

When your unspoiled eyes haven't soaked in the sheen and color of modern technology, it cannot be fathomed even in your best dream. When your ears are accustomed to answering a message transmitted by scant and often stale dialogue, when you still live on the edge of the woods, one fine day, someone comes along with a radio that says in big letters: RCA Victor. Then, maybe, without knowing it, a treasure has been given, magic itself. News, up-to-date and sensational news, is what grownups want, and the youngsters, music, loud music.

It was a time when a man ran Cuba for the second time. He took power by means of a military coup. The situation was troubled and complicated. All hope was placed on a young lawyer with sharp claws who had demonstrated the willingness to go for broke. He arrived on the Cuban coasts with eighty-two followers from Mexico. The difficult voyage hindered their arrival on the appointed date, and they couldn't reach the desired port of entry. The swamp, with its undergrowth, offered a grueling path, fraught with dizziness, vomiting, and fatigue. Injured by boots worn for the first time, and besieged by bad weather, a dreadful scene awaited.

Despite the setback and the reduced number of surviving young men, with much skill and help from local farmers, he managed to find protection in the mountains of the Sierra Maestra.

The famous American journalist, Herbert Lionel Matthews, met with the guerillas. The followers of these bearded warriors, who believed their leader dead, were encouraged by Matthews' work published in The New York Times, the first article on February 24, 1957 titled: "Cuban Rebel is Visited in Hideout" and two other postings on the 25th and the 26th, in addition to the revealing photograph of the 28th where he appears with Fidel Castro still in the fight. Tulopío was right: "Saints don't lie." It was all on radio news.

Now began the conflagration. Prieta felt supported not that she had taken to the battle with all her energy. And I inadvertently started to get involved. I used my trips to the village as a traveling salesman to run errands. Every day more and more abandoned the underground and marched to the mountains or any other hideout. The dawn wasn't at all peaceful. It brought action, always something new. Propaganda was necessary for it enabled participation from farmers, or at least, compliance with given direction. Ideas spread through the air like clouds of smoke, and though almost everybody knew where they came from, they wouldn't dare say either out of fear or out of complicity.
The entire country boiled. Women also participated with enthusiasm and desire for victory. I met two who after many stumbles found proper refuge.

Cuca the mare was confirmed as my unquestionable accomplice in my new adventure. She had the greatest task, carrying the women, and mine was to be cautious and scared. We had to move the women to the Canalta woods so they would be protected. In tight situations, they could make use of a natural cave that I thought only I knew. The greatest danger was in traveling through places unprotected by trees, so we always moved before the day brightened. In the afternoons, we returned by foot. I would have no justification if found on the mare at that time; it wasn't customary and could awaken suspicion. I took them to a tobacco house for some restless sleep unbeknownst to the owner. He never found out as we were careful to come into the house last and sneak out before the goats and the cow with its calf, leaving no trace.

Based on my parameters of youth in those days, the two girls seemed quite old. One of them was doubly persecuted because she could serve as bait to capture her boyfriend, a guerrilla chief fighting in the mountains. Among the most intense memories she held was of her last night in her village.

She was alone. An intermittent sound startled her, pebbles hitting her kitchen wall from the yard. With extreme caution, she opened the door, and from the trunk of the papaya tree came Alberto's unmistakable whistle. Her boyfriend had come at great risk. He had been in the city a few days waiting, never giving up on his goal. He needed to establish contact, evaluate battle strategies.

The night before it had become impossible to ignore the hunger. In near darkness, he approached an inn. Two intelligence officers appeared. One pointed a flashlight at the patrons while the other compared their faces to a photograph. They never saw him. He continued to scarf down the scarce hot food pretending not to notice them. He fooled death that time.

He had been followed from the moment he left the mountain, and to compromise someone else in such a difficult situation would have been his last option. But the desire to see his beloved was strong, he longed to touch her hair. Ana Maria didn't hesitate. He was there, and she knew that her man was weak and hungry. She brought him a glass of water and a plate with the food she had barely touched and went back quickly for a cup of coffee and a few cigarettes. There wasn't even time to quench the thirst. The house was surrounded. She woke up under a neighbor's coal stove not knowing that Alberto had escaped by running across the rooftops.

To be the refuge and custodian of two girls was an extension of what I was already doing. The delivery of messages and stocking of some foods for the guerrillas that were determined to open a new front in Guayabo was my strength in such adventurous activities. They had improvised an encampment on a lot filled with marabú with only one access, a path no wider than a thread, pregnant with thorns on both sides. They were careful to protect the entrance. They placed guards to deal with anyone coming in or anything unexpected. I went to "the heights" only a few times not wanting to complicate my life even more, and I was well warned by Prieta: "Don't tell them about the two women, and much less tell the women about them." And as I said, there was much contact with these and those, so I bore in mind that loose lips sink ships and to never go where you're not wanted.

I preferred dealing with men because I learned a lot. Each day I came out of the shell more and working with them was interesting. I even learned to shoot in those woods. Near the river where they practiced, I pulled my first trigger. A woodpecker was busy making a hole high up a royal palm, maybe for the female to nest. When it fell nearly fleeced from the bullet, I thought myself a good shot and ready to enter combat, though I felt guilty for killing the poor animal. It lost its life in the accomplishment of a noble task.

Only Prieta and I oversaw the transfer of whatever was riskiest, most compromising, from the village. From a house in the city, I managed to take a box full of ammunition. It was essential for the battle, but I had to pass the jail that held many youngsters detained for insurrection. While in transit and thinking I had cleared out safely, Corporal Bellón stopped me before I reached the place where I had left Cuca to ask me what I had in the sack. I said mangos, but they were green, they were heavy and bruising my back, that's why I had put them in a box and was carrying them over the shoulder. I felt some relief at hearing my own credible answer and his face didn't show any sign of doubt. Out of laziness, not wanting to bend over, he didn't look. He asked my name. I told him, and he wrote it down. He also wanted to know my two last names. I immediately reached the conclusion that I had made a mistake that could result in grave consequences. Calmly, he inspected me from top to bottom. He also asked me if I was related to the folks selling flowers. I felt harassed and I stretched my answer as much as I could with the intention of diverting his attention.

"No, just Hi and Bye. We sell white and yellow mangos and red guavas, and they almost always bring flowers for dead people and turkey snot, sometimes sunflowers or roses. Almost every time I go by the cemetery, I see them near the door leaning against the wall of the deceased that were rich in life. They hide from the sun and their flowers always look wilted in their vases. I don't trust any of them."

I knew them as well as my shoes, and really some relation existed, but I couldn't get embroiled any further. The box remained on the floor. From the effort I needed to make to lift it, he might've been able to tell I was carrying lead. I pretended not to have any trouble. That's when it all went to hell. He asked me about Aurelio. Bellón's face probably changed color when I answered no that the name didn't sound familiar. Aurelio was the chief of the Guayabo front, quite well-known among the farmers, and I'm sure the answer didn't convince him, because he pulled out the pencil and paper again, wrote something down, and with a scowl told me to disappear.

A few steps away, a young man of pleasant appearance carrying something like rolled up papers in his pants pocket, the right hand in the other, gave me a half-smile when I walked by. He had a brave stance, and was inconspicuous, but I'm sure he remained attentive to the questioning by Corporal Bellón. I watched him from the corner of my eye for quite a distance, almost all the way to Cuca, where I felt safe. I went into alleys, tight little paths where we barely fit, she and I, but it was the only alternative until we arrived at the thick pine grove. I ran away. They were probably following me to learn my destination. I was almost dead when I arrived at the appointed place. My balls, "guevos" as old Arsenio used to say, were up in my throat, and my friends were waiting for me with theirs under their hats. I decided to say nothing about what happened. Then they wouldn't know that I was flagged; that could have been my last trip in those adventures. I'd screwed up and I alone had to find a way to fix it.

The activities and trips continued. I felt stronger after each one, and I considered myself a person of importance, and if I wasn't, at least my work spoke for itself. Before solving one problem, I'd stumble upon another. The task of blowing up the Guayabo bridge was urgent for the purpose of cutting off communications between the big town and the village, and to advertise the vitality of that guerrilla group willing to accomplish great tasks and be victorious in combat.

The conclusion was that I was ideal to save their necks when needed. No one was to know that this time I was to meet two guerrillas that would be waiting for me in a house not far from the barracks in the big town.

I went in the direction indicated with no mishaps along the way. I had combed that place while hawking my merchandise. A blond woman who looked about sixty, according to my calculations, but was still firm and shapely, greeted me in the living room of her house. After offering me a cup of coffee worth five, she took me into a bedroom where she introduced me to a tall youth with a classic farmer's face who looked as if he hadn't had a hot meal in a week. The other blond man obviously hadn't been working in the sun and spoke in a particular way I recognized. Very quickly I realized that he was American. Since I was a boy I could pick them out from a mile away. He seemed brand new. He looked at me with tender eyes, puzzled perhaps to see me so scrawny and involved in grown men's problems. He demonstrated much knowledge and I felt a great desire to go with him. Perhaps he would've preferred to come with me to Guayabo with my people, but in Havana they had placed him in another front, a place more troublesome and superior in number of guerrillas and objectives to meet. They gave me a little package, and I ran hell for leather out of there.

I couldn't help myself and told the chief about the American. I was afraid I might've fallen into a raid. They had asked me a lot of questions and the skinny one with him, who smoked a lot, perhaps out of fear or to abate his hunger, even knew what corner of the knoll I lived in; besides, they told me soon they would be paying a visit to the folks in Guayabo, but not before they established contact with me so I could serve as their mediator. I also told Aurelio how they were interested in obtaining information on the whereabouts of La Mora. I knew she was in prison, but I played dumb; talking too much isn't good and much less when you don't know the people and you're scared. I had a sudden eerie feeling. Aurelio was discreet, or probably didn't believe my story about the American, but I stayed silent, I kept to myself my intentions of leaving with those who were better positioned if I felt threatened. Improving in any way possible had been in my sights since I was a boy.

Everything was in place to blow up the bridge. I didn't want to miss the event for which I had worked so hard. The weapons were greased and ready in case we had to fight, but Aurelio was always two steps ahead and he noticed that the munitions weren't ready. If things got ugly, they would search for them like a needle in a haystack, and no amount of camouflage would keep them from getting caught like wet chicks if airplane squadrons discovered their encampment in the marabú. Total annihilation due to lack of prevention would be a shame. They didn't know I had been flagged, so I was the best choice to complete the mission. Taking a chance was my only option; after all, if you do it once, you do it twice.

This time I went in my good clothes, low-cut shoes, plenty of Palmolive pomade in my hair, well-parted on the side. When the folks on the bus saw me, they started whistling and catcalling. And I went along with it by saying I was going to ask for a girlfriend who lived in Sampollo, and that's why I was leaving early and with no other means of transportation. Cheo Totí hollered from the last seat:

"You're a lazy freeloader and you play dumb, but you know more than you let on, and when you least expect it, they're gonna beat the tar out of you! I smiled at him with no malice and didn't respond. The sly old dog, as always, fucking around.

The munitions were in the Los Criollitos hardware store. I was supposed to give the owner a note. I was told he was a large blond man, but it turned out there were two blond men and they were both large. When I finally decided on the older one, I quickly realized that once again, the little peasant failed. The note said: "Send me the matches to stir this fire." That man began to shake when he read the note. What a big coward!

The night before had been a big night. Eleven bombs exploded in different places in the village and everyone was drowsy and startled. I had to tell him that the note was sent by the baker in the corner, but my story failed, he didn't give me the matches. The other blond man, who heard us from nearby, and knowing that I had made a mistake, gave a sign only I noticed. He waited for me in the next block with "the matches" I wanted.

There were two boxes. I would take them just as the blond man gave them to me. I'd learned the more you hide something, the easier it is to be seen. Walking up a street, I saw police officers across from the bivouac bringing in the two women I hadn't been able to transport that morning.

My skin must've been olive. Pomade dripped down my neck, though to my relief, no one even noticed me. Everyone was focused on the two women. With heads held high, they went willingly. I was anguished by my inability to do anything. As soon as I had a chance, I disappeared, as always, imagining that my steps were being followed. Cuca's trot on dry earth made me think someone was behind us. I tried not to think. Get there, get there, I needed to reach my people.

My troubles made me forget the appointed place to deliver the boxes. I didn't stop until I got to the actual rebel encampment. They must've thought I was a weakling because the words wouldn't come out, but I wasn't worried. I'd have time to show them who I was.

Aurelio was right. After blowing up the bridge, there was an almighty mess. New strategies were needed. The airplanes wouldn't stop circling. The men, fenced in by the marabú, would be exposed to death by fire if the planes threw flames all around. They were all willing to die "a necessary death;" still, not one would be left standing. It would've been criminal for that to happen, and I couldn't just sit idly by.

Tata was a part of the siege. He had become a "casquito[19];" he was in great need and the Army paid him. I had no alternative but to talk to Grandfather, who had a good horse, but I don't remember with what excuse I asked for it. If the Royal Guard saw me, they would notice the horse and not me. I would've preferred to stay with the other kids flying kites on Las Cañas hill, but my sense of duty wouldn't allow it. As I did frequently, I rode bareback for lack of a saddle.

I went to see Tata to tell him the truth. Those young men of extraordinary valor hadn't thought of the consequences. They would resist and were willing to be burned alive like the colonists did to that brave Indian, Hatuey[20]. Their desire for victory was strong, but the truth was that sooner or later they would be making desperate calls on God's help having no conceived way to organize a retreat.

Tata hadn't estimated what could happen either. No. He did so because, I, his cousin, asked him. There was great tension, but to everyone's relief, playing the Yuka Drums had not been suspended. Inherited from the African culture, every Saturday night whites and blacks danced, which on this occasion served to detract from the reality and ease the strain of the dismal atmosphere. Without wasting a single minute or missing a detail, I

---

[19] Term used by the populace in reference to members of the Army, based on the frequent use of military helmets (cascos).
[20] Leader of the first native rebellion against Spanish colonization; he was burned alive.

gave the coordinates to Aurelio. "The rebels" opened the footpath during the night at the spot Tata was assigned to cover the siege. And by the time the moon rose, without a fixed course, they had all escaped in single file.

The worst moment was when Alberto returned from the mountain to make contact with the rebels of another guerrilla front. Perhaps the contact he sought was Macaulay, the American I had seen at the house of the woman of sixty. However, it was easy to tell from far away that the man was not Cuban and surely they wouldn't expose him so many times.

In a jeep, inside a metal barrel the owner used to pick up food for the pigs, Alberto waited and waited impatiently. This time he didn't fail. At the appointed time, he retreated to his hideout, a little wooden house with a thatched roof. The road was a few steps away, but it was a lonely place with little traffic. I lived two diagonal kilometers away. I'd brought him some food that day and a letter, but he wasn't there. I left everything in the place and manner agreed. I didn't take the wide path but crossed the woods and the guava orchards. Two unknown men were walking away from the crossroads. Once near me, I heard parts of a whispered conversation: "The nightmare is over. Today is the day."

A sad feeling came over me. It was a heavy load I carried in a mind and body still fragile. The image of Alberto took hold of me. He was pale skinned, black hair, perfect teeth always showing in a cheerful smile.

All the girls wanted to win him over when he worked in the cafeteria. He always had a compliment at the ready for them. But on that day, I saw him weakened, no strength left in him. When I got home, I told Mamma and added that I wouldn't return to that place. She must've been happy with my decision, even if she didn't know the half of my involvement. She said to let go of bad thoughts, that good mangos and avocados were ready for me to sell in the village the next day, and that I should leave at dawn. Try as I might, I couldn't let go of the unpleasant images.

It was the first weekend in December. The starry night was cool. I was supposed to catch some fire beetles so I could have a competition with the neighborhood kids to see who was the owner of the bug with the brightest green light. We'd put them on their backs to find out which one could jump and land on its feet to continue living free. If I won, for a week they'd have to call me Champion.

I heard the buzzing of bullets coming from where I had been searching for bugs. It was around nine when the shooting started. No one could sleep. In the darkness, the desperate voices of farmers traveled trying to learn what was happening. We knew what it was. It couldn't be anything else. The moment was increasingly painful as we understood what great resistance that man had offered, alone under a blitz. Alberto didn't stop fighting until the last shot. When he thought everything was lost and convinced there was no way out, he sought protection behind the front door as if he wanted to grab by the neck the first man who dared come in or maybe snatch his weapon and continue the fight.

Certain of their success in battle, the men removed Alberto's body riddled with bullet holes. Even the vase he used as a urinal was pockmarked, and the white rose bush in the yard refused to continue living.

The next morning, talk about the events quickly circulated. "Corporal Bellón participated in the operation because he wanted his mistress to see him photographed in such situations." The news made the headline of the village newspaper with a picture of the Corporal's delighted face.

Prieta had to leave in a hurry. Not many days later, after I finished my sales, I went to the jail to bring cigarettes for the two women. They weren't there, and no one could tell me why. I suspected they had set them free and I couldn't imagine they knew what had happened. A few days earlier, Bellón had given the order not to lose sight of me anytime I came into the village. He was certain I was looking for trouble. He caught me just as I was about to merge onto the street. I looked him in the eye in spite of my thirteen years, and wouldn't you know it, with a small body and scant flesh on it, I felt big. He felt defied, and just like that, he locked me up.

I fell in with a group of insubordinate youths, and I learned about a list with the names of the most implicated, and of the possibility that mine might be among them. It was the result of putting my foot in my mouth and giving my name and last name in a moment of difficulty. On Holy Innocents' Day, after much negotiation, a friend of Uncle Manuel's saved me from my Calvary.

Those were the last days of the year 1958. The city of Santiago de Cuba was fenced in by rebel troops. Two columns had arrived from the east to the center. Che Guevara was traveling the country for the first time after two years of battle in Sierra Maestra. Once he had made agreements with other rebel forces in the mountains, and all the village towns in the city were under his control, he prepared to take the city of Santa Clara. He examined the situation and planned each detail. And after a short time, he began with the derailment of the armored train that carried the trappings of war toward the east. He had opened an entryway and from there he led the combat. He placed defenses, defied the snipers, and inch by inch, he advanced leading his men. He was in the most important central city: Santa Clara surrendered to him. It was the end, the mortal blow, and the greatest feat of his life as a guerrilla. The President of the Republic had no other recourse but to flee. He couldn't bear the great blow and at dawn he left with his closest circle.

Chapter 7

A kapok tree announced entry to the village from the west. It brought us riders and our beasts soft breezes and abundant shade to begin our street cries while wandering around in search of buyers. Our fresh fruits and vegetables, carried from far away, represented the livelihood of many families.

I had been initiated into these tasks with quite a bit of success when I still needed help to get on Cuca and had the reins handed to me, which made it difficult for me to sell because I couldn't get off the animal. I was required to educate my voice, to give strength to my lungs, and develop cries that would be inviting so the housewives would come looking for me. Our dialogue was entertaining. They haggled to no end, and I would lose innocently in the beginning, and sometimes returned home with the merchandise on the mare's back. When I grew a little, I fought back like a tiger, I went door to door and fixed my prices according to the buyer's appearance. They were almost always women. I liked my trade. I saw results when I returned home with some money or something to eat. And most importantly, I learned, I learned a lot; it was my first and greatest school.

That day wasn't a good one, sales were poor. Tired and hungry, I decided to go to Calle Real. I would treat myself to some rest. My saddlebags, worn by time and heavy loads, embarrassed me. Among so many well-dressed, nice-smelling people with cheerful faces, I thought myself smaller and more slouched than I actually was. The hat I wore wasn't a good fit. The stretch I walked gave me the impression that this section of the village was not right for salesmen like me. I noticed they didn't have what I carried, but no one seemed interested in buying my mangos. There were elegant stores, trinket stores, and grocery stores of a different sort, well displayed. I thought I should be one of those clean and well-dressed men in new green strolling down the street, but for now I had to resign myself to visiting the village and tell everyone what I saw.

With the load over my shoulders and shame on my forehead, I arrived at the door of the store La Colosal. In one go, the saddlebags and I fell to the floor without noticing that we were in the way of those coming to the stall for magazines and newspapers. It would be unforgivable if someone tripped because of my carelessness, so I moved. Unintentionally, the change in location was more favorable for the panorama I wanted to survey, the comings and goings of people.

From there I observed how the "olive greens," some of which I knew, gave the women eager looks. They found all of them pretty and they flirted with every one of them. They were anxious to win them over. Many of the women had walked great distances, early in the morning, to see the men, and if possible to acquiesce: it was a fever.

Two bearded men came in a military vehicle looking for newspapers. The first one out was the military chief of the province. The other, in a black beret with a star on the forehead, stood in front of me. He seemed older, just another soldier, but something different in his gaze startled me, and then I had no doubt. He didn't need identification. I recognized him in a flash. It was Che, always with his shirt pockets full of cigars and papers. He looked tired, I thought. I hadn't quite composed myself enough to greet him when a burst of questions came at me: how much for the mangos, where did I bring them from, how much money did I make... He made a comment about coming from the same direction where I told him I lived, as I understood, having just inspected the production of copper.

"You live in a forest. You must not have time to go to school."

"No, I stopped going a long time ago.".

"The Revolution didn't happen for this, you have to go to school, you have lots to learn." He wrote down the information I gave him. I offered him the best mangos, he thanked me but didn't accept them.

"Sell them, sell them and earn your money," he said while he rubbed my head, and with urgency, always pressed for time, he took his newspapers and disappeared with a wave as the village was beginning to congregate.

It took me a while to shake off the surprise, and I speculated that I should have told him who I was and all the tap dancing I did to help with his victory but, on second thought, it was best I didn't. It could be presumptuous of me and cunning where it didn't belong. I'd been taught that things should be done at the right time and shouldn't be exploited for personal gain.

A week later, I received a document signed by the Minister of Education that allowed me to continue my studies in the capital. I knew Che's hand was in it. Bienvenido was right. I was growing up in a hurry and in trouble. Perhaps that was why I frequently had to take a step back. But now the doors of Heaven had opened for me. My farmer head was in a mighty muddle, but I had no right to waver.

I left home with tears nearly running down my cheeks from fear of the unknown and how far away I was being taken. I looked ridiculous lowering my head as we went under the tunnel in the bay of Havana because I thought it would fall on me. I paid dearly for that and other crude peasant moments that I won't tell out of embarrassment. My insecurities were reinforced by the multiple stops made by the novice omnibus driver to ask for directions so we could continue toward our destination with no further loss of time. It was his first long trip too.

According to someone who knew the place, we were leaving Havana behind. Within the group of eastern beaches, appeared Tarará, with its white and ultra-fine

98

sand, our destination. A residential vacation area turned educational city. That northern sea had no connection with the southern sea in Maria La Gorda where I first noticed the difference between swimming in the fresh water of creeks, and salt water, where you swim light as a fish. This ocean seemed calmer and of softer tones, enchanting.

The first few days, I sat under a pine and watched everything that surrounded me without forgetting the memory of La Esperanza. My eyes, not used to what they were seeing now, were restless and astonished wanting to capture everything.

In my eagerness to investigate, I learned that the beautiful house where they had brought me, and which I already called "mine," was the first one inhabited by Ernesto Guevara in Havana for more than two months. According to my friend Homero, he came for some rest to recover from pulmonary emphysema, possibly caused by prolonged time as a guerrilla and a bout of asthma he had just brought under control, but he was not made for rest.

The bedrooms seemed to me excessive in size. I was given an enormous one upstairs, with a huge marble bathroom, and another tiny room next to it. In time, I came to know that it was a walk-in closet. There were many bedrooms, but that one, my room, was the one Che had chosen for his repose. I don't know how, but Homero appeared to know everything on good authority. When I went downstairs every day, I found myself in a great living room, the one Che used for his meetings and contacts. Day by day, I began to adapt to the place. It is said, and it's true, that it's easy to get used to the good life.

Not far from my house/ hostel, was the vacation home of Carlos Prio Socarró, former President of the Republic of Cuba. It was located in the heights, as was mine, and it was possibly more beautiful. I was proud of its proximity because he was from the province where I was born, and even if I never got to see him, his name was familiar. A teenager enjoying every detail and incorporating them into my legacy, I saw and lived unimaginable things. I thought I was in Paradise. Tarará changed my life. My longing for home didn't keep me from hunting for new possibilities. And as always, I idealized the future.

I won't deny that I underestimated those adolescents with stories similar to mine. I arrived with an inflated ego believing my story and the registration letter with Che's recommendation gave me an advantage in overcoming obstacles and placed me at a superior level than the rest. I had no qualms; from that point on, I wanted to rise. Celia Cruz said it: "Nothing compares to Havana."

It all started at the time of registration when they asked me about my level of education. Without thinking, I answered "eighth." I was following Catulo's principle, who once said: "Fear nothing, cutting balls is how you learn to geld."

100

It's fortunate that God squeezes but he doesn't strangle. I shared my bedroom with my roommate Homero, The Odyssey always under his arm, a book that I and so many like me, didn't even know existed. Through Homero the student, we learned that the Homer said to be the author of the book, also wrote The Iliad, and that we shouldn't envy Greek and Trojan heroes because we too were epic and each one of us had a little of Aquiles and Odysseus. The only differences were that we were all vulnerable, our Penelopes would not wait that long for us, and our stories would die in anonymity.

I never asked him if that was his real name, but Homero was truly admirable. He was my tutor and I never paid him a cent. Everything I asked, which was plenty, he could answer: How does the water get into the coconut? What came first, the chicken or the egg? Why does the crab walk backwards, and why is the turtle never in a hurry? He knew everything. And to leave no unanswered question, he also knew where the gnat laid its eggs. He was the one who, one problem after another, took me from a failing fourth grade all the way to a grade higher than the one I had claimed. I made efforts and I also did what I do best. I created funny situations to make me look good when the teachers asked their questions, since it all often sounded like Chinese to me.

But I wasn't the only one to benefit from Homero's knowledge and good will. Some were troublemakers not easy to beat, and we all had reasons for thanking him.

One night there was a big dust-up. It so happened that he was explaining the cause for the war between Greeks and Trojans:

"Helen, the most beautiful woman in all of Greece, and the wife of King Menelaus, took off with Paris, son of the King of Troy. It was a famous kidnapping." Homero told us.

"So the war started because of a whore, because of cheating. My father's right: this whoring thing comes from way back, way, way back," Pedro defiantly intervened.

We all wanted to give our opinions, and the pandemonium was endless. No matter how much good ol' Homero tried to keep the matter serious, ignorance was ahead of the legend. He couldn't quiet such blazing sentiments. That was one of the few times he decided not to finish the lesson.

Each one from his bunk would blurt some tasteless joke, quite racy at times. I wasn't sleepy, and I remembered La Esperanza with everything in it, and Miss Montaner, my Margarita, my beloved little flower, intelligent and kind. Her simplicity was such that it was impossible for her to leave the bubble in which she had been raised. How I would've liked to see the ocean and everything around me with her by my side, filling me with questions, and I pretending I knew everything! No one had told me about Socrates, from whom I learned that we would begin to know that we would know nothing once we knew something. How much we would learn together! Her letters were limited in vocabulary, but tender, with drawings of little wild flowers that filled me with memories and nostalgia.

Then, to boast to the boys in my mischief team and to convince them of my skills as a ladies' man, I encouraged them to get up so I could read them the letters from my Margarita, which they would greatly enjoy. Without a doubt, humans are self-sufficient by nature and attack if they find a breach.

Said and done, they had a great time. They were so captivated by my initiative, that soon the activity became habitual. Those rascals waited for the mailman as anxiously as I did. What interest they had in my readings! Perhaps to imitate Homero, I would read them once and again; more than read, I dramatized them. On the night of the latest reading, when my inspiration had risen to its highest point, I understood the reason for their deep silence, including our "teacher's." They were falling in love with Margarita, I saw it in their eyes. Out of breath, I opened the window, nearly choking to death, trapped. I had taken myself to the slaughter house.

But some things are like the devil and keep a rope around your neck, sometimes tighter, sometimes looser. One evening we escaped to Taramar to a café located on the avenue that leads to the city of Havana from the west, and to Varadero beach from the east. We intended to stop there to scope out the females, more than to eat.

Perhaps influenced by Paris, son of Priam and brother of Hector, the one Homero spoke of again and again, I fell into love's web. It was a stroke of luck. I justified Adam's weakness. No rib was better sacrificed! I found a pair of dark eyes that could split a coconut with a single look. Clarita, she said was her name. I attacked on all fronts and with all the artillery I had acquired by way of knock downs and thumps. I couldn't fail. I told her she was the most beautiful of all flowers, that I would take her to see the Capitol, the Morro and San Carlos de la Cabaña inside and out, that we would stroll Havana's pier from start to finish, and to clinch it, I told her "she was the most beautiful cowgirl in La Hinojosa". When I was done, out of breath and nearly faint, Clarita answered that all the others said exactly the same thing or very similar. I thought I would die. I would not be able to repeat so many beautiful phrases and I didn't have any others. I was disappointed. I, who could lasso the little peasant girls in one shot, failed. With pursed lips and furrowed brow, I let my eyes fixate on her well-rounded legs until I could find a way to withdraw.

The next day, at the same time, Clarita came, but I had arrived a few minutes earlier. After that day, we wouldn't make dates, but we were rigorously punctual to the encounters. We talked about everything, she more than I because I was concentrating on the attack so the king wouldn't suffer another check mate. A few days later, disappointed again, exhausted from the useless effort, I searched for patience, I invoked Napoleon Bonaparte. A timely disengagement would mean victory in battle. I was thinking of an excuse to disappear like a scared dog, when unexpectedly, she surprised me with a new approach, pure honey. Now my ego inflated even more. I had captured her.

Tarará became my celestial palace and I was the archangel Saint Rafael. Clarita's nearly constant company wasn't enough. All the beautiful things I was seeing, even the air I breathed, the sea, any pieces of sky I could reach, I wanted to give her. It was a state of ecstasy I had never experienced. Stimulants abounded. Every day we learned or discovered something new. It all exceeded my expectations.

Morales, the principal of the educational city, a cultured man and good pedagogue, spoke to us about our need for a formal education. He formed sports teams and workshops so that in addition to academics, we would develop other skills. Excited, I participated in anything and everything. Sports were my best option. I was good with the bat and I was throwing good pitches, so I thought myself in the big leagues. I was always the pitcher, and when I didn't win, at least I tied. And as you might think, I would join whatever workshop resulted most attractive to me. Painting won out. Morales promoted a contest and said all the workshop members had to participate. The piece selected for first place would be given to Fidel Castro, who would be visiting in the near future. That was enough rope to move me.

I took to the task with all my strength. Clarita would be my inspiration. I would paint her portrait. I felt such tenderness toward her when she smiled that sometimes I stopped painting to get involved in other more amusing activities. Those were unforgettable moments charged also with immaturity and juvenile notions. A week later, the face, which up to now had no connection to the original, began to gather such power that it concerned me. It became an abstract of the Cuban brunette. The memory of what happened with Margarita's letters and the infatuation of my classmates hammered on my mind to the point of stealing my hunger for food, my sleep.

I entered the workshop expecting to be alone. I intended to spend the afternoon making the final modifications: the position of the neck, highlights on her curly black hair whicht reached her waist. From the door, her keen gaze startled me. As if escaping from the canvas, Clarita's expression transmitted a message, her big black amber eyes rebuked me. I knew what she was trying to tell me, malice threatened. With one angry pull of my hands, I took the canvas down from the easel and hid it as quickly as possible where no one could find it. I couldn't trip over the same stone twice. If I wasn't careful, Fidel himself would fall in love with her, and I'd be fighting a losing battle. The little peasant boy would be left sitting on the bench once more.

No one gave credit to my excuse for the withdrawal of the painting, but Clarita, in keeping with the premise that "sane love is not love", justified my desire to paint something different, one of the beautiful landscapes of Guayabo. I was sure Fidel had knowledge about the guerrilla front that opened there during the period of struggle. I would have the opportunity to tell him that I had been a guerrilla, or better said, "a little of everything". Convinced that I would win, I saw an opportunity to inform him that it was urgent he rebuilt the bridge we demolished. The farmers still had to use a detour under awful conditions. The truck turned bus by the Chinchilla family couldn't go all the way to El Fangal. The peasants had to walk a great deal, and I felt complicit in the blasting. I knew that a chain is only as strong as its weakest link, and they didn't deserve such punishment. Likewise, I took for granted that the painting I now planned to paint would bring Fidel memories of the Sierra Maestra. Besides, since thinking costs nothing, I even believed that he might be quite pleased with such a special gift.

Once calm, that's what I painted, a bucolic landscape. The canvas showed a high hill in the background, La Chiva, in the shape of a grayish Egyptian pyramid. On the right side, the river, the royal palm with clusters of palmiche, and a bunch of fronds with the fiber still hanging. The oxen and the farmer plowing turned out extremely well thanks to Clarita's critique.

Principal Morales visited often. He would stop to look at my painting and insisted that I should have anything I needed. I tried to act as natural as possible, I asked for nothing. I needed to make a great impression.

The contest grew in significance. We all anxiously waited for the moment when the award would be presented. Myself, I planned trips to the beach and long walks with Clarita to ease the nerves. We went all the way to the Capitol one Sunday. We toured many of its beautiful rooms and we saw the original twenty-five carat diamond belonging to Tsar Nicholas II of Russia. It marked the zero point in the network of Cuban roads.

I had been led to believe that I was good at painting and, always the optimist, I assumed it was true. The day of the award was indescribable. I took first place, I hit the nail right on the head. Painting became an obsession. But since life's roads tend to twist more than wet ropes, as my grandmother used to say, and I needed to plant my feet firmly on the ground, when I received a transfer to another education center, I went. I had no way of learning the fate of the first landscape I painted and gave me so much joy.

Chapter 8

Every day brought something new in the form of motivation or a variety of new activities. At some point I learned that all the students of the new school were taking a long trip in a sugar cane train toward the East to harvest coffee.

With a pouch at the waist, every morning we'd go deep into Sierra Maestra to collect what would become, as they say, the black nectar of white gods. We considered ourselves fortunate. We were distributed around the hamlet of El Hombrito and were eager to learn about Che's presence there during the war. He had surely left his mark, so finding a shell of his Browning machine gun would've been a great prize. We found some others, but not his.

Even with the missile crisis already in progress, we remained at our posts. A severe case of the flu almost wiped me out. They decided to send me home. I was forced to travel across the country under maximum defense readiness warning. Unrecognizable from the illness, gangly, and sounding like a rooster in heat, I arrived home.

La Esperanza was nothing but weapons and men in olive green that blended with nature that rainy October. I found my family not quite scared but expecting to disappear at any moment like Matías Pérez[21].

I became one more in that human swarm blanketed by thick shrubbery wet from the rain. It was probably ignorance that allowed me to enjoy such mobilization with confidence. I remember with delight, on the dining room table, a little red flower in a glass jar with water that Ñata had the sense to put in because, according to her, the house should be pleasant to the eyes of so many people, young people primarily. Lucky for me, the sanitation personnel encampment, where I was given immediate medical treatment, was located on the left edge of the trail, at around three hundred meters from my house. Among all the happenings, the enigmatic theft of the American church bell is what I remember most clearly. René, a hairstylist not well adapted to extreme situations, also disappeared. Such things could not be imagined by people willing to give their lives for socialism, worse even, at the precise moment when death crept right under our noses. The central military kitchen was in close proximity to the portico that served as entrance to the place known to be the church. Che had been there two days after the commotion to find the disappeared valuable item had begun. But everyone maintained their silence when faced with the Western Chief, who was dealing with the grave situation in Cuba.

---

[21] Cuban historical figure who disappeared in a hot air balloon in the nineteenth century.

And fortunately, especially for his superiors, he learned nothing about the bell. The reason for his visit, it was said, was to check on supplies and to review combat readiness. "The high-ranked" made sure not to let him know about the intrigue afoot.

The task of investigating fell on Sargent Marín. One by one he interviewed every recruit that might've had any connection with the event. During questioning, the balance tipped in favor of René as possible architect of the deed.

"Juan, who do you think was the bell theft instigator?"

"Sargent, I can't put my hands over the fire for anyone. I participated in conversations about it, but that's a long way from taking what is not mine. I really have no idea. That's sickening."

"Can you recall what René said about it?"

"Sargent, René said that the bell here was not as big as others he had seen, that almost all bells in Cuba come from other countries and he was told that when we heard this one ring, it would mean that bombs were falling from one end of the island to another. I think that would be a sign that we were lost. But let me tell you, that doesn't mean I was happy to see it gone. Between you and me, Sargent, at the precise moment of my death, I don't want to hear it. But again, I don't think it's as easy as he said. We're ready and we'll win. These days, when you hear Fidel speak, he sounds more pissed off than ever. And he's not gonna swallow that pill their forcing on him. Haven't you noticed that he just as easily puts down Americans than Russians? He's like a bucking colt demanding his Five Points. I don't know who would do it, but they'll have to take his throat stones and his nuts before he gives up Cuba. And Che doesn't talk, but don't be fooled, they say he bites in silence. Didn't you see him when he was here? He didn't bare his teeth for anyone, not even to light his cigar with an ember. He didn't even want anyone to hand him one or offer him coffee. I got the impression that he didn't believe half of what they told him, or he was thinking of something else. He liked even less all the scrambling to see him, he was very serious, surly even. Not me. I went to pick up a huge pile of yucca shells for Rupertino to throw in the trash. Pigs can't eat them, yucca shells are poison to them, they make their insides burst. But about what I was saying, to tell you the truth, I was blown away by Che. My heart skipped a beat because I could tell that he's quick on the trigger. Everybody straightened up if he looked in their eyes, though he didn't seem bigheaded. Now I have something to tell in this dry life of mine. What a man, Sargent, what a man!"

"Yes, Juan, I know, I saw him, but please return to the question and be brief. What did René say about the bell?"

"Chief, every morning René had a different story to tell, what he dreamed that night, which I thought was made up, about the blessed bell; it was a daily feeding. I think he's a big, spineless coward. What can I tell you,

112

he's not good people! You never knew if he was telling the truth or lying. One morning, I heard Rungo, the old man that almost drags himself around carrying a little stew from the kitchen for his pigs, he was saying that it's true that the bell sounds beautiful, but there was only one person who rang it right. It was the bell's caretaker. But he said that man also took off with the Americans when he saw that everything was equal for everybody. See ya later. Really, that's all I know. Sargent, don't get your head twisted, folks tend to talk nonsense and be wicked so as not to think about what's coming."

"Thank you for the information. You're dismissed, and please, tell comrade Ruperto to come in immediately."

"Ruperto, do you understand the gravity of the case we're working on?"

"Hold on, Sargent. According to my father, on paper I'm Ruperto, but I answer to Rupertino. Also, I know nothing about nobody having any gravity or illness."

"Please, Ruperto, calm down, take your time before you answer. What do you know about the missing bell?

"Sargent, René said that the bell here was not as big as others he had seen, that almost all bells in Cuba come from other countries and he was told that when we heard this one ring, it would mean that bombs were falling from one end of the island to another. I think that would be a sign that we were lost. But let me tell you, that doesn't mean I was happy to see it gone. Between you and me, Sargent, at the precise moment of my death, I don't want to hear it. But again, I don't think it's as easy as he said. We're ready and we'll win. These days, when you hear Fidel speak, he sounds more pissed off than ever. And he's not gonna swallow that pill their forcing on him. Haven't you noticed that he just as easily puts down Americans than Russians? He's like a bucking colt demanding his Five Points. I don't know who would do it, but they'll have to take his throat stones and his nuts before he gives up Cuba. And Che doesn't talk, but don't be fooled, they say he bites in silence. Didn't you see him when he was here? He didn't bare his teeth for anyone, not even to light his cigar with an ember. He didn't even want anyone to hand him one or offer him coffee. I got the impression that he didn't believe half of what they told him, or he was thinking of something else. He liked even less all the scrambling to see him, he was very serious, surly even. Not me. I went to pick up a huge pile of yucca shells for Rupertino to throw in the trash. Pigs can't eat them, yucca shells are poison to them, they make their insides burst. But about what I was saying, to tell you the truth, I was blown away by Che. My heart skipped a beat because I could tell that he's quick on the trigger. Everybody straightened up if he looked in their eyes, though he didn't seem bigheaded. Now I have something to tell in this dry life of mine. What a man, Sargent, what a man!"

"Yes, Juan, I know, I saw him, but please return to the question and be brief. What did René say about the bell?"

"Chief, every morning René had a different story to tell, what he dreamed that night, which I thought was made up, about the blessed bell; it was a daily feeding. I think he's a big, spineless coward. What can I tell you, he's not good people! You never knew if he was telling the truth or lying. One morning, I heard Rungo, the old man that almost drags himself around carrying a little stew from the kitchen for his pigs, he was saying that it's true that the bell sounds beautiful, but there was only one person who rang it right. It was the bell's caretaker. But he said that man also took off with the Americans when he saw that everything was equal for everybody. See ya later. Really, that's all I know. Sargent, don't get your head twisted, folks tend to talk nonsense and be wicked so as not to think about what's coming."

"Thank you for the information. You're dismissed, and please, tell comrade Ruperto to come in immediately."

"Sargent, René said that the bell here was not as big as others he had seen, that almost all bells in Cuba come from other countries and he was told that when we heard this one ring, it would mean that bombs were falling from one end of the island to another. I think that would be a sign that we were lost. But let me tell you, that doesn't mean I was happy to see it gone. Between you and me, Sargent, at the precise moment of my death,

115

I don't want to hear it. But again, I don't think it's as easy as he said. We're ready and we'll win. These days, when you hear Fidel speak, he sounds more pissed off than ever. And he's not gonna swallow that pill their forcing on him. Haven't you noticed that he just as easily puts down Americans than Russians? He's like a bucking colt demanding his Five Points. I don't know who would do it, but they'll have to take his throat stones and his nuts before he gives up Cuba. And Che doesn't talk, but don't be fooled, they say he bites in silence. Didn't you see him when he was here? He didn't bare his teeth for anyone, not even to light his cigar with an ember. He didn't even want anyone to hand him one or offer him coffee. I got the impression that he didn't believe half of what they told him, or he was thinking of something else. He liked even less all the scrambling to see him, he was very serious, surly even. Not me. I went to pick up a huge pile of yucca shells for Rupertino to throw in the trash. Pigs can't eat them, yucca shells are poison to them, they make their insides burst. But about what I was saying, to tell you the truth, I was blown away by Che. My heart skipped a beat because I could tell that he's quick on the trigger. Everybody straightened up if he looked in their eyes, though he didn't seem bigheaded. Now I have something to tell in this dry life of mine. What a man, Sargent, what a man!"

"Yes, Juan, I know, I saw him, but please return to the question and be brief. What did René say about the bell?"

"Chief, every morning René had a different story to tell, what he dreamed that night, which I thought was made up, about the blessed bell; it was a daily feeding. I think he's a big, spineless coward. What can I tell you, he's not good people! You never knew if he was telling the truth or lying. One morning, I heard Rungo, the old man that almost drags himself around carrying a little stew from the kitchen for his pigs, he was saying that it's true that the bell sounds beautiful, but there was only one person who rang it right. It was the bell's caretaker. But he said that man also took off with the Americans when he saw that everything was equal for everybody. See ya later. Really, that's all I know. Sargent, don't get your head twisted, folks tend to talk nonsense and be wicked so as not to think about what's coming."

"Thank you for the information. You're dismissed, and please, tell comrade Ruperto to come in immediately."

"I can't say nothing for sure, Sargent. Here, everyone talked about it. I won't lie, it rubbed me the wrong way that I couldn't hear it, because in San Simón de las Cuchillas, where I live, forget about it! The horn, and that's it. And the chiefs here are obsessed. You can't make noise and they were hell-bent on not ringing it until the bombs were right over us. Can you believe it? They say you're from the East, and you know about bells, you've heard them. I haven't, comrade, not even one peal. There's none of that where I live. My father talks about little bells he's seen hanging from the necks of oxen when they're out hauling, but I haven't even seen that in my thirty-three years. We don't get nothing where I live. It'd be nice if a bell rang up in that hillside to tell Pipe, and Tote, and Coto, and all the people from around there, to drop the hoe and go home to throw something warm into their bellies at lunchtime. That would be nice, real nice."

"Ruperto, let's move on to another subject."

"Don't go moving me nowhere! Let me sit here and ask me what you want right here where we are."

"You didn't understand what I said, but it doesn't matter. What other relevant information can you give me?"

"Listen, from the moment I came through the door downstairs, my thing is to throw out trash on the horse cart. I do know about that. I know about horses and oxen. No matter how vicious they are, I can break them. Besides, I make good on carrying the rifle and wearing the leafage, which turns out they call that camouflage now. Yeah, they call the leafage camouflage. Can I tell you something, Sargent? This situation's got me all shook up, and then some. I'm 'bout to run into the woods. Maybe that's what happened to René, the notion of not being able to ring the bell. He knows bells."

"We're finished, Ruperto. You're dismissed, I'll call you if there's anything else."

"Listen to me carefully, Sargent Marín, my day is shot. If you call me again, I already know what I'm gonna do. I'll get lost like René did. The only difference is that they'll find me 'cause of the smell or the vultures."

"Don't say such things, comrade. You may leave, and please tell Pedro that I'm waiting for him."

"And you, Pedro, what can you tell me about the church bell? The stolen bell, to be clear."

"Chief, I'll give you the long and short of it; it was René. You must know that's why he disappeared. Every day he had some gripe about the blessed bells. Besides being a thief, he must have some mental problem. The one who calls himself a barber is strange too. I wouldn't let him cut my hair for nothin'. I don't know what side he's on. I'm sure René took the bell that morning in a truck in collusion with the driver. The last thing he was thinking about is what's coming. Although let me tell you, grimy and all, when it's clean it must be like the sun. I rubbed off a smidgen with a knife and it dazzled. But see here, René said that in the village the bells are in the church spires, and these Americans decided to put it at the height of a large goat, and away from the church by 100 meters. Do you see how anyone could feel envy and be tempted?"

"Thank you, good Pedro."

"José, I need your help, but you must be precise and convincing. I must find the author of the theft. We're on maximum alert, it's a difficult situation, and my boss is demanding. Please tell me, do you know anything about the driver of the truck that left that morning?"

"Chief, about being precise, I only have a far-fetched idea, and I can't take a chance. I don't want to get mixed up, so I'll talk my way. I need to get this mess out of my head. Don't even ask, I was on shift that night and no car came in or left until dawn. We couldn't smoke, or turn on the lights, or make any racket. Not a hay straw moved all night, I swear on this little saint my mom gave me the night they came to get me. I was scared from dusk to dawn, I didn't sleep a wink, that's why I remember it. That's all I can say."

"Pardon me, José, I know, I know. With all these problems, I forgot to confirm that. Thanks for the clarification."

None of those interrogated gave any clues that could lead to the truth. "The dead would continue needing blood."

Eventually, the Sargent had to present the report to the captain. He warned him that, in effect, although no one spoke clearly, and the thief left no trace, all evidence pointed toward René as the author of the shameless act. The captain, a veteran of the war having fought in Sierra Maestra, wasn't about to let some impertinent small-time thief smear him. He gave his men four hours to locate the bell and those who had taken part in such a grave crime. According to what he said, besides thievery, the deed was considered an ideological deviation,

120

counterrevolutionary, and would have political consequences.

It was mid-afternoon when they found René in his house, in bed and with his head under the covers. He had no time to react. Two men exposed him in one yank and confirmed his fear that this was the end of his existence. He thought the entire day how he hadn't heard a single peal of the bell.

It was raining hard when they put him in a military truck. Thunder followed them all the way to the encampment. His captors said nothing. His stomach turned incessantly, he had chills, probably from fear of approaching death. He would die because he left without permission, he would be tried as a deserter, and his family in the United States would never know the truth about his stupid death. He'd stayed behind when they left, like a dumbass, his nose always in the books, never knowing what was going on. He deserved his lot. If he escaped alive somehow, he'd want nothing to do with olive green uniforms again. After all, he'd never shot a gun, ever.

A lieutenant, Sargent Marín, and two militia oversaw the questioning.

Frightened, he asked permission to dry his perspiration. He seemed ready to speak, yet he remained silent. It didn't look as if he would say anything, He guzzled the water they gave him in a large jug. He was told they would repeat the two questions they had asked only one more time. Believing that compliance was his only salvation, he braced himself to speak.

He said he had left because they didn't have access to bathrooms and he couldn't answer nature's call in the woods for many days, regardless of effort. He'd tried to sit on the twisted trunk of a mango tree, like his friend the barber, who had the same problem, but not even a dingleberry came out. He was about to blow and that's why he left. He'd barely opened the door to the living room in his house, didn't have time to take off his pants, and didn't quite make it to the toilet to do what they knew he was talking about. And with respect to the bell, he thought it unbelievable, unforgivable. For him, bells were as sacred as mothers, and that one should be where it belonged, in the church, even if they hadn't seen a worshiper around for a long time. He couldn't conceive of a church without a bell or grasp how someone could think of committing the sacrilege of stealing it. As a great admirer of and fascinated as he was by bells, he relished their sound. He'd always lived near the Cathedral, and he would never leave. He couldn't conceive of living where he couldn't hear the daily ringing from his bed, the intoxicating sound that reaches deep in the heart.

The investigators looked at each other as if wanting to comment. That last phrase had sounded quite strange to them. No matter how much they encouraged René to tell the truth, he offered no new details. So, unsurprisingly, he couldn't avoid incarceration.

A few days later, old Rungo arrived hobbling, as usual, and eager to speak to Sargent Marín. He came under heavy rain, worried because while moving his pig, he'd heard a sound he thought familiar coming from a thicket near the garbage dump. It sounded like the bell from the American church. Or rather, it had to be, but he didn't dare approach in case the enemy was planning something in the woods.

When Rupertino learned about Rungo's declaration, he decided to confess. Although nearly illiterate, he was shrewd enough to know they would find him no matter where he went. They'd caught René easy and he wouldn't have any better luck. Besides, rumor had it that the chiefs said in times of war, the bell issue would be paid with the life of the sinner, and he felt it was preferable to have a Christian burial than to give the vultures the satisfaction of a bellyful. Rupertino didn't think twice: no use crying over spilled moonshine. He appeared before Sargent Marín to tell the truth, clearly, no dodging.

He'd been so interested in what René had said about the instrument, that he thought he might be right. It would be beautiful to hear it. It couldn't be the same to hear a big bell, ringing pretty and loud, as a horn or a güira that you play by putting your hands together tightly and letting air go through a small space. He decided to take it to the woods and hide it near the dump. That way, between trips, he could amuse himself by giving it soft jangles. And who knows, if the Americans didn't come forward, he could get away with taking it to San Simón de las Cuchillas. That was his intent. What joy he would bring to those who remained back there! What good is a bell in an abandoned church?

Then, with no other recourse, they let René go and locked up Rupertino.

A few days after the lockup, Rupertino began to hear the bell ringing non-stop from his cell. It rang, it rang loud and pretty to no end. It was the announcement that now the island was no longer on the brink of war. All was rejoicing and happiness. He was happy too. Khrushchev had spoken to Kennedy about his "little sausage factory", among other things. In short, they ended the missile crisis. They applied less severe measures with Rupertino.

And I, telling the story from well-informed sources, and being Rupertino's nephew, returned to El Hombrito to finish the coffee harvest. No doubt exists that I went through hell, but I didn't stop until I became a doctor.

Chapter 9

Dr. Cuní's libido kept him stuck in a protracted lethargy. He thought about his wife and calculated the distance between them. Gripped by those ruminations and romanticizing the ever more desired encounter, he enjoyed the air conditioning not available in his country. He recalled childhood moments when he, Emiliano Alfonso Cuní, slept in the raw and relished the warmth of a good blanket. That nakedness would have scandalized Ana's modesty. Ana, her one and only, whom he never convinced to sleep in the nude. Her religious education imposed on them some obstacles that still, at 60 years of age, tormented him. In other times, he had felt deeply ashamed of the sexual experiences he needed.

Cuní was the oldest of the Cuban doctors in the Seychelles archipelago serving in compliance with an accord between both governments. He did not believe opportunities for a romance, however fleeting, were available to him. Besides, he was horrified by the possibility of any slip being construed as a bad example and tarnishing his image of a serious and respectable man.

Just two months after his arrival in Victoria, Doctor Rafael, much younger than Doctor Cuní, sometimes had the impression that he had landed at the ass-end of space. With a full agenda, he devoted great passion to all his endeavors including a presidential order that appointed him as chief of medical services for the armed forces in the archipelago.

The truth was that in Victoria he climbed stairs in a rush, but eventually he moved like a fish in water, and whatever he lacked in knowledge about any given subject, he made up with ingenuity and extraordinary audacity when facing the most difficult situations. He was convinced that opportunities should never be wasted and always, better a bird in hand. Not even Sancho Panza himself could surpass him at that. Also, a jokester, lively, unpredictable, and quite charming, his company was entertaining and unwittingly, he began to look like a Seychellois, and always questioned why things were the way they were and not the way they should be.

Soon, Rafael began a hurried attempt to find himself a good female, to alleviate his homesickness and the longing for former attachments. He met Elizabeth Lemieux, her maiden name, of French origin but fluent in Spanish, in a fashion store in Victoria one afternoon out on the hunt with a friend. The young lady, of gracious gestures and sweet voice, wore a green dress somewhat darker than her eyes with elegance, tied at the waist with a black silk piece that matched her shoes perfectly. It showcased all the curves of her delicate figure. It was a blissful encounter for the doctor and more than enough reason to wander around longer.

Once out of the establishment, the doctors talked about the beauty of that woman who could well have been the daughter of the owner, since after a certain shyness, she was quick to make them understand that she wasn't simply an employee. Showing them a catalogue with prices was a sign of deference toward them. They agreed to return later to see if she was still there. On second thought, Rafael made no further comments, convinced that if the opportunity for an approach existed, he couldn't waste it. There was no room for a mistake, he wanted to live in her gaze.

From that moment, and with the greatest discretion, he learned several details about Elizabeth. The places she frequented, the probable times in which she did, anything related to her that could give him an advantage. A relationship with her could be beneficial. He was careful to make their encounters seem fortuitous no matter how well planned. He didn't want, or didn't think useful, to know her marital status.

With every expectation of fulfilling his purpose, every day he became ever more certain that a companion in those circumstances would be ideal. He examined formulas to accomplish the desired convergence. To be with a cultured woman, liberal, and a business owner, would allow him to be at his leisure and fully enjoy everything that was beautiful in a place he was now beginning to discover. Also, he didn't discard the idea of seeking the company of influential friends when they visited the private beaches and other places for rest and relaxation.

Although Rafael enjoyed the beach, Mahé has sixty of them, and he didn't know which one the young lady would prefer. In one weekend, he visited Anse Forbans and Anse Royale trying to find her with no success.

One sunny and breeze Saturday afternoon, he decided to visit the Botanical Gardens, one of the main attractions in Victoria, capital city of the islands. The impressive vegetation, the presence of giant turtles, and the variety of palm trees fascinated him. There, at sunset, at the foot of the mountain, in that magnificent environment, he got his chance.

It wasn't his first time roaming the place and he was alone, tired, and discouraged. He leaned on a tree trunk to light a cigarette before leaving, but he remembered that smoking was not allowed. The craving was torture. He picked up a yellowish leaf, inexplicably beautiful, and inspected it while thinking of the nearest exit when refined and cheerful laughter stopped him. Two female figures approached, the one he suspected he knew tossed the red flower she held in her hand and arranged her hair under a small hat. There she was. The young lady with the pretty gaze was in the company of a friend whose name turned out to be Laura. She didn't pretend not to see him. She turned her face over her left shoulder until her eyes found Rafael.

She was sweet, attractive. She smiled. Rafael had never looked better and she noticed. To his great pleasure, their conversation lasted a good long time. She was totally uninhibited and willing to take advantage of any opportunity for further contact.

That evening, he was late to dinner. He sat across from Doctor Cuní, who, alone and almost finished, opted for keeping him company. The colleagues shared conversation topics and enjoyed stimulating moments, perhaps due to the kinship between east and far west Cubans. Rafael wasted no time in informing him that he believed himself near the beginning of an intriguing adventure with a determined girl akin to a star fallen from the sky. He'd met her recently in a store, and he had just shared a moment of familiarity with her that he thought quite fruitful, a possible consolidation of a glorious relationship, but he wasn't sure the entire deck was stacked in his favor.

"I've told you, and you well know, that we are in a country with very different customs from ours. You must be prudent in any type of relation you establish; don't rush."

"I'll consider your advice, but I'm burning with desire to enjoy my life and this tremendous opportunity."

Rafael made sure not to explain too much, given the severe discipline to which he was subject. He hardly paid attention to his delectable food. But he couldn't help sharing the happiness he felt for having been invited to a dance the following weekend hosted by the lady. He was

129

determined not to waste the opportunity. The island's elite sector was sure to attend the birthday celebration of such an attractive woman.

The idea of making a fool of himself pounded him relentlessly. He wanted to dance with Elizabeth, and it was always expected that Cubans would do it with flavor. Without giving it a second thought, he expressed his doubts to Cuní, as he truly didn't feel able to meet that expectation.

"Count on me. We can practice several of our rhythms and dances; no doubt we're good at that."

"Thanks! And don't worry. I'll make you look good."
"I'm sure you will."
"When do we start rehearsing? The anxiety is killing me."

"As soon as tomorrow."

"I will always be grateful."

The dance lessons he received every day for a week from Doctor Cuní were masterful. That tall man with sophisticated manners became transformed when he gave instruction and danced, yet he wouldn't do it in public. Too bad he was such an extreme introvert!

Everything should work out like a charm.
On time and in impeccable appearance, Rafael arrived at the event hall. The place was spectacular. He saw himself living moments so sublime he would nearly touch the clouds. He knew about love and its wounds,

but now would be different, a great celebration, a beautiful woman.

In the company of her disagreeable husband, Frederick Shaw, Elizabeth welcomed her guests. To see her with that tall redheaded man, with a trimmed beard, and an elegance not surpassed within the venue, was soul-crushing for Rafael. Since his conversation with Doctor Cuní about the events at the Botanical Gardens, he looked upon this as his great night. Leaving was an option, perhaps undignified, but he decided to remain serene. Soon he found a safe corner. A large window served to turn his gaze in feigned distraction. The sea, in the darkness of night only brightened by yellowish streetlights, brought the whisper of the waves that arrived to meet the shore. He remained taciturn until he felt it necessary to take in the pleasant atmosphere in the hall. Soon, he began to concentrate on the music until a desire for juvenile vengeance filled him.

The moment had come. He would not allow himself to be rejected one more minute, and he set out to show her the kind of man she was overlooking. All the fear of looking foolish disappeared by force of will. He would dance until he became the focal point among so many distinguished people. He would catch the attention of the hostess to make her fume, under the assumption that she had intended to make him a laughing-stock.

Without delay, he found a lady willing to be led so he could inflict the stab wound. He remembered the recent instruction received from his friend and made

131

himself noticed with a great sense of rhythm in the Caribbean way, the Cuban way.

Rafael and his partner began to gain space and admiration, increasingly nearing the spot where Elizabeth and Frederick were dancing. He saw how she pretended not to notice, but perhaps she felt provoked, incited to dance with him. It wouldn't be a bad idea. What a pleasure that would be! No one there, on that night, could dance better, but on second thought, he wouldn't ask nor accept if she asked.

But then, on the cusp of glory, he looked up and met Elizabeth's stony gaze. All his confidence went down the drain. Without saying goodbye, or getting any information from his new friend, he left upset and disoriented. The party was ruined.

He spent a week looking for reasons. How could it be that the one who had awakened so much hope in him from the first day could be married and totally indifferent to him? He wanted to take her to the most remote place she'd ever seen, tell her about her ridiculous behavior, insult her, speak whatever viciousness he could think of and force her to listen. She would never dare proceed in such manner again. Unfortunately, such things would not change the course of events, the deed was done.

He struggled with his demons and to avoid the torment, he loaded himself with even more work. He didn't visit the beaches or sit in the park. His eyes were dull. He circumvented the square with the famous Tower

Clock, a replica of London's Big Ben, near one of her stores. He isolated himself in his work routine and the less time off he had, the better he felt.

At night, he would walk over to places where humble people talked about the islands' possibilities for enrichment with the search for gold, pearls, hidden treasure, and many other things. There was always someone who placed his hopes on an ancestor's charitable gesture, and on receiving notification of an inheritance from the Continent. It was a way to forget the hard labor the new day would bring.

The doubt that all those worn paths "led to Rome" had troubled him since he was a boy; nevertheless, the was silent. He couldn't keep from becoming flushed at the mention of inheritances. He was baffled by the memory of Nene, who never missed an opportunity to ask him in her letters to take an interest in the topic regardless of his efforts to evade it. She was sure, and it was common knowledge according to cousin Cosita, that the family name appeared on a London list which confirmed everything we already knew. She was even determined to locate the blue book with the gold letters that Grandfather received from the priest's hands when he returned from a visit to Valladolid. Now was the time! She was more certain than ever of being close to making her dream a reality, if God did his part, and Rafael put his feet on the ground.

But Rafael listened to similar stories from those people who also had a right to dream. Certainly, the difference was scant or none at all. Even in dreaming men are united despite the distance that separates them. Here and there, men dream. He'd wait for exhaustion to defeat him so he could retire and fall like lead on his bed and ease the pain of his failed dreams, scare away the yearning for that woman he tried to win over from their first encounter.

Elizabeth became ever more excited with the idea of finding him. Not even as a teenager had she been so impetuous about a boy; it was something strong now. A little rough and indiscreet yet friendly. Something different from what she was used to burst forth from that man. She had made the determination to show him that she was a married woman after their meeting at the Botanical Gardens, thinking it impractical to tell him then. She had been coquettish enough to let him know quite clearly that she was interested. She believed in the strength of actions more than words, and she had to seize the opportunity offered by her husband's arrival from Australia for her birthday to put her cards on the table.

Frustrated upon noticing the bewilderment in his face when she received him, she cursed the human habit of assuming others think as we do. The aim was to make him understand that her marriage was in name only, but it didn't work. She followed him with her gaze, more would've been impossible. She kept her composure fearing the doctor would presume this much-needed relationship finished.

She wouldn't give up. Her purpose was to make all efforts to salvage what seemed a potential romantic affair. She recalled how her friend Laura had taken the time to lavish Rafael with attention during the party while he responded with reticence. Elizabeth needed him, and she had no other option but to use Laura. Under the pretense of a strong pain in her chest provoked by a fight with Charlie, her chihuahua, she would visit the military clinic where the Cuban doctor held consultations.

Knowing full well the reasons for Beth's behavior, her friend showed no reluctance to helping her. The next day, watched by the puzzled eyes of the usual patients, Laura surprised the doctor with a visit. With her characteristic astuteness, she was immediately on the hunt for an opportunity to reveal her real symptoms, the reason for the visit.

Rafael was careful not to show concern. The complex psychology used by such a distinguished lady required the highest level of reasoning. He listened with patience as she did not mention Beth as the designer of the scheme, which would be so divergent from her character and good demeanor. Regardless of how serious he presented himself, she remained lighthearted as she told him without inhibition the grounds for the senseless end to the party. Politely, he concluded the consultation.

His prospects revived, he no longer believed in his original suspicions; everything pointed to circumstances being primarily responsible. But what the hell! He had solid reasons for telling her off. Now he would be the one to take his time. He wouldn't force an encounter, he would try not to see her. He made efforts to remain unnoticed for a few more days, and with the assurance of one who knows he is wanted, he resumed his visits to the places where they would "casually" coincide. Only God or the devil know what story she would feed him. In that city everything was abloom, and any event was over in a flash. Today a beach was uninhabited, tomorrow it would be taken over by nudists or some rich guy.

Their encounters became more and more promising before the hasty and furious explosion of passion on the last day of December in Grand beach on the island of La Digue.

It was hard to know how many tests would befall a relationship already difficult, but the truth was that he needed her flesh more each time they met, and her company was becoming essential. The woman never spoke about the future, she enjoyed the present as if it were her first or last day.

It became known, in a city where everyone knew almost everything about everyone except tourists, that a complicated web quickly weaved itself around them with threads of truth and falsehoods. Through scares and obstacles, day by day, a certain bond consolidated and threatened to become vital; love was a serious game.

They talked often about Europe and its wonders. Paris, the place where Beth was born, would always be their target. They cooked up the trip to "la belle Paris" on a hot fire of passion, and it was set for a few months before his return from his vacation in Cuba, since he was unable to resist the desire to walk the streets of the city that lovers of culture and art aspire to visit. Most definitely, he wanted to explore and admire it.

He wouldn't achieve his purpose if he didn't bet on success. Whatever he had accomplished in his life had been just like that: taking leaps without knowing where he might fall or rise. Now he wouldn't stop, the only option was to leap. No detail would be missed. Excellent idea to give his life a little glamour. To travel the capital of the world in the company of a lover was an opportunity that was worth any risk.

Nothing could be left to chance, he couldn't miss a shot or leave any evidence that might cause suspicion. The flight itinerary that would take him to Spain included a stop in Paris. Elizabeth would take the same flight in Djibutí where she would spend a few days prior conducting merchandising business and would arrive in Paris with the pretense of visiting her great-aunt.

Chapter 10

After several hours of longing, arousal, and sleeplessness, the insistent ringing of the telephone brought Doctor Cuní back to the reality he was trying so hard to avoid. He would have to peel back the blanket that swathed him, get up, dress, and go from warmth to the overwhelming cold regulated by the thermostat. All of it was hard to swallow. He'd manage to do it, but at 18 degrees Centigrade, naked, old, and flabby, it seemed insurmountable.

He remembered the heart attack his youngest son triggered two years before. Back in his native Santiago de Cuba, he had cracked the skull of a trumpet player in the group Los Hoyos with a bottle of rum in a drunken brawl at the carnival. It fell on him, the parent after all, to call on favors owed him by people with certain influence. The gratitude card was one he only played as a last resort, but he put body and soul into keeping his offspring from going to jail. He got the unexpected call at four in the morning on July 27. It was the hospital where he worked notifying him of his son's behavior and the status of the victim. From then on, Cuní detested the telephone, and if it rang in the middle of the night, his hair stood on end.

Now he felt that tightness in his chest again. Besieged by a morbid feeling, he presaged an inevitable fall preceded by severe dizziness the moment he got up. Everyone in the house was quiet. He knew they couldn't be asleep with that impertinent ringing at dawn, but they were determined to ignore it.

With no other alternative, his anxious hand searched for the receiver.

"Good evening, how can I help you?" he heard himself say.

"Good evening, I need to speak to Doctor Rafael, I'm his brother."

"He went on vacation to Cuba two weeks ago."

Threatening silence at the other end of the line.

"Asshole! Son-of-a-bitch! We've been waiting for him since the 29th. Who knows where he is that…!"

After listening to a never-ending torrent of improprieties leveled at his friend, Doctor Cuní felt obligated to hang up while the speaker continued to stew in his own fire. Already the experience had been bothersome enough to let a stranger continue to torture him more than was permissible.

Comfortable back in his bed, Cuní tried to calm himself. He aligned his arms to his body and breathed slowly and deeply in an attempt to recover. Certainly, he was irritated by what happened and it took him a while to arrive at the conclusion that it was vital for him to consider the most rational idea possible.

He assumed that Doctor Rafael had remained in Spain, since he'd heard him talk once about his interest in visiting Barcelona and Basque Country. He also deemed it his duty to communicate the incident to the Cuban consulate promptly, nearly convinced that they would be informed of the matter and kept quiet for some purpose he couldn't imagine.

The issue seemed simple, but the doctor's sixth sense gave him signs that something presumably serious would follow. In the morning, he would do his part to come out as clean as he could from what already smelled like a quagmire. Perhaps he would never know the truth. Times were complicated and Rafael a man who didn't hesitate to take risks. If he was up to something, surely he was walking around as fresh as a lettuce doing as he pleased who knows where.

Unintentionally, Doctor Cuní had become the only owner of the news item; the scoop was his and he would keep silent. No one forced him to tell it. Neither did he want to make conjectures about someone he thought trustworthy. The colleagues who shared the house would be embarrassed to ask about the matter regarding that call at dawn: It could implicate them. No doubt enquiries would fall on him given his responsibility as group chief.

To tell the truth, Cuní couldn't provide the smallest clue. Another headache! He would be accused of not exercising any functional political influence, of inability to control his subordinates. Also, the possibility of guilt by complicity existed, taking into account the good relationship between them and the coined pretext that as much fault lies on the one who stills the cow as on the one who kills it.

The time he spent in his bed trying to forget the incident and fall asleep seemed endless. Then, from the street, he heard voices singing off key in French a song from Edith Piaf's time. It must've been tourists returning from Pirate Arms, the most glamorous nightclub in Victoria. That night, Doctor Cuní couldn't sleep. Even before dawn, he longed for the next sunset. The tropical paradise would distract him with its countless wonders.

The first three days of the week were spent traveling to Praslin for medical consultations. He liked walking along the beach in solitude and look at the shape of the coconut trees, so different from the ones he knew. Not even the ones in Baracoa intrigued him as much. There, in his maternal grandparents' farm, he savored the coconut water and the sweetness of the meat. Now he found something different in the Praslin coconuts, considerably different.

A strange habit took him there and he always did the same thing. He roamed the same trails until he discovered the coconuts in the distance, hanging from the mother that birthed them. As he neared, his eyes would fix upon the biggest fruit that had fallen to the ground. He'd take a female coconut, but impulsively return it, anxious to witness the moment in which the natives changed its configuration with strikes or with their teeth and then see the inevitable, two white female buttocks, the peeled coconut. He continued to be as surprised as the first day. He picked up the bare female coconut without realizing in the least that time passed, and malicious looks fell on the respectable doctor.

When Cuní unwillingly tried to retreat, he couldn't ignore the male coconuts, which almost no one ever noticed. Many grow near the females, but with their huge pods, their threatening and imposing phalli, they're inedible. He always refused to leave until the light of day blew out. A great yearning excited that male who seemed still able to satisfy a woman.

Everything went according to plan. From the moment the plane began to gain altitude, Rafael enjoyed watching land and water from above. He recalled the work calls he made by helicopter to the islands of the archipelago that always left him looking forward to the next opportunity. From this moment, a discreet gesture of annoyance would show on his face from time to time. He pretended not to know her when Elizabeth went up the aircraft stairs and settled some distance from him. She noticed him, and without quite understanding the reasons for such secrecy, she complied with the agreed caution.

Elated by how his wishes were being carried out, he felt himself soaring into infinity. When the flight was almost completed after two stops, the anticipation at the idea of the short distance left to travel showed in him.

There, Paris at night. "The City of Lights" as they call it, resplendent as if all the stars had confabulated to appear in one immense beam. Under different conditions he would've been euphoric; however, the moment was not appropriate for showing joyous ebullience.

They left the airport as quickly as possible. The drizzle, the cold air of that new autumn, and the pressure from the choices made, overcame him. He could hardly speak. He hid a dry ache he felt for the first time that began to tighten his throat.

They arrived at the Hotel d'Argenson located on the 8th Arrondissement between the Champs-Élysées and L' Opéra. Once in the room he felt more secure, and slowly passion opened its doors. He was there. He wouldn't waste one second. That victory became part of the success he craved.

That charming woman who from the beginning loved him in a way not at all senseless, was worn out, beaten by fatigue and accumulated strain. He, who mostly wanted to follow her example, didn't even try to lay his head on the pillow. He couldn't. He surveyed her face and body now illuminated by the city lights softly perched on her sheer nightgown, and barely touching her, he covered her with a blanket. A strange look came over his face when, caught between desire and indecision, he opted for letting her sleep. In that moment, he asked himself if he truly loved her.

He settled into an armchair and skimmed over some destination maps with the intention of planning outings for the holiday. He made calculations, previewed and evaluated each detail of the places to begin their

143

exploration of Paris. That's how she found him, still smelling of the islands, the next morning, one of fine drizzle and cool air.

"Ici repose un soldat français mort pour la patrie 1914-1918." When they arrived at the Arc de Triomphe, Rafael's eyes fixed on the inscription. It's wise this English idea of the unknown soldier. It has strong symbolic spirit, because after all, it's the nameless that leave their lives where they least expect it, they save the nation, or they sink it, but they deserve the credit anyway.

How many stories could be summarized there! How many soldiers X of the Great War! The obsession with reaching the root of things hounded him. Wanting to channel in one direction the force of emotion that weighed on him, confounded by the idea of unraveling the symbolism of that inscription, he would follow one thread, the story of a young man who could be called Jean Pierre. He didn't know if he had existed or not, but it didn't matter. "On the eve of the attack, he remembered the sweet routine with which he had grown up. Within the encampment, it was said that the chief was planning a strategy that would liberate them from the German siege. Once the troops were arranged, there was no other option but to wait for the end of that suffering. The result couldn't be otherwise: a scorching hell. The surprise attack had stopped being so when, while at dinner with beautiful ladies, the commander's ego didn't deter him from demonstrating his ingenuity. The enemy knew that a giant wave of soldiers would come forward and they did nothing but wait. Fifteen minutes of agony later, Jean Pierre died, a machine-gun blast exposing his bowels."

Beth remained in absolute silence. She just stared at the monument. It wasn't out of indifference. On the contrary, she knew ahead of time that the selected location to begin their visit was not a random choice. Early on she had observed in Rafael a fascination with the heroic, with worthiness, with valor, things that didn't mean that much to her. In childhood, after the death of her mother, her father had impressed upon her a profound aversion to politics and belligerence. She didn't have a precise idea why she liked to see him participate in that moment that brought him God knows what memories. Meanwhile, he thought about the words Napoleon spoke to his men: "You will return home through arches of triumph."

Skirting the monument and stopping at the statues of each of the four pillars (Le Triomphe, La Résistance, La Paix and La Marseillaise), none seemed as alive as the last one. He stared at it. He remembered his childhood fondness for making clay figurines that he thought were perfect. Three-dimensional shapes always impressed him, and sculpture was a monster for which he had deep respect and a healthy envy of great sculptors. He had seen works by Rodin and many others in books and catalogues, but he would never forget Laocoon and

145

His Sons. He shuddered thinking of the abilities of those who transcend their humanity and approach the divine, that which man does not think himself capable of until he achieves it, and when he does, he bequeaths it to others. Inventiveness is never common. If it were, it would no longer be what it is. Therein lies its greatness. The sculpture facing him now consecrated François Rude for all time.

Already spent, they considered complete their exploration of the Arc de Triomphe museum of history and construction. They agreed they couldn't leave without going up to the lookout from where dazzled visitors admired the majesty that appeared before their eyes.

They finished their cigarettes as they reached the top. Beth searched for somewhere to discard the butt while he caressed her hair with his left hand. Then, a dissonant noise forced them to face an disturbing reality. Surprised and frightened voices reached them along with the roar of an approaching airplane. The noise was dreadful, violent, dangerous; it was right over them. Time seemed to rush, they were paralyzed, their senses recoiled. Beth was unable to discern if he was holding her tightly or if it was the other way around. She was shaking. Their bodies fused together in the embrace to await the worst. How cowardly are those who lie when they say they have never felt fear! A few seconds later, a bold pilot thrust his small plane through the Arc de Triomphe.

Rafael struggled to take a pack of cigarettes out of his pocket. He put one in his mouth and offered one to Beth.

"Smoke, it will help, it will relax you."

"But after I'll need fresh air. Don't let go of my hand."

"It was a rough moment. Cheer up, it's all over and we're okay. It'll be a unique part of our story. I'll get a taxi."

That terrifying experience left them breathless. After living the horror of being face to face with death, they felt the need for a pause to renew their energy. Rest and reflection became imperative. Beth's interest in reviewing the fashion stores in Paris to compare with what she offered on the islands, did not require immediate attention, so they decided to spend a week in more pleasurable activities in the French Riviera and give the recent experience its final repose.

The mild weather of the Côte d'Azure would do them good. A paradise where nature and the hand of man work together to create a marvel of the Mediterranean motivated long sessions of lovemaking. Rafael felt for the first time in his life that he had burst the bubble of rural provincialism. That intimate closeness bonded them day by day. Neither entertained anything that didn't have to do with the two of them. They didn't even think about the immediate future. That magic world of fine sands, always in harmony with the shades of the sea, brought breezes laden with happiness. The long dialogues and laughter burst forth at any triviality as if everything that was positive about their lives converged. They enjoyed their adventure to the fullest.

Splendid was that piece of our planet, yet Beth, as if happiness came with conflictive thorns in need of pricking, couldn't keep from making conjectures on the day before their farewell to the blue coast. Perhaps saying goodbye to the sea brought closer the memory of Anse Forbans, perhaps she missed her cats. She couldn't help speculating about the possibility of her husband arriving early from Australia.

It wouldn't be the first time. On several occasions, Frederick had been forced to interrupt the research that so attracted him; or perhaps he might use the interruptiont as an excuse to go to Victoria. For a while, he'd been coming to see her with unusual frequency. He probably sensed the reality he refused to accept. Perhaps he preferred to keep a lock on that Pandora's box. He would be who he is, naturally phlegmatic. Choosing to mistrust not knowing exactly what was going on would be taking a risk on making an irreparable mistake. He'd have no defense. As soon as Beth returned to Paris, she would speak with her friend Laura on the telephone and get an update on the situation.

Back in Cité Lumiere felt like being home. The Quartier Latin welcomed them the next day. Rafael had imagined it different from what he found. Pithy in his answers to Beth, who couldn't stand to see him absent from their shared moment, he gave the impression that

148

the Sorbonne seemed as common to him as the University of Havana. He seemed a total stranger and she tried to entice him. She was jealous of how the young crowd that cheered the weak morning sun could divert his attention away from her and toward girls with smiling faces and distinctive attire. She wasn't entirely wrong, although it was simply a part of the whole. He also tried to go back in time. Nearly no Chinese were left in Havana's Chinatown, but the Chinese bugle continued to blow. In Paris, long after the Middle Ages, those in the educational neighborhood communicated in Latin, the ancient academic language. Other hurried youngsters possibly late for class, now walked the same streets.

They strolled the Boulevard Saint-Michel and crossed Rue Bievre, they walked other backstreets neighboring the Seine and the Cathedral of Notre Dame. Their jaunt was nothing like the hurried Parisian pace in a drizzle that foreshadowed heavy rain. Their purpose was no other but to continue enraptured by the allure of the most beautiful capital in Europe. One more couple among so many French and tourists protected under a sea of umbrellas and dark capes, their resolve to have fun would not wane for any reason.

Time did not conspire to play tricks on them, but the days were fleeting, and they both enjoyed every instant. They strolled down an ample avenue tinged by the colors on the stores' signage and the profusion of fashionable clothes. Beth was well informed about modern trends. She was interested in promoting the latest in women's fashion, visible lingerie. They entered the stores, examined tags and prices to compare with other markets, especially the Asian. With some pride, Beth confirmed that her business was on the right track. Fashion takes its time to spread around the world, but she stocked merchandise still sold in Paris. Dressing well was something Rafael had learned by observation. He was convinced that novelty was attractive but dressing well set the individual apart. He could tell the difference without fail. But since shopping wasn't one of their objectives, they decided not to waste time on inconsequential matters.

They were crossing the Place de la Concorde when Beth walked ahead. She invited him to stop and look at the monolith made of rose granite of Aswan, from the namesake temple in Egypt. With her index finger, she showed him the highest point of the obelisk of Luxor, where reality and legend interweave in a piece that has no connection to the history of its location. After almost a year of traveling downstream on the Nile, it was returned to its place of origin until the following year when it finally made the voyage successfully. Obstacles could not stand in the way of its placement in its current spot. That was not the only case of Egyptian obelisks taken to other important cities in Europe and America, like so many other historical relics, under the assumption that this is where they indeed ought to be.

"How much slave blood and sweat infused so that one fine day any Joe can dispose of what he believes his.

The gods cannot remain unmoved in the face of these dirty tricks," commented Rafael.

Coincidentally, while Doctor Rafael and Elizabeth explored the city, news broke that President François Miterrand would officially "return" to Egypt another monolith also extracted from Luxor. It's nice to know that some treasured relics return to their original home.

"We're standing in an infamous square. You know," Beth said animated, "the unbridled massacre unleashed here during the Revolution makes me question its objectives. Despite the majority being devout Christians, one of the things they sought was a vengeance they exacted with cruelty. This place became a carnival in which the populace saw heads fall, the heads of people whose feet they would've wanted to kiss not long before."

"Sadly, the struggle was among the French themselves, they were so tired of the injustice, but in the Caribbean islands the Spanish arrived and exterminated the natives. Only a few people of native blood are left, not counting the losses of thirty years of wars. They didn't escape the feared guillotine, either. It was taken to Guadeloupe among other places, but it didn't do much more than travel. In Cuba, firing squads, hangings, the vile club were "instruments of justice" that took many lives."

"Many say that Guillotin, a man who can only be credited for the emblematic use of the machine, which could've a been any other though not as frightening, died by his own tool."

"My understanding is that Guillotin's death was not so, that there was a mix up with another man of the same last name, and the event happened in your beloved Lyon. Can you imagine the horror those souls must've experienced looking at the baskets where their heads would fall?"

Beth tossed back the hair that covered part of her face. While she looked at him with suspicion and gestures of revulsion. He knew the joke had not worked as he thought.

Now their walk was reluctant, not usual for them. Revisiting those events perhaps contributed to the intensity of their fatigue. That night they had planned dinner at Café de Flore and later a stroll t the hrough Luxembourg Gardens, but they wanted something more intimate.

They would dine on the Rue de la Huchette. The soft music heard in Caveau de la Huchette provided a warm atmosphere. Rafael found a special spot to give wings to his memories, but he kept his feelings to himself. Unexpectedly, Beth asked:

"Other than a doctor, what would you have liked to be?"

"A painter."

"Will you paint me someday?"

"I don't think I would succeed. I couldn't capture your charms, those that make you a desirable woman."

152

"And after Paris?"

"Always Paris."

He wanted to return to his memories, but he couldn't stand so much silence. He had the need to break it, to tell her an important part of his interior world. He told Beth about his family, his childhood, the contrast between his prior life and that mantle now unveiled before his brown eyes, which she insisted were black and slanted. His voice was soft, with cadenced intimacy; nevertheless, his sometimes-childish words didn't appear nostalgic, but they were charged with sincerity. In his remembrances there was a mixture of pride and gratitude to life. Like loose pearls from a broken necklace, rolling on a polished floor, he evoked times past. His first years were a precious treasure of charmed good fortune. If he shared them with her on such sublime moments, it wasn't merely for emotional relief.

In every phrase and every word, she found reason enough to feel extraordinary admiration for that man, who other than for the century between them, resembled a new type of Rastignac, exploring the streets of Paris, always stopping to remember his past. She believed herself knowledgeable in human psychology from learning it in books and experiences, and she was moved. She didn't want to distract him with questions that could distance him from the intimacy or investigate the circumstances that led him to become a doctor, but she was certain that from his emotional transparency emerged immense spiritual strength.

The person in her company was capable of feeling moved by man-made wonders and savor them like few could. He was the result of the pastoral environment he had just drawn with eloquent words. He was forged like iron and he proved to her that he wasn't engaging in naïve mischief. His commitment to continuing his life's path was irrevocable.

Still under the spell of his redolent confession, they decided to return to the hotel earlier than expected. They would need to be ready in the early hours of the morning for their trip to Lyon where Beth's great-aunt awaited.

Chapter 11

From the Lyon airport exit to Mrs. Durand's residence, quite close to "the hill that prays," great pride registered in Beth for that slice of France, ancient capital of Gaul during the roman empire, now distinguished by the development of textile and pharmaceutical industries. She blushed when she spoke of episodes and memories of long holidays when she came with her family.

They caught sight of a large house defiant of the trees that surrounded it to reveal itself to the traveler. Rafael felt an invitation to wander and marvel at the fluttering yellowish leaves that already carpeted the ground. It should be beautiful to see snowflakes clinging to the branches when completely exposed. His curiosity for the authentic French residence was sparked. He imagined the Durand generations established there since the mid-nineteenth century; nevertheless, he tried to live in the present.

Detained for some time at the entrance, the wait and weariness from the trip were irritating. Rafael thought the visit might not have been expected. Job himself would've been exasperated in such a situation. Fatigue from the trip and the useless waiting made him fidgety. In the meantime, Beth tried to mollify him by telling him anecdotes similar to the current circumstance, as on one of her birthdays her aunt kept the entire family waiting in that same spot for more than two hours claiming she was not finished with some details of her personal appearance. She was the type of person never in a rush and who takes their time on that which others might consider trivial.

Rafael tried to peek through the windows, but it was pointless. The humidity wouldn't allow him to see anything but static, blurry shapes. It was late. He wanted to persuade Beth to go back to the city, stay in a hotel, and return in the early morning. When he thought her convinced, Aunt Durand appeared bedecked in an elegant gray dress, a black scarf tied around the neck, and her white hair perfectly styled, framing a face brightened by round eyes, unbelievably blue. Everything sparkled in her. She gave no excuse. She welcomed them as if she had been waiting for them. The octogenarian remained firmly attached to her habits.

Madame Durand politely led them into the house through a wide hallway with a wood frieze at waist height. Small, diffused, and judging by their appearance, rather old photographs hung from the walls. Midway, a door looked onto a passageway toward two bedrooms, followed by a staircase to the upper floor of the dwelling. At the end, the drawing room, where they would spend the greater part of the afternoon. A large painting presided. It showed a man of late middle age in a royal blue frock-coat. Below, it was escorted by two auburn damask armchairs with green silk throw pillows facing the antique divan where Rafael sat.

The doctor suffered through an hour of monotonous conversation with a dose of intrigue about family matters to which he had nothing to contribute. He felt strange in that somewhat somber, lifeless house. Always a man of spark, here he seemed like the living embodiment of disinclination. Beth tried to ignore it. She saw it, but she didn't dare interrupt. It would be an indiscretion on her part. The great-aunt took great pains in pleasing her despite some digressions and the time it took for her to express each idea.

Suddenly, Rafael rose. He had already memorized the pattern on the rug. The carpentry seemed attractive, but the most valuable items in the entire house were the furnishings. He reviewed each painting and estimated they had only sentimental value. He stopped at the large one, the one presiding over the conversation between the two women occupying the armchairs; it must've been the deceased husband. His gaze pulled him in and repelled him equally. He couldn't explain it.

Aunt and niece continued their conversation. Beth was interested in getting an update on the subject of Lyon silks, but she soon perceived that the elderly woman was still committed to the past, she had no present. She wasn't the right person with whom to discuss the topic.

Rafael couldn't find anything to do or ways to exploit the spare time. He felt the need to walk, look at trees, breathe fresh air, but he didn't chance it. With no other way to entertain himself, he kept looking at the man in the painting.

Enough time had elapsed for him to evaluate that woman of deliberate speech and elegant gestures. He paused at the name Durand, probably her husband's name; it sounded familiar. He recalled a vivid scene in Lyon during the Commune. The first echo from the provinces had sounded there with the necessary resonance. It's been said that the people centered their attention on the bulletins written by Mr. Thiers himself, after they were deprived of the Paris newspapers. Finally, instinct prevailed and they refused to stand by uselessly. The multitude filled the streets while cheering the Commune. Lyon had become a stronghold.

He believed he was right. Durand must've had some relation to the lady now sitting before him. He thought about interrupting them to clarify the mystery that pestered him, but he didn't. He appealed to his patience to wait for the proper moment. He felt a mixture of tiredness and boredom. He went on with his contemplations.

Indeed, a certain Durand along with Crestin, Bouvatier, Peret, and Velay had formed part of the five named as communal councilors when the municipal commission was dissolved. It would've been interesting to engage in a dialogue about that topic, though in reality, his greatest interest was in listening to any facts relating to the man who flew the red flag from the balcony of Lyon's City Hall palace.

He was convinced that Madame Durand was a great reservoir of that rich history. On further thought, all of Lyon was laden with extremely interesting names and surnames. It would be unthinkable to miss such a valuable opportunity. He wanted the women to discontinue the drawn-out conversation, but it wouldn't be prudent to remove them from the shared pleasure of their strong ties and countless memories. He wouldn't even make a comment to Beth about his interest in visiting Terreaux Square and St. Peter's Palace.

Just a few seconds after he finished his review of the events in Lyon, the two women seemed ready to devote all their time to him.

"You don't have the appearance of someone skilled in the use of weapons. My husband was an excellent shot, a distinguished and admirable Frenchman."

"It would've been an honor to meet him. I'm sorry for your loss. Your pride for him magnifies you, my compliments."

"Thank you, thank you."

"I'm really not knowledgeable about the use of weapons. I like to paint, hunting is also entertaining. Being a doctor, restoring health to the sick is my function. I get pleasure from that practice."

Madame Durand pretended not to give importance to his last remarks, yet from that moment, she was fairly interested in him, more than is customary with any person met for the first time and for whom one scarcely has any references. Maybe loneliness and longing, brought on by talking to Beth, the dearest of her remaining family members, drove her interest. But the mere fact that her new guest was a doctor was enough for her to like him and made it easy to engage in rewarding conversation. For his part, Rafael delicately endeavored to inquire about that which had kept him occupied for so long while they talked, and from that moment would cease to be a simple assumption.

The three of them enjoyed a stroll in the garden and rested on a bench under a weeping willow already spreading its first long shadow of the evening. The elderly woman asked him about some aches and pains befitting her age and others he didn't understand altogether. The recommendation was simple: short walks in the fresh air as she was doing now. That environment would serve her well to oxygenate her tired lungs.

After a frugal dinner and brief table talk, they played cards before retiring. Rafael cheated mischievously at the game to the elderly woman's initial chagrin as she didn't expect such behavior from the doctor, but once she discovered his intent, she found it amusing. He was just trying to entertain the ladies.

When time came to withdraw to their rooms, and since the niece had taken the precaution of not mentioning her relationship with her companion, the hostess deemed it suitable that they sleep in separate bedrooms. He would settle on the second floor in an ample and well-ventilated bedroom, evidently the master suite.

While Madame Durand ran inspection to ensure that no detail would be overlooked that could hinder the rest and wellbeing of the guest, they were distracted looking out of a window. The moon, on its last crescent days, made its way amid the virtually motionless clouds.

"I haven't been able to sleep here again…"

The pair, still on the moon, were delayed in turning to face her, after she left the idea incomplete, muffled, as if a knot tightened her throat.

Beth was fearful that the elderly woman would reveal the grim events that caused the death of old man Durand. The entire family had been involved, especially her only brother.

"Life is not the same after something like that, Aunt, but you are strong enough."

"Poor man, it was all so sudden, so inexplicable. What happened to your mother couldn't be helped. But yes, it was imprudent of Bennett to insist on traveling in such a severe blizzard. Dead and all he wouldn't forgive him. Much less your brother after what he did."

"Aunt, where will I sleep?"

"Downstairs, in the room where you used to sleep with me when you were still a baby."

Her niece didn't object, but she had the impression that her great-aunt was suffering from dementia. She

161

sometimes mistook her for her mother or spoke of visits from her husband.

"Don't you worry, Doctor, not everything that is said about this room is true. It's the best in location and comfort. As you can see, it extends the length of the façade, that's why there are so many windows. It was my husband's favorite place. It is most natural that you sleep here. I offer it with pleasure. Your presence is an honor. I wish you a pleasant night."

"Merci, Madame. Merci."

With no further remarks, both women left for their bedrooms.

The unfamiliar house, which he found forbidding and unfriendly from the first moment and without a clear idea why, unnerved him and worse, he would have to sleep alone. Although the lady's words had left him in a state of vigilance, worn out from the draining day, he settled into bed.

The silence bothered him. He tried several different solutions to no avail. He would get up, turn on the light, and walk around the room which seemed several times larger than it was. He walked barefoot. Sometimes he walked in concentric circles, other times he made the shape of some parallelogram or other not to be repetitive. Weariness should bring him sleep. He couldn't break away from his fixation on the painting in the drawing room that came to life in his intermittent somnolence.

All at once, he began looking for something undefined. He grabbed the cigarettes from the nightstand. Did he really feel like smoking? He lit one, exhaled an enormous puff, and tried to distract himself by watching the smoke drift slowly over a window reluctant to let it out; the sleepy air forbade it. In that same spot he found a large book, bound in dark, old leather. He skimmed through its pages. It was a history book.

He had managed to fall asleep when the ringing telephone startled him. It might be Beth unable to sleep and intending to come to him, but no, it wasn't Beth. He answered but no one spoke. It happened several times. He tried to ignore the incident, but his eyes, like headlights, were once again nailed to the ceiling.

He had enough time to think about the things he wanted and about things he didn't like to remember. He began to wonder if Victor Hugo had spoken with the ghost of Leopoldina in Guernsey, he pondered on how Marco Polo avowed that certain birds can fly while carrying elephants in their claws, how Lutero saw the devil before him and threw an inkwell at his head... Cirilo, Rungo, Rufino, all those who went to his house in the evenings, spoke of lights and visions, though sometimes they became confused and said that the large flying beetle was a spirit looking for something, and others had seen the dead man wrapped in a sheet, leaning on a palm tree near the creek. Then, it was plausible that the man in the royal blue frock-coat could appear when least expected to question why someone from Remanganagua[22], was so brazenly lying on his bed, enjoying what wasn't his.

Awake or not, the fact is that the dead and the lights of his childhood bubbled from within him as if he were looking at them for the first time. Like the soldier on guard duty whose panic makes him see an enemy he has no time to avoid, with hairs on end and a fistful of good luck, he would wait for dawn.

Restless, he got up to find a way out of his condition. He devoted himself to the examination of what could be hidden behind a large armoire located to the right of the armchair. He smelled old age in the suits and costumes he quickly removed. He thought they might serve him in his purpose. After thrashing about and putting the contents in complete disarray, he surprised himself by choosing something he found adequate to show up in Beth's bedroom and end the night in laughter and jest.

He didn't count on the devil's perpetual insomnia. He took the frock-coat worn by the man in the painting on the wall and chose the best of several walking canes. Then, his paternal grandfather, who had belonged to the world of the dead for more than two decades, came to reprimand him for fooling with things that were not of the living. He came sulky and offended, cracking his leather in the air. Rafael saw him move away, still

---

[22] Colloquialism that indicates a remote and isolated place.

irritated, with a cane made from an ordinary branch, the same one he used when roaming the paddock and the crops.

Rafael reflected. Hemingway too, during his last years of life, roamed slowly around the entire Vigía farm and the streets of San Francisco de Paula leaning on a cane made of unpolished güira wood with knots in plain sight. However, Rafael had selected the most luxurious, and maybe too elegant for the occasion, made of ebony with filigree ends.

Carefully, he went in the direction of the bedroom where he assumed he would find Beth longing for him. He snuck all the way in socked feet so she wouldn't notice him until he was snuggled beside her. He thought it remarkable to find the door ajar and a faint light illuminating the bedroom. He looked ahead but didn't stop to discern if someone was in the bed. It was empty. To his left, sitting in a wicker armchair, he found the foggy presence of Madame Durand.

She wasn't disturbed, as if this was a familiar visit. She looked at her watch, exactly two o'clock in the morning. Was he early? She found him younger, robust, and strangely, he had grown a mustache. She didn't believe that such things happened after so many years, much less from someone she'd just seen the night before and had made no mention of such a decision. She didn't like the mustache at all, she wanted him as he always had been. Abruptly, she rose from her seat and left the room. The apparition wouldn't move. He was petrified.

Time passed. Still at the threshold, Rafael decided to sit while he waited. There had been curiosity in the woman's face caused perhaps by the royal blue frock. He didn't know where she went or why. Presumably, the place to which she disappeared was a bathroom. The calmness with which she had welcomed him indicated that the delay had some justification. She would come back. Not even the slightest idea came to mind as to what she would do with him. He would be obligated to look for her if she were gone much longer: Something serious might've happened to her. No doubt about it, this was a strange household.

As exasperation set in Rafael, the Durand woman returned without making a sound. She had changed into a nightgown and perfume that smelled of roses flooded the bedroom. Still she didn't show the least expression of fright or worry. Carefully, she approached with an expression on her face that indicated her intent to please as she caught her prey. Brazenly, she made to recline the visitor's head to accomplish her objective more comfortably. Meanwhile, with her right hand, she took out a blade from a pocket of her flannel nightgown. But the new Durand stood, removed the object from her hand, sat her in the armchair he had just left, and ran out. She just wanted to shave his mustache. She didn't like it.

In great haste and alarmed by the incident, Rafael fled down a hallway flanked by hanging weapons belonging to the Frenchman, but there was no time to waste, no time for stopping no matter how interesting

166

they seemed. He tried to find the staircase, but at the end of the hallway, he was confronted by the real Durand. They struggled, the dead man pressed on, but no strategy worked. Then, he gained advantage when the living man realized who he was fighting, the man in the large painting! The battle continued, both on the brink of surrendering, particularly the one with the beating heart; men have had heart attacks for much less. The dead man persisted until he snatched the blade from the living man's hand. There wasn't much he could do. He hadn't strength enough to rip off the royal blue frock, and he was already late for his rendezvous.

Somewhat stunned and with no other option, the dead man had no time to recover his strength but continue his path toward the bedroom from where the living man had exited. He was horrified to think he might be late to his meeting with the implacable woman.

Evidently, the living man thought himself dead, and the dead man thought himself alive. With his heart pounding, the living man went into "his bedroom". He felt some rest had been well earned, so he sat, lit a cigarette and did some relaxation exercises in hopeless attempts to recover his composure. In need of fresh air, he walked to the window from which he had admired the moon next to Beth. It was no longer there, and the night was black.

Beth didn't sleep either. She felt uneasy about wasting one of the few nights she had left to savor the company of her lover. Also, knowing well every detail

167

of the house and the unpleasant memories of the chamber where she had left him, kept her from sleep. They all awoke as if thrashed for one reason or another.

He waited for breakfast with anticipation. He wanted to be in the dining room, which he found so lovely during dinner, and because it was detached from any other part of the house. It would be a nice respite from the tension of the previous night. When they arrived, the Durand woman was already sitting and not exactly in the same place as the day before. Her topic of conversation only centered on her wish that they would enjoy the specially prepared breakfast. She seemed self-assured and never showed any evidence of having participated in any unpleasant events during the night. She spoke of her taste for tropical fruit, their delectable flavor, but nothing about the nocturnal happenings.

No matter how much they tried to listen, their gazes hung on the dagger on Madame Durand's napkin, which she didn't appear to notice. Beth lost her appetite, she was nauseated, horrible memories overwhelmed her, those the lady of the house had been about to extract from within herself while she arranged the room for Rafael.

Not to mention what Rafael had endured, face to face combat. He confirmed the relationship between this living woman and the dead man who still needed her. He judged that enough time had been allotted to the visit. He had no interest in learning anything further. The goodbye was a great pleasure.

They would return to Paris on the afternoon flight. Beth didn't pass up on lunch at a restaurant in the gastronomic capital of France and made a quick tour of the city before heading to the airport. They didn't sleep that night either.

Chapter 12

Laura and her husband, who had been on holiday in the Seychelles, would be making a two-day stop in Paris before continuing to Scotland. Rafael wouldn't say it, but he was looking forward to her company and, if possible, to finding out if any speculations had been made in Mahé about his destination.

Laura arrived on time and alone. She excused the absent Inukai, who had been forced to travel to Japan to resolve some family issues. She looked like those blondes from the movies. Beautiful and cheerful as always, from first contact, she made her good mood contagious. She didn't waste any time in telling them about the latest novelty, the opening of nudist beaches in some of the uninhabited islands. Anse Royale and Anse Etoile were full of tourists like never before, to say nothing of Victoria with its superb atmosphere, though she preferred the tranquility of Praslin. From the moment they began the exchange, she scarcely took a breath, eloquent and amusing she talked non-stop. A great conversationalist and knowledgeable as she was about Paris since her time as a student, she only granted them a turn to tell charming narratives or hair-raising experiences.

Laura related, ever so delicately, that according to Doctor Cuní, it was quite serious for Rafael not to have gone to Cuba on vacation, and worse even, that no one knew his whereabouts. Apparently, she commented, as she wouldn't venture an opinion, she chalked it up to difficulties in communication, since they spoke in English and there was a possibility that the doctor had not made himself clear. As for her, she didn't find it reprehensible for anyone to decide where to best spend their vacation after so long at an arduous job. She found Beth's call somewhat amusing and in great taste for them to be in Paris, away from gossip and intrigue. She pronounced in perfect Spanish what Rafael would say when it was appropriate: small village, big hell.

She also told how one afternoon in Praslin, when Beth had already revealed to her where they were, she tried to walk unnoticed by Doctor Cuní who was on his way to the beach. Amusingly, she told the story of how she discovered the Cuban Doctor's mysterious ritual by mere coincidence. One of her housekeepers had informed her about how the elusive native women had followed him to watch him at the foot of the coconut trees. More and more female patients came to him for consultation. There was also speculation about a relationship with some mystery of the gods, with something divine.

In private, Laura informed Beth of Frederick's sudden return to the Seychelles. Normally a laconic man, this time she was intrigued by his unusual behavior asking insistently for his wife, amazed that she hadn't told him where she was. He also had the audacity to reveal the concern he felt because lately his wife preferred to stay in Victoria, an absurd place, according to him, at certain times of the year. He added his intention to wait for her and propose that they settle down together permanently in Sidney. He had purchased a beautiful house in Bondi where she would enjoy the magnificent beach and he could stay in this wonderful world where fish lived, to enjoy their diversity, and find new species, without worry. He was obsessed with his research in Australia, and his life would lack meaning if he couldn't explore those marine depths; but he also didn't want to lose his wife, though the two had very little to do with each other.

They had made a reservation for dinner in the restaurant-lounge "La Candelaria" specializing in Mexican food. They opted for tacos and spicy chiles. Rafael added white rice and fried eggs. All was good cheer, their eyes looked upon everything through a prism of happiness. Dinner was long, not for being abundant, but because they found it impossible to stop talking. They would enjoy Laura's company for only two days, and each instant seemed precious.

Had he gone to France alone, he wouldn't have appreciated all the charms the country offered in the same way; without someone to share it with, everything would be different. Having another with whom to evoke those days was marvelous, now he had two by his side and felt an incomparable sense of elation.

After a stretch of time much longer than average for anyone to have dinner, they concluded the repast. The food had lost too much of its flavor and they didn't feel the need to continue further. They headed toward the bar intent on having some drinks. Rafael made the women laugh heartily when he was startled by his first shot of aged rum, which he guzzled, and let out the Cuban expression "Coñooó!" Those hours were unforgettable. Laura, who would not join them in their adventures around Paris the next morning, surrendered. She needed to rest before moving on to Scotland to visit her parents.

The Eiffel Tower was their next destination. While they waited for a taxi, Rafael said he had forgotten his travel documents as an excuse to go back to the room. He took the opportunity to make an important call to London and returned downstairs quickly.

The tour would take whatever direction the driver thought most convenient to arrive at the tower. The man smiled his assent while looking at them on his rear-view mirror. He repositioned himself on the driver's seat and put chest to steering wheel. He endeavored to be polite, always a kind expression on his face knowing this fare would guarantee a loaded tip. When they arrived at the Seine, he slowed down at Notre Dame Cathedral. He skirted the river with its discreetly running waters. They identified the Louvre, passed by the Orsay railway station, which had recently begun its transformation into a museum. The taxi driver couldn't help shooting looks at the couple. Since their departure he had noticed that the girl made some comments in Spanish, while the man just opened his eyes and made faces of amazement. They approached Palais Bourbon. Then, the car turned in search of Champ du Mars to drop the tourists ahead of the Eiffel Tower.

Right out of the taxi, Rafael seemed breathless from so much contentment. He had no need to speak. His expression revealed that this was his first visit to those parts. With his inherited habit from childhood of making measurements "by eyeballing," he surveyed the tower from top to bottom and bottom to top and calculated how many royal palms could fit in its height. Its true dimensions cannot be appreciated until standing right in front of it: "It's a molten iron titan," he remarked.

They bought the tickets and went up to the first floor. Again, Rafael was astonished. He thought he could see more than a thousand people, in small groups or dispersed, in that circular gallery and still space remained for twice that number. A couple spoke in loud voices, and quite rudely, in convoluted French. Evidently, they hadn't selected the right place, but Rafael didn't flinch, he concentrated on reviewing the inscribed names of the scientific world's main personalities. Beth took advantage of the radiant day to observe Paris through the telescopes and fascinated, invited Rafael to the second floor.

He found no words to describe the scene before him, Paris, the city of his dreams. Yet memories of the unmatched tropical vegetation, his inseparable friend, from where he dreamed of raining coins and fought for a more decorous life, haunted him. He abandoned the deep meditation and tried to concentrate on the scene Paris displayed when Beth touched his back and brought him back to reality. Both immersed themselves in the panorama the city offered.

They conquered the third and last level by elevator. They wanted to visit the restoration of the Grevin museum, which displays the moment when Gustave Eiffel welcomed Thomas Alva Edison, the man with more than a thousand inventions. From that viewpoint, the city of lights amazed them once again.

Lethargy presented no obstacle to a new day that looked to be especially intense. Rafael left the bed covers faster than usual, he needed more time. Beth would be leaving Paris the next morning, Sunday, with bad weather predicted, but she could not delay her trip. She had to return to the Seychelles. He wanted to wake her but wouldn't interrupt her much needed rest. Besides, their night had been wonderful. He sat near her for quite some time. She had slept soundly. Her eyelids were still heavy and her mouth slightly open when she whispered:

"I leave when I need you most."

"When we need each other most."

"We never intended for the game to get so serious."

"A game we both bet on and we still don't know who risked more. We're sailing, and we're far from shore, but it'll be alright, we're determined."

"Are you worried about staying here alone?"

"I'm worried about you, about letting you go. But let's not think about that now. Come, let me help you get up. Let's hurry. The sun is trying to defy the clouds. A great day is ahead, maybe the most interesting."

The decision to make the Louvre Palace the last place in the city they would visit together was not made casually. From the first night at the hotel, he had promised himself to defer the emotion he knew would overtake him. That year the expansion of the Palace had begun with the addition of the Richelieu wing while still open to the public.

Majestic, beauty like nothing he could ever envision. They were in ecstasy taking in the scene that welcomed them. Before they knew it, they were at the entrance. They joined a group of tourists eager to visit the place. Rafael's greatest reason for the trip: to face the most famous piece of artwork in the world with all the assumptions and mysteries that surround it.

When his eyes and soul penetrated the legendary Mona Lisa, he observed it with a sincerity he wouldn't have imagined. He thought it a beautiful painting and a lovely woman. He'd forgotten certain things, as is common on great occasions. He'd forgotten what he already knew, her expression and her smile. Gradually he began to withdraw in contemplation. He moved

176

slightly to the right to better appreciate the enigmatic painting that provoked so much debate. Surprisingly, something was missing. Something he'd noticed in art books and in the most beautiful replicas was missing. Until then, he had judged the woman as simply lovely, but now she looked at him with a changing expression, somewhat sad and with a delicate smile.

So vocal in similar situations, now Rafael said nothing, he had no words. He felt an excessive desire to seize the image, to concentrate on the most minute detail. When he thought himself on the apex of his hunger, a shadow intruded. He returned to his original position uncomfortably; something was grazing his pants' leg and held on to his left knee. It gave way to his impatience. He lowered his gaze as if wasting precious time of life. Impossible. His son! His dear son was next to him! He took him in his arms to share this singular moment. With large eyes that now turned grayish green, the boy looked at the woman with great attention, perhaps because he found some similarity with his mother or because of the natural wisdom in children. He wanted to touch her. Then he placed his soft hands on his father's face and smiled widely.

Within that complicity in pure love, as if not wanting to pluck the petals of a beautiful flower, Rafael placed a kiss on his small forehead, and his haunted father's arms extended to their highest to give him wings. May he gallop once again with his grandfather along the guardrails! May he make castles in the sand!

Not before he swore to him, to God, and to DaVinci, that he would continue making progress one step at a time, and sooner rather than later, he would paint again.

Not unlike Vincent Van Gogh, who couldn't slide his brush without the presence of a sunflower, or, according to Goethe, could Frederick Schiller write without the smell of rotten apples, he suspected that his brush too would not run along the canvas if not in his native land. He hadn't decided to leave medicine. He didn't look at it as pure science but believed in the art of healing. For now, taking painting up seriously again seemed a distant notion. He wished, at the right moment, to paint in Cuba, its landscapes and its circumstances.

He didn't dismiss the memory of the last hours. Who knows if on any given day, one of his paintings might appear on the wall of an important gallery. Men like him, when they find what they want, plunge into a period of nonconformity that drives them to set new goals.

In the first hours of the morning, Elizabeth would return to Victoria. She was quite definite in her reaction to her husband's proposition; completely determined to make a clean break, as Rafael liked to say. The flood of happiness during that holiday, now at its end, was in direct contrast to the times yet to face, possibly troubled by yearning and setbacks.

Neither one dared speak. Rafael feigned a degree of self-possession seldom achieved. Beth seemed driven to undo her marriage. He thought it cruel to allow such a resolution when she couldn't count on him to make any offers, not even the possibility of seeing her again. Much as he would have wanted, the consequences of that trip could not be ignored.

A shared omen that this would be the last night they would spend together wounded them. They maintained dialogue only with their eyes. They remembered the night before but said nothing. The last should've been the best, but they feared the bed. Something trivial had to be added to her carryon bag, a reminder that came in the form of a brief word or two, a frivolous phrase.

Beth clung to her decision. She had to bide her time and feared that some inconvenience or simply her failing nerve, might interfere, and that her weakness might make her lose forever the chance of other encounters with him. In a few hours she would have to confront problematic Frederick. She longed to lie down as soon as possible and get enough rest. Always so composed, now she unraveled in a fit of sobs until dawn brought them the inevitable farewell.

Paris, the city worth contemplating every second, its bustling streets, its unique gastronomy, the greatest tourist destination in the world. None of this seems to steal the serenity of the Parisian. However, in the span of a few days, for Rafael, Paris was not the same. He felt devastated, nostalgic for the sun, the loneliness was painful, and the cold air stung him. He missed Beth.

He didn't hesitate. He packed his bags and went to Charles de Gaulle airport. His eyes fixed on nothing in particular, he observed the actions of the human mass that populated the hallways and elegant lounges. People seemed to travel in groups, yet they weren't. Perhaps some of them felt as lonely and disoriented as he did, but they showed no signs of concern. He was determined to imitate them, to portray endurance.

He found a place to sit and ponder the prescient ideas that hounded him. An emergency room in Calixto García Hospital in Havana called him insistently; he must come as soon as possible. Perhaps his paternal instincts influenced him, but in any case, he made efforts to recover and find an answer. The most immediate consideration was to take an Air France flight to Spain, and from there, an Iberia flight to Cuba. Fruitless inquiries resulted in the realization that he couldn't buy that ticket or any other. He masked his anxiety until he came up with an answer. In any case, where was he going? He simply needed to travel.

He returned to the hotel completely disconcerted. Three days later he made a call to London and was advised, as a possible solution, to contact the Cuban consulate in Paris. He accepted the proposition. He had no other option. He wouldn't give excessive explanations as the result would be the same. He would take the bull by the horns. The two people he spoke to were not as helpful as he expected and treated the issue like a hot potato burning their hands. It would take some time to get a response. Paris darkened in his eyes, anxiety weighed on him.

Before the appointed date, he received a visa to return to the Seychelles. Besides the desired reunion, he wanted to conclude his vacation in Victoria and return to work. He arrived at the Point Larue airport as unruffled as the most serene of mortals. And while the devil was distracted plucking hairs from his beard, under a sun hot enough to fry eggs on the sidewalk, at two o'clock he knocked on Elizabeth's door.

She was paralyzed, coffee pot in hand, apparently trying to make a Cuban coffee "colada". She was alone. Both swallowed hard to recover, they needed to be together.

A few days later, Beth still couldn't establish a serious conversation, so she told him about a call from her great-aunt, Madame Durand, to inform her that she had named her sole heir in her will. The elderly woman had been jovial during their conversation, and although her announcement did not come as a surprise, Beth was pleased to hear it. Also, she sent Rafael greetings and thanks. His visit had much improved her mood and she longed for another encounter at the earliest possible time. She prayed every night for his return but asked in advance that he remove his mustache before the anticipated meeting.

Her aunt's attitude didn't seem at all proper to Beth, but she refrained from telling her. Given her advanced age, she was happy and sure that one day, when she knew the truth about her relationship with the Cuban, she would approve without reservation, since she no longer cared about how much capital he held. Also, the invitation confirmed the suspicion that she had never thought well of her marriage to the arrogant Australian. She probably already assumed the existence of a relationship between Beth and the doctor.

In the meantime, Rafael, trying to hide his surprise at the darkness toward the end of the lady's message, looked out a window at the sea. He watched the waves rock a yacht sailing toward port, and remembered what happened that night in Lyon, which by the way, he had never confessed to Beth. Now it caused him as much mirth as concern.

"Very nice, very nice, send your aunt my thanks." Lucky for him, Beth didn't notice the delayed response.

He settled in the couch unable to focus on reading the newspaper, so he watched the white cat sleeping placidly in the corner. Madame Durand also had a cat. It was a female, he knew, because he had always been told that male cats are no more than two colors and that one was white, black, and gold. Besides, now he remembered its face being small. He would've liked to see its eyes, but it had spent all its time sleeping next to its owner on the Persian rug that covered a great section of the bedroom.

He felt special affection for cats, had them for company since he was a boy, ginger almost all of them and dynamic. They didn't spend much time in the house, mostly climbing where no one would imagine, defending their survival. They chased mice, lizards, stole food. They were always on the prowl. He thought about a newspaper article on the Intra-Sciences prize awarded to Michel Jouvet for his study of sleep phases based on observations of these animals.

Beth, sitting next to him, tried to entertain him with tales of some of the things Laura did to compensate for the mischief of her two boys, still young, but Rafael wouldn't react, not even with a smile. He didn't try to fake it either. He would've preferred to continue meditating on the small docile animals. He had just noticed that Beth was wearing the bracelet her husband had given her at the birthday party. No comments had been made regarding Fréderick. Strange woman. She was silent about her past, didn't talk about the present or gave a clue about the future. What the fuck did she think? He wanted to tell her that she was a shameless bitch, that from that moment their affair was over, to never come looking for him. It was easier to deal with ardent, explosive Latin women who didn't waste any time, and, like uncorked champagne, release it all in rants and raves and to hell with everything, or start all over, blank slate. He was sick of so much silence, so much bullshit.

It took him a while to snap out of it. That afternoon he had karate practice, but he had lost interest. Neither

183

did he tell her that he didn't want to delay a visit to his colleagues any longer, who had all returned from their vacations to get back to work. He began to think of life in a different way. He would concentrate all his efforts into the task of disease prevention and healing. He also hid his desire for the days to go by swiftly. In the meantime, he would endeavor to spend some of his time reading the books he had purchased in Paris.

Chapter 13

The doctor went to Antananarivo by Beth's urgent request to treat the son of Manhakanony, a business man and known personality, who would be waiting for him at the airport with his translator, Tante. From there, they would have to cover 571 kilometers by car to reach Mahajanga.

Rafael was impressed with the island, the fourth largest in the world since its separation from the African continent eighty million years ago. A diverse landscape displays its wonders, which explains why ecologists call Madagascar the eighth continent.

Manhakanony didn't waste any time in telling the doctor about his son Mandrika's grave condition, afflicted by prolonged fevers, vomiting, and intolerable headaches that brought him to delirium. Those were the weakened child's most persistent symptoms. The tests administered did not concur with the physical examination, and his appearance deteriorated daily. There was no clear diagnosis. Evidently, the fevers were unfamiliar to that region. The truth was the boy's health required urgent and effective treatment.

With unbelieving looks, frowns, and darkened countenances, tense and dispirited, the Manhakanony welcomed Doctor Rafael, who didn't look as they expected at the start. He didn't fit the ideal in whom they had prematurely deposited so much faith. The young man, white of skin and thick black mustache, didn't seem as elegant as others. In blue jeans, short sleeved red checkered shirt and flip flops, he appeared incredibly simple. Nonetheless, with reservations, his presence was hopeful, perhaps because he was serious, of few words, extremely attentive to any interesting fact they could reveal regarding the patient.

Words of welcome and introduction had been scarce, and soon gave way to the father's request for the doctor and the translator to go into the next bedroom where the boy lied. Malala, the wife, and Andrasamara, the eldest daughter, would accompany them. As they approached the bedroom, all eyes were focused on Rafael. Anxious and nervous they observed the gestures and movements of the doctor while he handled the unconscious, unmoving patient.

Time elapsed without an answer to the case as had befallen others before him who had come to relieve the boy of his grave condition. The doctor peered at all present. He didn't dare tell them how difficult the situation was and that he couldn't find an answer. He was ready to appeal to Hippocrates to intercede for him, or to "the little enchanted crustacean to get him out of the situation," when Aunt Iluminada presented herself in the form of a strange insect on his shirt sleeve, but it wasn't her. No. It was dead Gregorio who came to his rescue.

Seemingly relaxed, the doctor took his time before running his hands along the patient's body from head to

186

toe and backwards with extreme gentleness. Three times he repeated the action. The silence was endless. At the edge of desperation, Malala, without understanding the spirituality of that moment, believed time was running away from them while her son's life hung in the balance. She recriminated the doctor in abrupt gestures and an aggressive tone for his passivity in the face of such urgency. His reluctance to act had disappointed them, and he would always be blamed for the death of her home's great treasure.

The mother's words still resonated when the boy made a push to open his eyes, but an instant later, they were closed again. According to her, that was the worst of the symptoms, and she was living the most dreadful moment of her life. The translator limited himself to communicating to the doctor only the necessary words, but he'd caught the entire message and continued without hesitation. In no haste, he removed some medicine from his bag, applied it to the patient, and instructed them on the schedule in which the dosage should be repeated.

The dismay was short-lived. In less time than anyone imagined, Mandrika began to feel energetic and hungry. The astonished faces of those present showed unbelief in what they witnessed. A miracle had been achieved. The doctor regarded the event as normal and made no comment: Saving lives was his job. It was almost common to accept the gratitude that comes after restoring the health of a loved one. Perhaps that is why

187

he changed the subject and set aside the inevitable compliments. The boy was the couple's only male of nine children. Soon there was a toast and the offer of a tour of the city and other attractive places of renown.

The next day, they began their drive with great enthusiasm on a pusse pusse (push-push) dragged by a black man who quite soon was sweating and nearly faint from the effort and energy expended. He had been at his hard labor since early in the morning. During the trip, looks, smiles, and poses from young women with the intent of provoking licentious thoughts in tourists didn't convince the doctor. Disappointing, unhappy that moment when he saw how it was their sad role to show the ugly face of poverty. He felt sorry for them.

They continued their progress through the narrowest and dustiest of alleyways from where appeared hawkers and stores with good quality pieces and original crafts. He became interested in the embroidered hand towels and tablecloths. They seemed similar to the ones made by the women farmers in his country. It was either pure coincidence or some unknown influence. He made no comments to his companion who seemed a pragmatic type of fellow.

He worried when the conductor of the pusse pusse was notably threatened by hypoglycemia. He asked the translator to let him know that he preferred to continue the trip on foot, or another possible solution could be for each one to drag the cart in turns. Thus, the weakened man would have the possibility of recovering as evidently, he could go no further.

Manhakanony gave no response. He presumed it was a flawed translation. The man continued trying to balance the load. One of his passengers was of physical mass superior to one hundred kilos, which hindered the driver from making turns without the coccyx and other parts of his customers' skeletons suffering more than was permissible.

The doctor was desperate traveling through the worst of those impassable alleyways. Decidedly, the driver's skin was turning yellowish, it stuck to his bones, he was done, defeated. With nothing left to do, dynamic as he usually was during stressful situations, he forced the man to stop with a few words incomprehensible to the Mahajanga people that included the obligatory dicks and other parts of the body not often mentioned in public, and much less in writing. With great effort, he managed a more measured tone and returned to the original proposition, considering how close they could be to the gates of hell if something wasn't done. It was quite probable that since he had come to assist him such a short time ago, Gregorio, so far away in space, would not be willing to save his nuts from the fire when he wanted to give life to someone all but finished.

Manhakanony immediately remembered that Mandrika, his little one, was alive and well thanks to the strange way in which this man saved him from near death. He thought that if the white man, who came from so far away, could give life in minutes, in seconds he could wipe out the best pigeon in the flock. He then gave the driver a few Malagasy ariarys to dismiss him, but the man refused them categorically because, faint and all, he needed the full fare, even if he arrived home in pieces. Such was the mental state of Mandrika's father, that he paid double the fare and became the new conductor of the vehicle.

No one spoke. The doctor brushed off the insult while drops of sweat ran down the body of the new driver. Never in Majinga, as the natives call the city, had so many people from who knows where mixed together in such a short time. Positioned on the edges of alleyways, they squeezed together to see the rich and famous merchants doing one of the most humiliating jobs imaginable. The exaggerated human swarm reminded the doctor of the first stages of the Cuban Revolution when credible rumors spread that Fidel Castro, Che Guevara, or Camilo Cienfuegos had surfaced suddenly in a given place. He made an extraordinary effort to contain his laughter.

To his great surprise, what pointed toward an affront, had a happy ending. The new driver, up to that moment focused on his task, decided to stop for a breather. It amused him that he was taken for a South African tourist with intentions to ingratiate himself. After declaring the tour finished, he invited the passengers to a few drinks before lunch at a traditional food restaurant.

The next day offered different overtones yet no less interesting. They set out on a trip around the seaside city, where a pier captivates the walker with "Le Jardin d'Amour," filled with flowers of varied shapes, colors, and fragrances. Lovers stop there to watch the sea and enjoy the pleasant aroma while others sit in rustic cement benches to declare their intentions. Just a few kilometers away they visited a sacred place where relics of King Andriamandsoarivo and his two wives, Andrinamisara and Andrimasara are kept.

The grateful father continued striving to make a good impression on the   intrigued doctor. He had seen on numerous occasions the reactions provoked by the exotic island on people not accustomed to it.

Outside the city, they stopped in the thick jungle to cover themselves in its refreshing shade. Strange marvel…on the branch of a tree, a lemur poked out its scared face and looked as if it were being followed by an intruder. Rafael thought it was their presence that disturbed it. The hutia also remains paralyzed when it spies a hunter, shotgun in hand. But no, two fossae lurked one meter from where they stood. These reddish-brown carnivores measure around eighty centimeters in length, the tail can reach ninety centimeters, and their favorite prey is the lemur.

Upon noticing the fossae, the men were as surprised as the lemur and remained still allowing time for resolution. In seconds, the predators could change their minds and turn them into their victims. Human flesh could be more appetizing. They could possibly be bored with lemur meat. It was prudent to remember the legend of how fossae kidnap newborns and devour them. Who knows? So much has been written about men killing off dragons and other colossal monsters, that in comparison, it wouldn't be far-fetched for the two small animals to try feasting on them. Besides, they had waited long for the jumpy monkey to descend. Nothing more to say, Filomeno knew it well. There's good and bad in the woods.

Further ahead, farmers appeared burning trees. With implacable yet innocent fire they bid farewell to precious wood, defying any living thing in their path. Rafael tried to hide the sadness in his heart. He remained quiet as he witnessed the death of a great treasure amassed by nature for centuries.

Manhakanony thought the doctor was still frightened by their encounter with the fossae. The African couldn't understand that he didn't speak because of the inevitable corrections to the translator who spoke Spanish similarly to Malagasy. It made him impatient. So he concentrated his attention on accepting something unpleasant: The farmers did what they could, burned their great fortune to feed their families, even if it gave them little to put in their mouths. Victory, should it be achieved, would be in the style of the Battle of Heraclea, perhaps conscious but with hands and feet tied. He compared such monstrosity with the burning of the library in Alexandria done with the knowledge that it was unforgivable. He was

192

exploring one of the countries with the most biodiversity in the planet and witnessing the inconceivable. The farmers were not to blame as their survival was at stake.

With his patience at an end, he continued the charge as he had done when traveling in the cart pulled by the man, so in a gentler tone he interrupted the silence of the forest:

"Why don't the powerful make an effort to improve the living conditions of these wretches, or is it allowed to destroy what is given by nature?"

The answer was not delayed.

"If we share what we have, we become poor like them."

No doubt the translation was correct. Manhakanony acted as he thought.

Rafael wished he hadn't heard such malicious words. The gentleman looked at his guest and believed he was offended. Both remembered what happened during the trip around the city. Both decided to distract themselves with the landscape and continue their progress.

The doctor was pleasantly surprised by a beautiful baobab a short distance from the trail. This and his words of admiration, spurred Manhakanony toward impressing him even further by showing him a great marvel and taking him to the largest and oldest on the island, a tree said to be one thousand years old.

Far in the distance, in solitude, the aged baobab displayed its immensity, its opulence. It reminded him of the Cuban silk-cotton trees, yet approximately three times taller and leafier. He thought himself before nature's perfection. Perhaps Antoine de Saint Exupéry had been there and seen the tree from an airplane. Many offerings surrounded the tree. The locals believe that it houses a spirit that must be kept alive and fed. A similar cult worships the Cuban silk-cotton tree, the sacred tree. Again, he was reminded of the premise that man is one and the same regardless of location, a superior unit to what he is able to conceive. That is why a ring, the precious token he carried, feeds the spirit of the Great Baobab since that afternoon.

Chapter 14

Only a few days were left for Rafael to conclude his vacation. The new evening offered a strange flavor. In Anse Forbans, the wind pushed in heavy rain. A tempest approached from the sea and ignited lightning. Rafael hadn't decided which newspaper page to read. He was thirsty. He went for a beer when a sustained ring at the door startled him. He reacted quickly as visitors seldom arrived without prior notice, and the service staff came in through the back door; besides, he had left work at four in the afternoon as usual. Some emergency would be the reason for such insistence.

Beth remained in the living room, eyes closed, breathing deeply while stroking one of her cats. That afternoon she had proven herself a good surfer.

Rafael didn't think further, went to answer the door, but no one was there. He heard a loud knock on the side door in the hallway to the garden. Somewhat concerned, he didn't move. He would wait calmly as long as necessary.

Two men evidently in a hurry asked to come in using the rain and the forecast announced as excuse. One unfamiliar, with a phony smile, somewhat ironic and arrogantly polite, extracted Cuban consulate credentials from his shirt pocket. He was in the company of Doctor Cuní who, visibly nervous, remained at a certain distance until finally approaching his colleague for a delayed handshake.

The unpleasant stranger proceeded to inform Rafael of the reason for his visit. They had sent him to make the doctor "a proposal", a post in the Cuban embassy in England. The messenger allowed no time for comment or objection, all facts delivered at once and only the minimum necessary. In the morning he would receive his ticket, and the man would be waiting for him at the airport at exactly ten o'clock, when Rafael would take the flight to Cuba.

Doctor Cuní took great pains to pretend he knew nothing of the matter, but he couldn't keep his eyes from widening so, that they seemed about to fall out of their sockets, like the sad look on a slaughtered calf. Not one

195

sign of astonishment showed on Rafael's face. Not one word uttered, with a tight handshake he said goodbye to the messengers.

Beth continued stroking the cat pretending to be unaware of the conversation. She didn't want to trouble him anymore than he already was. He, however, showed no sign of worry. He probably didn't give much credence to the words spoken, and he thought it prudent not to act prematurely.

That night he was supposed to play chess with a Croatian friend. He decided not to go, to remain alone. He wouldn't even say goodbye to his closest friends. After dinner, still at the table, he was visibly disgruntled and stared at the interesting embroidery on the tablecloth he brought her from Madagascar. They were both mindful of the fact that something strange was happening, and as one who needs support to find the truth, he obtained an affirmative answer to the question of whether she had paid attention to the instructions from the consulate. He then said he wasn't interested in the proposal, that he didn't appreciate the idea of working in England. He would like to visit, experience their millennial culture, their climate so different from the tropics, everything that it represents in the European and global context, yet all so unlike his idiosyncrasy, his nature. He would always feel as if he were wearing a tight suit, uncomfortable. With a side smile he said, "Here, in Victoria, I've already seen Big Ben. I'm satisfied to have seen it in your company, even if it's just a replica."

Beth tried to find a pleasant conversation topic to share in such a difficult moment. She hated her consternation, she hated her stupid behavior. She remembered with some envy how her friend Laura would skirt around trouble gracefully. She also decided not to comment on the recent wedding of Princess Diana and Prince Charles of Wales because it wasn't the right moment.

After the meal, neither spoke, as if they had all the time in the world. Adept at creating situations and providing the most unexpected responses, it was Rafael who decided to tell her about the first great wedding he attended, his Aunt Iluminada's.

Aunt Iluminada was tall, elegant, and renowned for being a beautiful woman, even if her legs were more gangly than thick; also, a famed seamstress and a good dancer. Every early Sunday morning, she waited under the carob tree for Benito Chinchilla's bus to take her to the village church where she had joined a group of catholic ladies. She enjoyed enough of a reputation to act as she did. Everyone came to her when the proverbial shoe pinched, showing no worry if she fell into a trance or prayed a rosary. Quite sure of herself, she took her time in finding a boyfriend, preferably someone who lived far away and of course, better built than her neighboring suitors. Most times, she didn't know about their interest, but they knew what the answer would be ahead of time.

When they all thought her already a spinster, at a dance on New Year's Eve, a tobacconist of poise and respectable presence arriving from San Juan de los Remedios appeared at the door of the improvised dance hall in a tobacco house. She deliberately hadn't committed to any of the dances that "the orchestra" would be playing. She didn't think twice when that tall, slim, blue-eyed man whom she was seeing for the first time, asked her to dance.

The music burst amid the anticipation, and the couple wasted no time in capturing the attention of those watching. Nearly everyone joined in a circle to admire or envy their rhythmic and graceful dance. The sanjuanero, as we later called him, followed the beat well, he carried it in his blood, and she, with her shoulder-length curly black hair, rejoiced at the adulation. In her bell-shaped white skirt with red floral print, she made ever larger circles on the dance floor. The entire neighborhood was kept awake by a night of music and bodies in rhythmic movement, now away from each other, now coming near as dictated by the chords on the guiro, the drum, the claves, and two guitars. Meanwhile, my grandmother, five of my aunts, and some cousins, spent our time eating roast pork sandwiches and drinking pineapple juice paid for by the tobacconist. And so, a happy idea emerged: The suitor, accompanied by his father, would visit on the first

198

Sunday of the following month to carry out the marriage proposal.

We urchins waited as anxiously as Aunt Iluminada for Sundays to come. From two to four in the afternoon the man in the guayabera would visit. Finally, in consideration of how far he had come from and that he was a good catch for their daughter, they granted him an additional half hour, always under watch by the cousins, who took turns. Sometimes, to get another candy, one of us would distract grandmother, and whoever had that task would pretend to go into the woods to pee so they could be alone a few minutes. For six years the sanjuanero courted her, not too many in comparison with Aunt Josefa's courtship by the circus man with his little cans and little dogs. That lasted fifteen years because he didn't have a pot to piss in or a window to empty it out of, just the cans.

The preparations for the wedding seemed endless. The women of the house spent much time on the painstaking hand embroidery. On all the towels, in great big letters, there had to be a "His" or "Hers"; on each doily, the weekday to be used and the corresponding function; the tablecloth with arrangements of poinsettias, all red with their stems wrapped in green thread. Overlays and embroidered hems were added to the bed linens. The backstitch, the raised cup stitch, the feather stitch, and the chain stitch were the least complicated. Intentionally, the trousseau was left until the last possible moment. They hoped by forcing brown sugar water on the bride, she would gain a few pounds.

I had never seen a bigger celebration, and nothing was more important to me than to station myself next to the cake on the long table located in a dining room that ran from the small saints' room to the kitchen door. I stood there under the pretext of scaring off any fly that tried to sit on the cake. In some old trunk must be the pictures of the moment when everyone fixed their eyes on the device the photographer placed on a tripod, put his head under a dark cloth where the camera was hidden, and closed one eye to look through the hole with the other. Finally, he asked us to smile. My eyes were pinned not on the camera nor the little plaster couple on top of the cake to make it look prettier, but on the white and pink frosting that covered it.

As soon as the glasses for the toast were distributed, grayish clouds threatened behind the palm grove, where some were quickly split by zigzagging lightning bolts that made them collapse with great force. The space turned out to be small for so many people with muddy feet who had no alternative but to seek shelter squeezed together under the same roof.

When the time came to leave, the rain still had not eased. Clemente, who had been one of my aunt's unsuccessful suitors many years before, had a 1948 Ford ready to drive them to the Lincoln Hotel, the best and located in the village center, with fifteen rooms, some with a view to Máximo Gómez Street. There they would spend the customary three days of their honeymoon.

Iluminada came out of the room in her reception outfit with all the accessories appropriate for the occasion. The sanjuanero had also taken off his oppressive black suit and returned to a guayabera in "monkey shit" color to match his beloved's attire.

The sendoff was about to happen. Everyone watched for the smallest movement, but no one moved, no one laughed. Big tears and great sobs began to develop when she kissed each person present. Later, Tata told me they cried because she would be moving out of the house, she would go far away, over yonder to the region of Cuban Land. I didn't understand her last words, but I didn't ask for further explanation. It must've been a nice place by the sound of its fancy name. From now on, she would only come to visit.

It was still raining, and all the goodbyes had been spoken, when Clemente grabbed the large brown suitcase with gold buckles and locks perfectly matched to the dressing case that Paco was carrying. Amid all the commotion grandmother's umbrella went missing. Both men under the same palm frond, they didn't stop until they reached the trunk of the car to place the luggage. Without alternative, the driver decided to get wet, he went to the driver's seat and readied himself to start the car. At that moment, Paco gave the frond to the newlyweds, so they could reach the backseat.

Tradition could not be ignored. At full thrust, fistfuls of rice fell soaked and violent over the frond turned cape. The nervous couple thought they were being pelted by hail and began to jump and scream. Fortunately, their voices mixed in with the ruckus and good wishes. However, we couldn't break through our sadness at the moment of the final goodbye. The dogs howled miserably, the cows mooed, the goats bleated. It might've been because of the thunder, the unfamiliar sound of the Ford, or because the best of that family was leaving. Now we were helpless.

A shrill voice that reverberated through the woods was heard calling for Clemente when he started the Ford.

"Clemente, honk the horn, honk the horn and don't stop honking until you get to the village. I'll pay, I'll pay anything. Honk the horn, Clemente."

It was Uncle Pepe, Aunt Iluminada's only brother, who had indulged in a few more glasses of punch than was sensible, sweating despite the rain and very excited, seemed willing to give up his negligible fortune so the day would be memorable. In those days few people knew that honking the horn was free, and consequently everyone took this seriously. No one laughed.

Short, with a scraggly mustache, and a gold tooth, Clemente still looked better than ever. Making sure he was noticed, he extracted his fob watch from the pocket of his 100% denim pants. He looked at the time, cracked a shifty smile to prove he would obey the command because his car could respond in any circumstance. He waved goodbye with his left hand and departed in the thunderstorm.

Even during the best moments, misfortunes announce themselves without permission. Two hundred meters away, while trying to merge into King's Road, the front tires became buried in the mud. We forgot the rain and in solidarity, we became one. We had to push, push hard, but the Ford wouldn't budge. We gave up. It was useless. The newlyweds, sweating buckets, were about to abandon their trip, but just in case, they kept their windows closed to keep from being drenched when they arrived at the Lincoln.

No better decision could've been made. Ambrosio yoked some oxen to drag the car to King's Road. We remained alert, listening to the horn. They were approaching the curve at Las Curritas when we thought the car dead. Clemente later assured us that he honked to the very center of town.

I was the first to see the rainbow behind the cedars, and all the little kids went after it, so that while we peed on the pumpkin leaf where it was born, we could make a wish. No one doubted that before nightfall all would be granted.

Rafael hated goodbyes; certainly, he couldn't avoid this one. Beth had a feeling this would be the final farewell and insisted on taking him to the airport.

He was used to driving when they were together, but this morning she drove. A few minutes after arriving in Victoria, he suggested that she merge onto Francis Rachel street. She complied. She knew him well enough to understand the reason. She drove to the exact spot, visibly lit from inside. Both extended their gaze past doors and windows. They had stopped opposite the store where they had seen each other for the first time.

They left the city behind and drove seventeen kilometers to Pointe Laure. The smell released by tea plants and cinnamon trees was increasingly penetrating owing to a violent wind in anticipation of rain. One of the six planes on the runway had just landed. It was the Air France flight that in a short time would take off toward Madrid.

A round clock hanging from a spacious wall signaled the time for goodbyes.

As expected, the intimidating consulate functionary was there waiting impatiently.

Approximately forty passengers, mostly tourists, would be on the flight. His lips now on fire and hidden by the black mustache kissed Beth with great passion. Visibly anguished, she followed every movement with her eyes until she watched the plane disappear among the storm clouds beginning to gather.

He was gone, perhaps forever, and with him the best season of her life. Beth didn't realize how troubled she was until she decided, finally, to start the car, how loneliness and sorrow had left her weak. She didn't know where to go. At one o'clock an Indian couple would be waiting for her to join them in a business lunch at the restaurant "Le Perle Noire". Nature had conspired against her on this sad moment. She would be self-conscious about her deplorable state of mind. She needed to be alone, to recover. She remembered an adage by a famed Cuban writer whose name didn't come to mind. Rafael used to say it: "It is a duty to cause pleasure and not pain." She was determined not to show her feelings, to take her time. When she arrived in Victoria, she canceled the lunch and continued to Anse Forbans.

A pillow covered her face from the moment she fell into her bed. Sharp chills forced her to seek protection under blankets. An insistent cold wouldn't relent. But rather than worry about those symptoms, she accepted them without anger. She was sick, and she would postpone all obligations until she recovered.

In the meantime, every night she read and reread the songs and poems Rafael used to dedicate to her in the moments before sleep would overtake them. She couldn't stop mourning his absence, she missed his way of giving their intimacy a special touch. He joked about authoring the words in riddles, décimas he said were his own, all a way to entertain himself and have fun. "I borrowed them from Neruda. I'm jealous of Lorca because he knew about your green eyes. I wrote it in a bit of a hurry, though to tell the truth, it was Whitman wishing to be like any man, who dictated these song verses to me."

She also remembered how she used to tell him the legends that circulated in those islands: the one about the three-meter giant of yore who walked in Mahé and is buried in Victoria. The obelisk erected in his memory in the city cemetery is of the same height. However, of all of them, the one Rafael paid the most attention to was the one about Anse Forbans: "Lights come and sit on the sand where there is a great treasure, and you can see how slowly the air takes them away. The treasure is most precious, so no one tries or dares to take it." When he heard it the first time, he laughed heartily. He said with some malice, like someone who has something up his sleeve, "The world is a nutshell!"

Beth willed herself to suffer for another week before she went to Doctor Cuní seeking information. Rafael had promised to call her as soon as he arrived in Cuba. Her concerns were not unjustified. She needed to speak to him urgently, to hear his voice. Someone had informed her unofficially about some reasonable conjectures, surely motivated by the insistent night calls from his relatives in Cuba. She became restless. Doubts about the destiny that forced Rafael into silence took flight.

Not even her taste for the sea filled the emptiness. She cursed herself for not going with him. Guilt invaded her. Impatiently, she stayed the two days left to fulfill her promise. She knew Doctor Cuní was punctual. At 8:30 in the morning he left his house to go into work. On Monday she would wait for him fifteen minutes before he arrived.

By fortunate coincidence, Doctor Cuní's car was moving in the same direction as she by the Benazel street sidewalk near the market. She stepped on the gas to reach him. She would make up an excuse so the encounter would appear casual.

The man had no choice. He couldn't escape Beth's presence. She was right in front of him. He swept his right hand over his bald head and breathed deeply. No matter how much he tried to seem calm, he couldn't manage it, his nerves won. It would be convenient to wait a few days, or even better, it should be someone else who told her the truth. It wasn't the appropriate time or place either. He improvised an answer to the expected question as best he could under the pretext of not having much time. "Nothing new, Elizabeth, really, I'm sorry, but count on me. I will share any information with you immediately. We're beginning to feel anxious too."

That night Cuní decided that the impertinence of someone on the other side of the planet would not disturb the sleep he needed to be at peace. Indispensable rest was the solution, sound sleep would be most appropriate.

Sadly, once again, the alliance was united, no one moved. They knew where the call came from and its purpose. In the last few days the telephone had always intruded at the same time. And it was always Cuní, the compulsive, who answered the familiar question.

Spread on his bed, he remained rigid, eyes open and hands crossed behind his neck. He couldn't avoid the insomnia, the goose bumps, the pity for the one who

207

made the phone ring again. It must be Doctor Rafael's older brother provoked by the lack of information. The last few times, his still youthful voice sounded listless, impotent.

Cuní, feeling as if something was pounding on his forehead, was in no condition to get up. He was glad he didn't pick up the phone. He would've told him to look for him first in Havana, they knew where. Besides, he witnessed firsthand the unexpected goodbye and knew what would come upon the doctor, but he didn't have the courage to tell his brother. If he opened his mouth, he would find himself in a complicated situation.

"It's a fucking mess what these people are going through!" The words escaped his lips unintentionally when almost everyone was awake.

It became increasingly difficult to answer the same question repeatedly. It was a never-ending story. Beth informed him with a phone call that she would visit him on the weekend. Difficult hours were to come, he was beset by doubt. He shouldn't avoid that meeting, but instead confront his reality this time. It was different with her, there was no tiptoeing around the issue. Certainly, she would use her influence.

The undesired drama disturbed the quietude he needed. The story of Doctor Rafael in Victoria must stay in the past as any other. He'd always heard that to kill a snake, you need to cut off the head, but the peace he sought would not come quickly. The guajiro turned doctor had left admiration and affection in his wake from those who knew him, he had everyone in his pocket. His disappearance would become a myth. Something made him think of the long road ahead. Cuní couldn't avoid another miserable night. Ana, his children, and his entire family crowded his mind. He thought of his work and how it was becoming dull, it caused him anguish. The mail took too long, and the Cuban government paid him thirty dollars monthly, not nearly enough to make long distance calls and pay other expenses. His trips to the coconut trees hardly motivated him as his appetite for female coconuts was declining.

"It's a fucking mess what these people are going through!" The words escaped once more.

Chapter 15

The hours in the air to arrive in Cuba seemed interminable to Rafael. The rough movement of the airplane caused by bad weather and the strange circumstances in which he had left the Seychelles wouldn't let him rest.

They flew over the east of Africa to land in Cairo at the worst moment and during the most tragic situation. President Anwar al Sadat had been assassinated. His life had been taken during a military parade. Chaos owned the city. Even the locals were ignorant of the facts. Information was scarce, but the reality was clear: The President had been killed, turmoil ruled. It wasn't the right moment to measure the possible consequences of that act. Egypt had been robbed of its most important man. The enemies of the government took defensive positions while the struggle increased.

All passengers agonized at the idea of not being able to leave such a troubled place; it was a tense moment. The crew negotiated to acquire fuel and permission to leave as quickly as possible and in the least danger. Finally, in manifest distrust, after many checkpoints, the plane was allowed to leave for Moscow. No one was prepared for its cold temperatures. There was plenty of flight time left, but the stops and plane changes diminished, the distance shortened, and Cuba was ever nearer.

Rafael began to think about the delayed reunion, the surprises that his arrival might offer. He was sorry to come with such light luggage. There had been no time. He cheered up when he saw the jeans he'd had in his travel bag since he bought them in Paris. They were the smallest size he was able to find. He thought it impossible that his son could already fit into them, but the letters said that he was beautiful and growing rapidly.

His blocked ears were the first to let him know the arrival was near. The clouds, drowsy from the noon sun, had remained below for some time, but now they were above him.

It was common for travelers to applaud an impending arrival. They all seemed to know each other, winked at each other, hugged each other. Someone had the initiative to start singing Guantanamera, and the rest sang in chorus. A large group were returning from studies or conducting business abroad and had felt great longing for such a special moment.

It was the first time that Rafael had seen his island from above, but he wasn't moved. The daunting part would come now, the rolling on the ground and the abrupt braking of the plane. Almost everyone's eyes swelled, and a cry of excitement, of happiness, was heard when José Martí Airport in Havana welcomed them on a humble red billboard. The smell of Cuban earth was unmistakable. Relatives and friends crowded together wanting to be the first to identify their own. However, his welcome involved other feelings, it was different. His two companions, whom he had but ignored during the trip, stopped him as soon as he descended the stairs. He felt someone shake him forcefully. He felt inscrutable looks followed him. The curtain had just fallen. The moniker Doctor Rafael disappeared. From now on, he would be a number.

Three men were waiting for him at the bottom of the airplane stairs. The heaviest of them, dark-skinned and ostensibly from the eastern side of the island, snatched his luggage from his hands. He decided to act ignorant. There was no time for questioning. There was confusion, and he broke his silence. In applying his knowledge of personal defense, he tried to lay on the charm. He struggled to keep them from leading him. Two of the strangers handcuffed him. Their vehicle was parked by the sidewalk, in front of the exit door. They pushed him into the back seat. It was a gray Lada. He didn't see the license plate. He had always thought himself sufficiently prepared to face the most difficult situation, but apparently it wasn't so. The scene in which he had been chosen to star was terrifying, and worse, he had no inkling of the tragic drama that had just begun.

The heavy-set man in dark glasses sitting in the front seat identified himself without making any moves to the left or to the right. He told him where they were

212

going and added a few other confusing phrases. The speed and the incessant siren put Rafael on alert; an olive-green jeep joined them when they reached the main avenue.

Once near their destination, Rafael sat up straight and tried to give a certain air of distinction. He chose to show his good side to the curious poking out to see what was happening. They would have good reason to ponder because the guy in question seemed to be well-fed and didn't look like a drunk. They would probably think it had to do with some big fish in trouble. The ride seemed endless until his destination appeared, faded and mistreated by time and lack of paint. It stood out from neighboring buildings for its large scale and quality of construction. He knew what it was. It had been famous since his days as a university student. He still couldn't avoid feeling unsettled.

The man from the east got out quickly while the other two continued their custody. Uniformed men appeared immediately. The three new companions said nothing. The one in the back was in charge of the luggage. A wide hallway led to the door through which entered everyone in similar situations. The start of the process was extremely unusual. They took him into a room, gave him a white uniform into which he should change so his belongings could be inventoried. His watch was last. His life disintegrated when he saw the exchange of intrusive looks of amazement. He remembered the moment when Manhakanony gave it to

213

him as a demonstration of friendship and gratitude for saving his son. Come to think of it, that unauthorized trip to Madagascar could stoke the fire of the situation he was in if they knew of it.

A broad staircase led to the great interior courtyard. From there, they took him into another room to be photographed.

"Stand straight and please look ahead at the camera. Don't smile. These are serious procedures."

That condescension didn't bother him, he found it rather funny. Profile pictures followed, they took his measurements with a tape measure while barefoot. The scale was broken, so they asked him his weight in pounds. He gave the answer in kilos, and not accurately. Before he left that room, he told the photographer in a stern tone that he would return for a photograph to have as a keepsake; the occasion deserved it.

He waited patiently in each of the departments through which they took him. Men of the most diverse social status, a great percentage black, the majority tall and slim, were there for different reasons. Each one he surveyed reminded him of Yayo, his childhood best friend.

He lifted his gaze reluctantly and noticed some windows with thick, rough iron bars. He knew where they were taking him. Bitter guards, perhaps because of the heat and the length of their shifts, from every point began to lay eyes on the new guest. The sun was setting when they put him in a cell by himself.

214

Rafael continued trying to decipher the reasons why he was there. The idea of mistaken identity came to mind. Perhaps they confused him with a drug smuggler or a counterrevolutionary. He rejected his circumstances and felt somewhat optimistic; such things were alien to him. Cigarettes or cigars would be ideal, but he didn't have any. The possibility that matured in his mind was that it all had to do with his vacation in Paris and the hasty trip to Madagascar. He didn't understand how compromising his transgressions could be to warrant that situation, fraught with displays of drastic security measures as if he were the worst of delinquents, and what's more, locking him up for God knows how long.

Terribly tired and without food for a long time, after the second interrogation session the next morning, he eagerly ate the incredible helping of breakfast they gave him. They opened the door once more and led him into another room where Sargent Anselmo and two officials, almost always the same ones during each interrogation, waited for him. He was beginning to feel like human garbage.

The great storm. It could be the title for a good novel, or one of the best and most scandalous paintings. His thinking was restless. They accused him of not returning to take his vacation as agreed, of attempting to get asylum in several countries, and of maintaining tight relations with an Asian and a Croatian who lived in Victoria seasonally. These individuals were big capitalists with ideas completely contrary to socialism, which could cause grave political consequences to the country. Anselmo insisted on knowing the reasons why those men stayed so long in Mahé.

He lived through insufferable moments. At any time of day or night they would take him to the interrogation room. The days of boredom at the Investigation Center seemed infinite, the difficult reality in which he was embroiled wreaked havoc on him, and memories of his family came to him like small rays of light and as quickly disappeared. He needed to sleep but couldn't. During the hours when all prisoners were fully active, he heard their voices and rowdiness, sometimes deafening, even if he didn't see them. They upheld a stereotypical behavior that was alien to him, yet too obvious. When he had company in his cell, almost always of people wanting to talk, talk about unpleasant things, nothing interesting, he preferred to stay silent.

It would take him a good long time to find an explanation, to discover the unsuspected truth. His days in captivity without a trial seemed to extend. Without alternative, he would have to accept it. It was a tangled mess, and he would have to summon strength to undo every knot, thread by thread. He began to believe Cheo Totí's saying: "No evil lasts one hundred years, and no one body could withstand it."

The moment could not have been more poignant when after forty days he welcomed two relatives for a few short minutes. They had been informed of the "severity" of the crime and persuaded to go forward with the long process. They brought him the novel Explosion in a Cathedral by Alejo Carpentier. A friend had sent it, but he was not allowed to receive it, not that his mood was favorable for such reading. Perhaps warned about the limitations on topics to discuss, he seemed less than communicative. However, the excitement, the limits on expression and time, were not obstacles impeding Prieta from playing her tricks and conveying her message. "Be strong as always, remember what old Arsenio said men in trouble should do. Gregorio has been visiting Aunt Iluminada a lot lately, he never fails."

Other meetings followed much the same as the first, although longer. After approximately one hundred days, spent almost always alone, on a most appropriate date, the 31st of December, they took him to a high security penitentiary. Evidence indicated extreme culpability; also, they needed time to declare the case closed. It was taken for granted that the court would decide on a severe sentence for him.

The change didn't bother him, it was change after all. The destination, San Carlos de la Cabaña. From there, he'd be able to secure an attorney. He would place his hopes on his family finding a capable one for his defense. Rafael remembered Clarita and the unkept promise he made when he courted her in Tarará, the visit he never paid to the same place where they were now taking him. The difficult times that awaited were far from his imagination, though they wouldn't be as cruel as the moments already lived.

From a hill located in east Havana, a fortress rises clinging to boulders that appear to be part of its walls. In the distance, ships know it as the faithful sentinel, its front in the shape of a crown, watching the sea, the bay, and the port, a relic of eighteenth-century colonial architecture.

Rafael was part of the group of prisoners that would be assigned to the new jail. They arrived at sunset, and as expected, those there had already been fed. The new group would have to wait for the next day's grim breakfast. Facing the dilemma every prisoner faces when moved to a new place, cheered by the hope of better conditions, the once guajiro found "a new year and a new life." The hope that future times had to be better encouraged him, and he believed impossible the idea of enduring seven more anguishing months before learning the verdict.

They led them through passages smelling of mold and extreme moisture. A depressing scene was common behind the balustrades: confined faces spewing mocking whistles, insults, smiles that looked more like masks. No one who has ever lived such moments can dismiss the unpleasant imprint they leave. It was the usual behavior when "the new ones" arrived. At the expense of those similar to them, the miserable men had found a good reason to bid farewell to the year. But Rafael, like others, lowered his eyes until he was made to stop at the fifth door in the right wing. The gallery had bunk beds for thirty-two people. Exactly five were unoccupied, the destination of the newly arrived.

He felt lucky when they placed him on the right side, somewhat distant from the door, on the third level of the bunk beds. He preferred it that way, removed from the constant bumping into people with whom he didn't want to socialize. He had come from extreme discomfort to take refuge in yet more of the same with the added inconvenience of being in more danger. He would not face that base world recklessly. He had enough time to collect adventures.

Even three months after his release, he couldn't forget the face of the first man he spoke to without reservation. They sat facing each other, except when his new neighbor went to the bathroom with unusual frequency that entire first night. Whether they wanted or not, from that moment they would be each other's company.

He was a white man of medium height. His head was shaved so close it had a certain shine, more noticeable in daylight, and he was in a permanent bad mood, but had a fine presence; nonetheless, he demonstrated appalling adaptability. He smoked the butts of cigarette butts desperately, and he stared at his sandals while he spoke. Several hours passed before they exchanged some words as neither showed interest in knowing anything about the other. The one already there, to avoid exploding into a litany of pains and sorrows, began to share some concerns at midnight.

"I'm a barber, and business wasn't bad, but in the United States I can get rich in a short time. My trade makes a lot of money there, people tell me. My wife's entire family left when they came to get her at El Mariel, but she stayed with me. She didn't want to leave me with my mother during the last days of her life; now, sadly, she's not with me anymore. I'm not sorry about losing the opportunity I had in hand, I couldn't leave my old lady, but my friend, life's a bitch. I'd prefer to be eaten by the sharks in the Florida Straits than to be suffering this calamity. Just when I'm feeling better, the stomachaches return to twist my insides. They won't stop. If they rear up again, I won't make it."

"Did they catch you in the jump?"

"Yes, disaster follows me, what bad luck I have, damn! I can't catch a break in this life."

"Was it your first try?"

"No way! Five in a few months."

"Were you alone?"

"Twice with the family and three alone. I was desperate, I couldn't hit the mark. They had guaranteed work for me, I didn't want to lose it. Bro, you can't imagine the thousands of "greens" that've been wasted on this, because in truth, rafters are pure mafia, goddamn nerve they have, but it's the only way to get to the big money. I've heard it floats in the air over there. And the kicker is that I have to pay as soon as I start working. If you missed the chance when they opened El Mariel, you're a loser. Leaving secretly costs a lot of pesos, a

220

fortune, and with no assurance that you'll get there alive. I'd been after a permit for almost ten years, and at that damn moment they come with the motherfucking paper.

"From what coast were you intending to leave, north or south?"

"Always north, the Keys are just a step from there. Do you have any family there?"

"No, I don't."

Rafael's mouth was dry, bitter acid burned his throat. He was glad the man didn't want to continue the dialogue. He needed to ruminate over his misfortune, return to his silence. He wasn't up to having the sons of bitches hear them and try to approach with their good boy act. Meanwhile, he would have to stay alert at all times. He felt sick in that intolerable environment.

Morning came. They were still sitting face to face, each twisted in his anguish, when he decided to speak to the barber.

"I'm a doctor, but please don't tell anyone. Call me Guajiro. I prefer it to my name."

"A doctor? Brother, you got fucked too! Look at that, a doctor and stuck in this damn shit. I'm only a barber, but I'm here for anything you need. No one's asked my name, and that's okay. I'm starting to see that everyone has a nickname. Call me Barber before they try to call me whatever they want, and I'm forced to send someone to hell and entangle myself in slaps and punches. If they think you're afraid of them, they'll beat you to a pulp, they're dogs when you don't do what they want.

Besides dealing with persistent bouts of diarrhea, the barber was shaky and emaciated, but he wouldn't ask for medical services, he refused everything and everybody. He expected to recover on his own having already experienced a similar situation during the first days of incarceration. That place was not for the weak. Feeling somewhat better, he said that visits lasted two hours. He had seen his wife and one of his daughters the day before. His wife brought a telegram from the Section of U.S. Interests in Cuba letting him know that he had received the "lottery." Besides the married couple, the daughters, the son-in-law, and two granddaughters, one four years old, the other six, could accompany them. He released as many profanities as he could think of and finished with a fuck on the damn hour of his birth. He said he'd been a skip from becoming rich, he wanted to die, everything had become salty water. Two huge tears ran down his face and he lashed out again.

"We were almost there, the Comet was in sight. It lifted the waves higher than itself with the tip of its nose, it was close. A few meters from Palmarito beach, the Coast Guard intercepted them, and they couldn't escape. In the darkness of night, it looked like daytime. Our group fell into the trap as we waited for the Comet, goddamn misfortune that follows me. There were twenty-one of us and only fourteen would fit, but my family and I would not be left behind or be thrown to the sharks either. When people started complaining because the little boat was filling with water, or whatever the hell else, that was my task. I know well how that jungle works, I have a lot of tricks, and family over there, but what's best is that I'm man enough to break anyone's neck."

The barber also said that women and children were sent home, and the men straight to La Cabaña in a truck. He was alone and knew nothing of the others.

"Buddy, I was that close from jumping the puddle, so you can imagine what it was like. That always happens to me; all the misery falls on me at once. My trial is pending and surely, they'll lock me up for a few years. It'll be because I was taking minors, they're gonna fuck me for that, block my dominoes. Every time I think about it, my guts twist and I have to go to that foul, putrid hole. Fortunately, my wife is thoughtful and brought me some of those newspapers made with soft paper. She knows me well. The diarrhea and the stomachaches were gone, and as soon as she showed me the telegram, they started to grip me again.

"It's said on good authority that the Comet's crew was captured, and they're holding them in the Tank at Combinado del Este. Man, they're in the Tank! Cubans who live Over There and are well-paid. They must be worse off than ten cats in a sack, afraid to even fart, goodbye to Miami and everything in it.

"I don't know what to do, what corner to sit in to calm myself down. I have no way to defend myself, they have the proof in their hands. Those assholes fucked me over good! My friend, I have plenty of reasons to feel miserable, don't I, Guajiro?"

"You know I just got here. I'm not in a position to give you advice."

Perhaps expressing himself freely to the imprisoned doctor would give the barber comfort, help him have a better time of it, the illusion of not being so stuck. Every so often, he'd charge again.

"I've been here fifteen days and you're the first person I talk to. Call me Barber, fuck, don't forget, it's the only thing I've ever done in my life. I'm gonna oblige you and always call you Guajiro, though come to think of it, that'll be a hard pill to swallow for the inmates. A mile away anyone can suspect that if you ever had "palm strips tied to your feet," you broke out of them a long time ago, and nobody could imagine that you're not a decent man, and that you're smart; you can't hide that. You and I both, hard as it is, we look people in the eye. Maybe they think that you're here to listen to the shit they say, and then things can get ugly. You can count on me. I don't look it, but I was a good boxer."

Guajiro was upset too. He admitted that feeble and all, if things got difficult, he could count on Barber in some way. He gasped at the strong body vapor, between bitter and salty, released by so many men with little exposure to soap, most of them without deodorant, mixed with the cold, the smell of the sea, and other excretions in that reduced space. His stomach turned

224

now and again, and he felt like retching. He made efforts to remain silent on the patience bench; they might think him a misfit, and he was. There had been turmoil until dawn which had a negative impact on his much-needed rest. He couldn't accept that such behavior could be sustained. It was more reasonable to convince himself that it was all because of New Year's.

Every day the two men strengthened and learned to coexist surrounded by so much human misery, such pestilent shit. They had plenty of time and stories to tell. Most interestingly, they began to apply order to their lives, and for a time they decided to assign their periods of rest. They would take turns every three hours until more practical solutions emerged.

Things were going relatively well when Rafael was allowed to receive visitors, and he began to cling to some optimism. He also took heed of suggestions and empirical knowledge shared by those already processed to find a way to regain his freedom as soon as possible, the main topic of conversation. He looked forward to each encounter. He had acquired the names of some attorneys who had earned the reputation of being among the best in Cuba, according to the collective.

Prieta always arrived loaded with good wishes, yet soon she understood that she would have to make a great effort not to show that she was aware of the battle her brother was fighting; few moments in life are worse. She didn't want to spend time on unpleasant things. Perhaps she couldn't conceptualize self-esteem, but to her way of thinking, she grasped the internal rage that corroded him no matter how he tried to stop it. He didn't waste any time in telling her about his desire to bolt like an unbridled horse, but he would contain himself until he could arrange his words better.

"Everybody's on it for you. Old Chila read your shells. A pretty woman is coming to see you with a red flower on her black hair. Don't worry, nothing bad will happen to you here. And the best news is that a release is coming soon, it must be from this place here. And can I tell you? Aunt Iluminada, night before last, screamed so loud it shook the house. She saw Gregorio, and he didn't talk about the weather, he told her other things, but she didn't want to get ahead of anything. She told me that happiness has to be spread in little pieces. I don't know your opinion, but she said that he's never lied to her. She seemed optimistic."

The jailer didn't seem to be hearing any of the conversation. At that moment he gave no sign of concern while looking out a small window in the visitors' room that faced the courtyard. Perhaps it was his way of finding relief. It was also possible that the type of deliberate language in which you try to say something, but say little in the end, was familiar to him.

His sister's words brought great comfort to Rafael. He wouldn't take Chila too seriously. He didn't have any faith in her task of reading shells. He remembered that Flor Divina, Bienvenido's daughter spent ten years waiting for an answer from Chila's shells, and in the end

226

her boyfriend Casimiro left her for the miserable Engracia. Dead Gregorio merited more confidence, although Rafael's interest should be placed on the attorney they secured. He would have enough time to dissect what Gregorio had said, who didn't speak of possible length of time or other good things to come. It wasn't exactly what he wished to hear, but still his next few days were more comfortable. His mood and the uncertainty in which he lived, required a more complete answer, yet for now he would have to accept it as it was. Many times, a prisoner has an extreme change of heart. He had settled on an interpretation of the message close enough to Prieta's intended meaning. It served him to refresh his mind in that degrading season of his life.

Chapter 16

He was isolated, locked behind several layers of iron and a thunderous ring of keys to open and close an equal number of locks. He heard them now. Yes, the keys jangled against the doors opening the locks. The sun was rising in other parts of the world, people began their workday, but he was confined, standing guard with eyes wide open. By his calculation, it was one thirty in the morning. Two unfamiliar officials came for him. As they walked, they treated him with uncommon politeness.

"You have a call from abroad. We can't understand the man too well, but he wants to speak with you. You must tell him that you feel well and that this telephone number is your office, your number. Encourage him to speak as much as he wants and to call you as many times as he wishes. It will be comforting for you to have someone to talk to; he must be a good friend. We have seen how even family can sometimes let the prisoners down and it's friends that come to their rescue."

"We can agree on that," answered Rafael about to put the receiver over his ear.

"Hello."

"Rafael, Rafael."

"Yes, it's me."

"Hello, Rafael, what pleasure. How are you?

"Fucked."

"No understand, no understand."

"I'm in jail in Havana. Do you understand now?"

"Unpleasant news, it's not possible, very unpleasant, no accepting."

"Me neither."

Rafael hung up. What came next, must not be retold.

Summary of a prisoner's life (were it not for unexpected complications): A man thinks his life useless, surviving without contact with the outside world, for a determined period of time deprived of the individual liberty granted by the rights of a citizen. Like the deacon of that disparate collective used to say: "In a fourth of land anyone can find a troublemaker. The gate closes, and you're on your way to another world."

None of the prisoners there considered himself a "shark", even if they were. The majority were there for being thieves, gamblers, street criminals, and some for crimes of passion, as was the case of Mocho. He killed his wife because she found her screwing around. Though the man hid under the bed, he found him, and cut off his dick. Mocho would not allow a taint, he demanded respect.

Rafael couldn't stay calm. During the first consultation with the attorney he was forced to reconstruct verbally the most important events.

Meanwhile, the attorney was all ears until the end, but displeased still with what he heard as he had a different version of the crime, he added three questions:

"Who were you calling in London from the hotel where you were staying in Paris?"

"A friend."

"Did the Japanese and the Croatian with whom you had relationships make any compromising propositions?"

"No, never."

"Why did those foreigners approach you, or you them?"

"I was interested to know if in Japan they like to fly kites like they do in China. I've wanted a big one since I was a boy. Homemade kites always fly low even if you're on the summit of a hill with good air; they lack support. And the Croatian was good in karate, but I beat him. We also played chess. I lost many times, but I'm stubborn."

The only fear that troubled Rafael when he finished answering the questions was that the attorney might bring up some intrigue regarding the sudden trip to Madagascar, but everything focused on Paris. One less flea in the sac.

The attorney closed his agenda and put away his pen. He didn't think it convenient to board that ship. He told him point-blank that he'd paid the visit as a favor and that he didn't have the time to take the case. Besides, that wasn't exactly his expertise. He would leave a card so Rafael could contact a colleague that he recommended as an excellent specialist in those matters.

From the beginning, Rafael didn't feel comfortable in the presence of the attorney, his fragmented thoughts on the potential benefits of his representation. Perhaps that had something to do with his decision not to take his case. Such decision surprised him. He deserved greater understanding, to feel someone's company during the difficult moment that awaited, but he had no alternative, the dominoes were blocked. A new opportunity would clear the way. He would bet it all on a promise made to himself. Enough with all the pessimism in that environment of uncertainty that little resembled reality! From that moment, we would take the matter seriously, he would make efforts to prepare himself, everyone would know his truth.

He needed to change the subject, to stay in the present. He would try to do something useful to kill time, avail himself of resources applied in his professional life that would benefit him. He had enough reasoning to evaluate human behavior while under conditions of imprisonment.

He dedicated a good part of his time to studying how to act in an environment where man is under so much influence, sometimes forced into assuming a demeanor learned out of necessity, out of the fear of giving an unfavorable impression. The newly arrived saw in the rest a potent enemy until marking their territory and creating factions. If a man insisted on isolating himself, sooner or later someone would pick a fight with him.

Even the worst of individuals tried to hold on to some values. Few liked talking about the anguish caused to their families, the crime committed, the moral deterioration; if they did, it was in a small group, quite confidentially. They seldom showed remorse, they shirked reality. They sought support in those they thought experienced, those forged in fire.

Guajiro he was called because he always liked to be so recognized, and because the Cuban guajiro is known for his honesty and courage. He was careful to set such precedents, to fight the good fight. Then they learned the added fact that he was a doctor, which he had achieved by having tough balls.

Rafael began to feel the needs of a prisoner, who once stripped away of all his belongings finds himself equal or worse off than others. Then, he looks for something that will distinguish him, that will give him some power or influence over the rest. Things as simple as a bit of sugar or a lighter could allow a guy to feel important for a moment within his small group if attentive to the law of supply and demand. Food, cigarettes, or other products considered indispensable, items "hustled" without being detected, became a great privilege. Some attained a certain amount of money and ran small businesses outside the prison, always true to the adage "no one can kill a Cuban."

The Magnate was one of them. He tried to approach Guajiro when he learned that he was a doctor. He hadn't been able to sleep for a while. One evening, when their meal was undergoing the process of digestion and the majority joined together to hide their nostalgia, he asked permission to go up to the bunk occupied by his one-time barber. He opened the book of his memories as a boy, a street kid. His mother worked and had no time to care for her children. He was there for illegal trafficking of merchandise purchased from the merchant marines. Even in jail he hadn't abandoned his trade.

According to what he revealed in conversation, he was born to do it: Sales, whatever fell into his hands, he could unload. He had built an attractive home, his children and wife were well cared for, and whether inside or out, he fared all right, he survived. Now he demanded the doctor's opinion. He asked for it directly, with no hesitation. Every night he dreamed that someone was trying to kill him. Sometimes the dream was interrupted by another nightmare, or worse, they linked together and seemed endless. During the day, unavoidably, he looked at everyone with desires to punch them all. He needed to solve that problem, or he would ruin himself. If he ever felt self-conscious, things could get dangerous and he might trample over a few. The scene would be dreadful. Lately he had felt sentimental. He had one year left and he didn't think he'd make it alive after doing five years with his head held high.

Rafael had listened to the prisoner and realized that the same syndrome afflicted a good number of men. After a long time on the inside and prolonged suffering, the collapse would come just when they seemed adapted. He would support the Magnate in the weightiest experience of his life.

The case of Alfredo Hernández González was rather strange as well. Not much of a conciliatory man, he would assert himself when anyone messed up his bed, or worse, tried to get cocky with him. Not too young, he had arrived at the prison to serve two months for a crime committed at the warehouse where he worked as dispatch. He was also made to pay for the value of the missing merchandise.

Everyone knew his story. Forty-five days after coming in, they took him into the interrogation room. Turns out that Alfredo Hernández González, believed disappeared, would serve ten years for receiving stolen property. Alfredo didn't lower his head or stammer; he always answered with a no to incisive and accusatory questions. They said he returned to his cell as fresh as a cucumber. He wasn't processed again, but he would have to serve the ten years plus the fifteen days left for his previous charge.

"This is shit, just shit, I'm telling you. Don't let anyone fool you, talk straight, look people in the eye. Without a trial they gave me ten years. It wasn't me. It's a lie. The gall, the people that make the laws are the real culprits. One day they'll find out that it wasn't me, it wasn't me."

With his disrespectful attitude, Alfredo, whom no one insisted on giving a nickname, was admired. The majority were glad that he spoke openly and with great force against authority. He'd been there eight years and twenty-five days, the equivalent of nine years and seven months considering his conduct. He had seventy-five days left when one early morning the jailers came for him, ordered him to pick up his belongings, and set him free. He couldn't believe it. Also, taking into account "the time he had left in the convent," as he said, it didn't come as big news.

They returned for him, but Alfredo wasn't ready. An hour later, he was still following his routine. Other jailers came, but Alfredo Hernández González wouldn't give credence to their senseless words, it wasn't worth it. This time they brought in a toothless old man in handcuffs. Then Alfredo looked at Erculiano with nostalgia. The old man's heart was breaking in half.

Someone recognized the new prisoner and yelled:

"Here we have Alfredo Hernández González A! Fuck man, life hasn't treated you well! You can't deny you've been running on flat tires for a long time." Looks from A to B broke the speed of light, as if attracted by a magnet. Neither knew the other existed, but they were face to face. B was the first to notice. A was the real thing. They brought him to serve ten years pending. "Coincidentally," he would occupy bunk B. The topic was discussed longer than usual, although new things happened all the time.

Time on lock up left traces that manifested in many ways. Some became slow in their speech to the point of losing interest in practicing expressive language, nearly forced to hunt for any other way of communication. Those who were rejected by their families or couldn't be helped by them, and to add to their misfortune, had no talent, made use of an even less orthodox method. They appealed to brute force and to their respective group of troglodytes, thus limiting those they had broken, a job they had performed plenty of times to perfect it.

There was no lack of destructive specimens. They kept the pavilion awake entire nights with fights and perverted games. No one knew how the problems with these beings began, but there was a clear idea of how they would end. The most bilious commonly created conflicts among themselves to attract attention toward the setting of the brawl, a morbid type of entertainment.

The impish demons that live within us battle with each other when the worst memory of life embeds itself deep inside like ivy on a wall. Rafael's demons made him remember that in one of those enclosures they kept those condemned to death. He had no idea exactly where they came from, nor where they took them. Talk became assumption as few knew more than what related to the reduced territory they traveled, but they were certain that the sad ones were taken toward the Foso de los Laureles.

A heavily barred window let in noise from cars. No one could sleep. Someone would take care of getting the pavilion on their feet on one of the few occasions in which time turned into generalized silence to listen to what always left an mark on us all. He is coming, Christ the King! Aim, fire. While we waited in a stupor of solidarity, the sound reverberated miserably, most miserably.

Rafael knew how the trial process worked. He predicted the attorney's prolonged absences, the no-shows on established dates, his attempts to make him think that time was on his side. Haste could handicap him, he must have confidence. Consequently, with marked interest in not being disturbed, he aimed at demonstrating an unlikely optimism.

In effect, the date was set, and few days were left. The attorney appeared in a rush to agree on his plea and how to answer the court's questions. Everything would go well, his defense wouldn't leave room for much questioning, he was an expert in such matters, probably just a few more months, no reason to worry. But the trial was just a formality. The law always has the last word. It always finds a way to be right.

Some time passed before Rafael could benefit from a more advantageous situation. He substituted for a colleague when he was set free. The infirmary became his compound. Also, the green shirt, a strong symbol, told everyone that at any given time they could depend on him. To earn small preferences, somewhat more respectful treatment, was his greatest interest.

One morning, Tiger approached him to say that he was glad his conditions had improved, that to be placed at a job was the best thing that could happen to a prisoner. They would be placing him in construction. Teaching would be better, but it wasn't up to him.

That shy boy read avidly from the early grades, and being a writer was his greatest aspiration. He blamed a crook for his failure. He was in eighth grade in a boarding school center when he lost his belt. His father didn't give him any option other than to return home the next weekend with another belt like his or resembling his. Quite afraid, he set out to comply with the warning. Not long after, he had taken ownership of other objects.

The father didn't censure this attitude since besides being intelligent, his son already demonstrated he was a fighter. Soon, he left his studies to devote his time to doing nothing, and then, another option, to making money by stealing and sacrificing cattle.

His youth was going downhill while he was still in jail. Once his sentence was served, he was free to return to "his trade": risk. Danger gave him a satisfaction superior to monetary gain. Once, he asked the doctor to save his plate and spoon since he wasn't prone to staying out of jail for long. The police sector chief would always have him under scrutinizing observation.

Prisoners recognize in doctors a certain dose of indulgence in their manner, they don't care what type of person is in need of their services. What's important at that moment is to help them regain their health as quickly as possible. Sometimes, particularly young people or rebels, try to find an escape to their substandard conditions, resistant to tolerating the load they carry. Unable to reason, fixations overtake them.

Jabao was a hard one. He was a young drunk, spoiled, and a coward. No one knew where he got the booze, but he managed to get drunk often and then confront anyone who disagreed with what he said or did. He decided that the doctor was obligated to send him to the hospital, and from there he would make a call to his girlfriend. He would be sent to the hospital because he damn well demanded it. When words didn't serve him, the doctor remembered his guajiro roots; he closed the infirmary. Jabao received kicks and punches all over. Once recovered, he came out asking to be left alone. They had given him anesthesia and a strong headache had kept him awake the night before.

For the doctor, as for almost all, the true saving grace was the time they spent in the courtyard, in the fresh air, where the smell was less acrid. They could stretch the skeleton, the view, and the mind. They gazed at the rectangular frame of the sky nearly always blue with a few whitish clouds making bets with the sun while they, desperate for it, lashed out at the clouds to make them go away, they needed the sun. Everyone took

239

pleasure in his own way. Some exercised, others strolled, and perhaps suddenly, someone became still, looking above, vulnerable, searching for space. It made the crushing reality less tense. There were always three or four in a corner near the wall, only they knew the reasons why. No one was exempt from becoming involved in roughhousing caused by some unfinished business, some seemingly random incident. However, family, friends, the liberating visits they received or were to receive, were favorite topics.

Rafael began to make portraits on construction paper with pieces of charcoal. He attempted to elevate the image of his model, to mask the bitterness in the jawline, the sadness, to improve him. It was interesting for the prisoners to see themselves in a portrait. They ignored details, they simply wanted to guarantee a gift for their mothers or wives. Others, like Barber and Magnate, didn't want to be drawn.

Chapter 17

Once rid of bars, chains, and locks, Rafael wagered on restarting his life. In a hospital where presumably, things would go spectacularly well for him given his purpose to devoting all his strength to the task of recovering the time lost, he would put his enterprising spirit to the test. Every day should bring a new possibility, but it must not be overlooked that once a rope gets wet, it twists.

He traveled the ample hallways to the ward where the psychiatric patients waited for him. For several reasons, many of his colleagues were familiar to him. Nonetheless, soon, a hostile atmosphere, disagreeably strange, set in. He was received with great apathy.

No matter how hard he tried to erase the traces of his recent past, surrender to the demands of a situation in which there were still insufficient specialists to care for so many patients, he couldn't do it. In the day to day routine, he discovered a certain obscuring in work relations; a fringe of intrigue began to weave itself around him.

Rumors reached him; some considered it an insult to accept him as an equal. Also, he sensed that his words were distorted, misinterpreted even in the simplest and most honest conversations engaged in by civilized people.

During syndicate meetings or shift changes, someone appeared ready to question him. He became the bearer of culpability, but he wasn't silent, he couldn't be silent. He wasn't made of malleable material, or sweet, or suitable for certain ears.

The dishonest conduct of those around made a dent in him. The integrity and dignified demeanor in citizens of that time would break apart when a domestic item arrived for those who had accumulated merits at work. All hell would break lose if it was a Lada car or approval to serve in another country. From the moment they entered the conference room, they all became die-hard enemies. In ceaseless dispute, any hidden dirty laundry would be aired out, frequently resorting to invectives. Whoever was on the dais, had the floor to prove his excellence, forgetting that, in an hour, or perhaps less, that person who had suddenly become his adversary, would be sitting across from him in the same place of work. Betrayal was pervasive.

"I don't need to be here, I'm not sick."

She stood up, took some steps, and made gestures pretending to leave.

"If you want to know anything about me, ask the big blonde that saw me yesterday. I told her everything, I said everything, you weren't here, I didn't see you."

That's how the consultation went on the last case Doctor Rafael treated in Cuba. Gladys Bárbara Nápoles

González sat down, stared at him, raised her index finger until she touched his nose.

"You think I'm a dyke too. Why did you call me? I'm going to make saint, so I can be protected like you. To make saint doesn't mean becoming a homosexual."

She rose again, came even nearer than before, and as if wanting to betray someone, she yelled:

"You're a doctor and you've been made saint! You don't want to say it because you're ashamed. What's your name?"

"My name is Rafael." Looking her straight in the eye, the doctor answered in a voice lower than usual.

"You must know I'm not a homosexual. A few days ago, they arrested some "fairy" friends of mine. They may have their flaws, but they're my friends. I'm afraid something will happen to me, very afraid. Everyone looks at me, they laugh and talk behind my back, but I'm not sick. I'm going to make saint, Saint Barbara, and even if you deny it, you've already been made saint. You said your name is Rafael, Saint Rafael. You don't say it because these things have to be done in hiding, or maybe you don't even know it, but I see it in your eyes and your hands. It's very true, I assure you, I know a lot about these things. I've been doing it since I was little."

Ángel Hurtado de los Santos was twenty-six years old, Gladys Bárbara's lover, from Guantánamo, and a maintenance worker in the industrial construction sector in San José de las Lajas. During the interview he seemed quick to reveal that he'd been suffering from diminished stamina for a long time because of a gastroduodenal ulcer and problems with anxiety. He'd met Bárbara in the home of a friend in Güines, and according to references, she was an extravagant girl who occasionally acquired some coins on her adventures, but he felt sorry for her. He thought it could be a product of her gang of friends, and poor thing, no one would throw her a bone.

Ángel also testified that Bárbara's mother engaged in witchcraft and he didn't doubt that she had put some curse on him. Lately he hadn't felt well, and he just couldn't move ahead in life.

"That woman's not easy," said Ángel. "Big brawls start up in her house and the police have to go all the time. That family is a disaster, but not her, Barbarita is different. The poor girl only gets to see her five-year-old son once a week when she goes to the store. She sees him in passing. His paternal grandfather doesn't want her to see him because he says that she's a tramp who disgraced his son, and that's why he's always in jail."

He declared he had no idea why Bárbara was acting that way. She just said not to hang around the "fairies", that it would hurt him, it would cause people to think badly of him, and he'd be on the lips of every person in the most gossip-filled village ever.
Bad luck followed him, and even his marriage broke down. Adela, his wife, was pure gold, but lately she didn't even want to see him, which made him feel even worse. His heart broke for his two small children. With

244

all that fuss, his head wasn't in a good place, and to add to the rotten luck, the curse Barbarita's mother put on him because she wouldn't accept their relationship affected his right leg so, that he couldn't manage to walk for the unbearable knee pain, but his heart wouldn't allow him to leave the girl. Besides, she was the prettiest little mulatta and the one he liked best from all the ones he'd had; none like her.

"I'm crazy about that little woman; the best pigeon in the flock would want her. She's pretty, real pretty and a trickster, and no one can beat her at dancing, she makes me drool. A thousand eyes are watching her, and if some wise ass comes along she might fall for him, and he'll snatch her from me quick as a frog's tongue. Maybe somethin's been done to 'er, and with some simple medicine she can be cured. When she gets better, I won't blink. Her son's father is always in jail, but he can't get her out of his head, and every time he gets out, everything gets fucked up. But I, Ángel Hurtado, I'm telling you man to man, I won't play the fool, even if I lose my head on the way. As long as I have strength, I'll fight for her, you can be sure of that."

De los Santos was pleased to have someone listen to him. He spoke leaving almost no time for breathing. He wasn't well either. He continued unabated.

"Barbarita is one of those "self-conscious" people, and when she sees a group together, she thinks they're talking about her; it makes her throw fits for no reason. I've tried to get her to lose the bad habit, but she just

245

won't listen. I even think that it's true what they say: When somethin's meant for you, there ain't no saint to pray to. These last few days I tried to distract her, I took her to the cabaret in Güines to dance and have a few drinks. When we left at dawn, she started to shake, to say that she wasn't gay, that the police should be told so they would leave her in peace, that she wanted her son. Then she wouldn't bathe, she would talk and pace incessantly, she had me fuddled, that's why I brought her to you."

Hurtado also was convinced that Ochún had to do with the problem, she was punishing the man for betraying his wife. His mother, "who knows a lot about these things," had warned him. She, descendant of Africans and Haitians, was lucumí although in Santiago de Cuba everyone prefers Babalu-ayé. In 1976, he was initiated into the Palo Mayombe cult.

This refers to the ritual in which a priest, also called Tata for his place in the hierarchy within the sect, is qualified to make incisions in the skin of the initiates with a sharp instrument. At the same time, the body is flagellated with a desiccated cow's tail to remove evil spirits. The belief is that the ceremony is the door to change, to forward motion and happiness, it is a pact with the creator that will make possible the fulfillment of every desire.

According to Hurtado and based on what he'd seen, people had a negative opinion of these priests. Also, soon he would remove himself from all of it because the government had forbidden it, and if they

246

caught him, they would take him to "the Tank" in less time than it takes a rooster to crow.

Adelaida Fajardo Almiñaque, age forty-five, mother of the patient, pointed out that the girl, Barbarita, had difficulties at birth and took longer than usual to speak. In elementary school, she was retained in several grades, she had problems with concentration and repeated disciplinary issues. When she was in sixth grade, at thirteen, she ran away with her boyfriend. They fought relentlessly. Barbarita wanted to return home because he beat her and abused her verbally, but she wouldn't take her back because the house was full, and her husband would have to find food for too many people. That wouldn't be fair, things would be difficult for him. For that reason, she found her a small room where she could stay. The girl went back to her boyfriend for more rows and fighting. They lasted more than three years together. But that man had nothing to do with these problems; they separated and each one went their own way.

According to Adelaida, the father of Bárbara's son was more troublesome than the first and all the others she'd had. Without blinking, she stated, "Once, the girl needed seven stitches on her right hand because of a machete he threw at her. It grazed her head, and cut her hand, but that can be mended. She almost didn't live to tell the tale. There was a trial and they took him to jail, he's in jail almost all the time. When Barbarita went to San José to ask for money to solve a problem with the boy, he took advantage and accused her. The charge was abandonment of a minor, they gave her a year, she appealed and didn't have to serve you-know-where. It's true that Barbarita wasn't on a good path and didn't take great care of the boy, but it wasn't that bad. Besides, he's a lazy bum. In jail, the other prisoners would take his care packages publicly and he wouldn't fight. The twist is that he refuses to lose her, whether the easy or the hard way, he wants her with him. When he comes out of jail again, if she's still with Ángel, someone's gonna end up dead, may God and the holy virgin keep my daughter from being the loser."

Adelaida declared she had much "clarity" and knowing that the problem would end in something diabolical, just in case, she had mobilized all the saints at her disposal; she had turned them to face the wall.

"I'm going to tell you the whole truth, I'll be frank. They weren't together, and he still bothered her. Then, I advised her to give the boy to José's father, the grandfather, so he wouldn't make her life a living hell. She also gave him the milk card, but since José's in jail, the boy's grandfather, an old man of nearly seventy whom no one can stand, recalcitrant and cantankerous, says he doesn't care about feeding one more mouth, but he demands the clothing and food ration book for the boy. Because of all that tangle, she's got a pending trial and she's behaving the way she is. The trial and not having the boy have made her sick. Of all my six children, she's the one that's given me the most trouble.

It's true that her friends are not the best lot and there's no way to separate her from that company. The man she has now is married, and they say his wife is a good woman, but she's always threatening my poor daughter. Maybe that's why she's been hanging out with those people that were taken to jail three days ago. And you can't imagine how much I've cared for that girl! Come to think of it, if she wasn't sick in the head, Barbarita could live with me, make a little money and give me half. To tell the truth, not 'cause she's my daughter, but that little mulatta is well built and she's pretty from top to bottom, real pretty."

The case before the doctor was interesting. Without delay, he began to put together, in the best way possible, the pieces of that complicated puzzle beginning with the patient's behavior and the relatives' reports. This was a psychiatric patient affected also by the environment in which she lived. Likewise, that family presented an abundant fountain of information on the subject of Afro-Cuban religions: what unites them and what distinguishes them, what can be defined and what causes confusion. In addition to applying scientific knowledge, he would rely on the study and investigation of African religions and its influences. A good diagnosis was essential.

In evaluating the information provided by the relatives, he recognized that Hurtado had incorrectly used the term witchcraft with a pejorative connotation when referring to Bárbara's mother, who in reality practiced the Lucumí religion: Santeria. Bárbara was also Lucumí, understandable since Santería was more ingrained in Havana than in other provinces in the country. Santeria and witchcraft should not be confused. Santeria is a new religion in the Afro-Cuban religious system, which in Cuba already transcended the whites and the mixed-race mestizos. The Saint is the deity that appears as a result of the syncretism between African beliefs and the Catholic religion.

The doctor intended to use an approach to the truth regarding those recognized as witches. He heard the term witchcraft repeatedly from patients and their relatives. It was also included in the oral tradition of narrating stories and legends kept alive especially in the most remote areas. He recognized it from his own childhood. The adults used it frequently to make children cease their mischief. One threat was enough. The witch would come for them, throw them in a sack, and make them disappear.

It wasn't a coincidence that when Rafael's paternal grandmother won the lottery with the number fifty, she entrusted him to the virgin of Las Mercedes, a deity syncretized with Obatalá, and since her children can receive any saint, there would be no problem. It is permitted to interchange between them and counteract any malevolent action. They receive from the godfather a necklace of white beads with sixteen "queens." Nearly every cult accepts the virgin of Las Mercedes as the mistress of the heads, and every person has its head or guardian angel.

From Filomeno he had also learned of other saints, at least the ones considered among the most important: Ochún, virgin of Caridad del Cobre, Cuba's patron saint, Changó's lover and favorite. She is like Venus, the goddess of water, love, and fertility, Holiest Mary who appeared floating on the sea miraculously to aid fishermen in danger of being swallowed by a violent storm near Santiago del Prado in El Cobre. She is luxurious and attracts gods and men with her libidinous dances, she fertilizes the ground and makes crops grow, she is mistress of coral and money, she symbolizes the richness of gold. If someone wishes to win Ochún's favor, they must deposit copper coins (north American cents) in small vases containing honey. If the person wants to conduct some financial operation, or to receive money suddenly, they will place a light floating in oil, which has previously been inside a pumpkin (for savings), within a hollow güira. The secret is love.

Likewise, he engaged in acquiring deep knowledge of other deities. Yemayá, or Aphrodite, is the goddess of salt water, patron of the Bay of Havana, faithful wife and obedient to her economic duties.

Changó, Saint Barbara, is a powerful character, lover of risky adventures and great accomplishments, patron of storms, holy warrior and warrior advocate, guardian angel of impulsive people.

Oggún, the holy whore, is wife to Changó and daughter of Obatalá, lover of all women.

Babalú-ayé, identified with Saint Lázaro, is worshipped by the entire country as one of the most important and respected deities.

It was possible that Ángel had decided to distance himself from Santería because the saints also committed sins, and he planned to protect Barbarita from all evil, so she could recover her lost mind. Also, he didn't seem to have the ability to face that complicated universe and its risky practices.

Rafael learned by reading, asking questions, and sometimes looking through slits and crannies where there was talk or some interesting ritual. He sought support from a babalao priest who always made him see the need for an education and a sense of discretion if he wanted to be like them, those who constitute the highest echelon in the hierarchy of Afro-Cuban priesthood. Men who do not earn the merited respect are forbidden to practice, as well as females. And so, he began to understand the magic key to Santería, how religion and folklore burst from deep within as a result of an ancestral culture and the experiences and conflicts of daily life.

The "Barbarita" case had almost concluded, but his work at the hospital wasn't going well. Lacking the skills appropriate for the work he was assigned, he couldn't avoid embarrassment, great resentment, too many obstacles, and exaggerated limitations. Another practitioner had to sign any documents he composed as he evidently did not deserve trust. More and more bureaucracy extended its hand, his job became unbearable, he could no longer summon patience. He found himself in a situation where the person authorized to sign a medical certificate was on vacation, and therefore, he would have to calmly await his return while his liver quietly rotted in anger. He had no option. He was sorry he couldn't continue his treatment of the patient Gladys Barbara Nápoles González.

Chapter 18

Big fish eat little fish. The Florida peninsula where Rafael intended to arrive penetrates the sea abruptly and descends as if wanting to continue its progress, as if pushed toward the search for something. However, almost at its end, the low and muddy coastline is surrounded by impressive keys that interrupt it. Then, it hides its path, perhaps because not far, ninety miles away, a green alligator with a northern tail peeks from its east to west position, its eastern head in imaginary slumber. For centuries, the governments of both territories have complained about each other without recognizing that their respective people need to stand in brotherhood to move forward and improve.

The North, a difficult port yet safe enough for those in the South that suffer and dream. Many times, willing to risk being devoured by sharks, the southerners search for El Dorado. Almost all live the paradox of coming from poor countries, or impoverished, indebted countries that have gone from abundance to dearth. The majority risk paying the high price of losing their lives on the way, anxious to reach "the American way of life."

Days went by and Rafael hadn't received the visa to enter the place that represented his last pitch, firmly on the box, ninth inning, zero runs on his side. The Office of U.S Interests in Havana had not answered his requests.

He asked for help desperately. Someone from Over There might take an interest in being his guarantor in his ill-starred intentions. With great insistence and tenacity, after a long period of time, he jumped.

What a mix of pride and gratitude he felt for that American, blond, tall, slim as always, an adult now, who didn't ask him if he was still faithful to the beliefs he had been taught. He waited for him at the Miami airport to offer him trust and solidarity. Barber too was there to welcome him. He still hadn't acquired the capital he desired.

Rafael arrived just in time for the privilege of joining those who would say their final goodbyes to Mister's wife, a woman whose memory would be indelible for all the good she did, for the daring she showed when she became the founder of what came to be a great ministry. A pleasant surprise made that wake a bit less painful. Neil Macaulay, the American guerilla he remembered so fondly, came with family and friends to pay his respects. It had been impossible to forget his face since the last time he saw him.

Macaulay too felt great happiness in his heart as Cuba was still present in his mind. His youth was linked to a notable part of its history. Once he completed his military service in South Korea, Macaulay, a first lieutenant, returned to his country, learned about the fight in the greater of the Antilles and the reasons that fueled it from the New York newspaper La Prensa. He only had one condition for the Cuban revolutionary: He would carry a Thompson machine gun and a carbine if he was accepted as a guerrilla. Stealthy and quite an exemplary fighter, he took on the responsibility of helping those, mostly illiterate, who remained in constant peril from the inequality in numbers and in fire power compared to the Cuban government forces. It wasn't long before the Key West radio station announced the escape of Fulgencio Batista, the President of the Republic and his closest circle. It was Macaulay who heard the news on his radio and told his fellow fighters in the mountains of western Cuba. The ex-fighter, now a Doctor of History and professor emeritus at the University of Florida for a long time, wrote about several Latin American countries. However, he dedicated most of his work to Cuba. Neither the landscape nor the moments he lived there ever left him.

At night, away from the conflict he had lived in for the last few years, in the intimacy of his room, Rafael reflected on his desires as they began to materialize. Once more he would put his conquering spirit to the test. He had loyal friends, and come to think of it, his arrival in the United States would not be like that of Juan Ponce de León, known through legend as a Spanish fighter, nearly convinced, among other things, that he had found the fountain of youth. He came from far away and thought he had stumbled upon a dazzling place. To his great surprise, his calculations had failed, and he found a great variety of indigenous people, the Appalachians, the Calusas, and the Matecumbes, in the territory of Florida.

It is said that Ponce de León tried to establish friendly relations. The Indians and "the visitors" attempted reciprocity in the beginning. Nevertheless, it appears the natives had a hard time buying that story and saw through the real motives. The white men had not come in peace and looking to help as they said. A Calusa poisoned arrow hit one of Ponce de León's legs or his shoulder, and he paid the consequences with his death in Havana where he had been taken.

Rafael got up. He was in no hurry. He lit a cigarette, went to the bathroom, and sitting on the toilet, he continued to dream. He was a dreamer even if his dreams didn't go as far as the Spanish conquistador. He didn't pretend to remain young forever. His aspirations were based on enjoying freedom, painting. He was enthusiastic about continuing his medical practice. Helping in the reestablishment of an individual's health, one of the most beautiful tasks a human can engage in, always moved him. His ambitions were not as exaggerated as those of Ponce de León's, but he would have to take on hard labor. In Miami, the Cuban influence since 1959 was jaw-dropping to even the most optimistic. Emigration had carried on its shoulders the future of that city which did not disparage the presence of so many immigrants, the majority from the Antilles or the southern part of the continent.

He got the impression that everything there was invented with the definite participation of those who preceded. He confirmed the idea that a man arriving in a strange land is more enterprising than the native. Miami, the great city of his dreams, now dazzled him and should not disappoint. He knew for a fact that all that glitters isn't gold, and that two can live as cheaply as one, if one doesn't eat. The possibility of immediate prosperity was slight. A greater letdown was the withdrawal of work permits for Cuban doctors coming into the country a few months before his arrival. The United States was in a great economic depression.

Still sitting, the heat on his fingers from the last cigarette startled him, he threw out the butt, and looked at the clock. It was the perfect time to sleep, but he stayed in the same place and position. He had almost forgotten the Spaniard who undertook his great adventure because he didn't want to get old when the thought of him came again, and he made comparisons. He thought his own situation but a trifle.

He would think about something else. He was troubled by the memory of Julia Tuttle, the rich widow who in 1891 bought 640 acres on the north bank of the Miami River. Using her art and wiles, she achieved her purpose. She convinced the railroad builder Henry Flagler to extend the tracks to an area where a hotel would be built and become her property. The lady's intention was to establish a town in that location which she founded in 1896. It was precisely where Rafael's feet were planted,

258

backside in comfort. He felt the urgency in the enterprising spirit of a woman. Rafael didn't know how much time passed or whether the wish that had brought him to this narrow room had been granted.

Where could Elizabeth be? A huge need for her sex and her creative impulse transported him, he wanted to take her to bed, wake up with her. Slowly, he calmed himself. His body numb, he finally managed to peel himself off the white ceramic seat. A cup of hot coffee could drive away sleep when he needed it, but he didn't think about it twice, went into the kitchen, made a good colada, and lit another cigarette.

Now reclined on the couch, he debated between imprecise concepts that began to take shape, though, in the end, man poses, and God disposes. With unusual optimism, he decided that his first task the next day would be, once again, to try his luck. He had never been interested in communicating with Elizabeth. It was reasonable to believe in the possibility that she had found another rolling stone in her path based on the assumption that the abysmal relations with Frederick would've played out a long time ago. He would ask Prieta to send him as quickly as possible the bale of letters Elizabeth had sent him. Everything would be different now, it was worth a new attempt, he needed her now.

Spent and sleepy, he would have nothing to discuss with the pillow. If anything, he would dream those dreams that were never as interesting as his waking dreams, but he dreamed. He dreamed something lovely, he dreamed of Beth, of them together in Paris.

Impatiently, he waited more than a month to receive the requested letters. He needed to know if he could find something specific in one of them. One by one he read them avidly, beginning with the latest.

His response covered two yellow sheets of paper, witnesses of all he wanted to unload. No complaints, no regrets, nor the scars in his heart left any trace on the paper. He spoke of the beautiful shared moments, of how clear the memory was of each episode that marked him so, and of the future according to his sense of confidence, a good one in his view. Once the envelope was sealed and mailed early in the morning, he purchased a bunch of yellow roses, the most beautiful he could find. The young saleswoman wished him a nice day, and he said his goodbye with a hesitant smile, almost mocking.

Forced to understand this new world, he perceived that a good number of Cuban immigrants kept their dreams alive by believing "the Americans" to be the only ones able to support them in their victorious return to their land; recovering their lost assets was an obsession. He also understood that regardless of how broken his fellow countrymen were, they wouldn't give up, chin up always. Citizens, residents, or illegals, the immigration status or the date of arrival mattered not, for nearly all showed abundant self-confidence, at least when they were retelling their adventures. They always outweighed the misadventures. In their recollections, the good

260

moments on the island sparkled, a place where everything seemed to indicate that previous governments had favored abundance equally distributed among all. Ironically, it was difficult to find someone who didn't have roots in El Vedado or other important location in Havana, their robust stories giving one to understand that everyone came from wealthy families.

Rafael also learned how the elite among the immigrants skillfully specialized in the unbeatable recipe for the tastiest little pastries a human can savor. Offered as a traditional treat, no candidate to the presidency of the country refuses to try them when visiting Florida during an electoral campaign. Later, without exception, the White House hopefuls feel obligated to fulfill the well-known formal commitment to overthrow the Castros once they have the upper hand. The clock still stands at three o'clock, as they say in Cuba, the day Lola was killed.

Every day Rafael would return home anxious to find a letter from Beth. He would freshen the water for the roses, watched them as if he could ask them for a clue.

He was relentless in his determination to find work, and his greatest wish was to accept the simplest of offers, for the moment. He had little to do other than kill time.

He played dominos with other Cubans, and when hungry, the memory of well-seasoned, traditional country-style Cuban food fueled his appetite even more. Cuban pizza is unavoidable. It's food that has become

261

popular, almost necessary, along the length and width of the island due to the speed of preparation and the reasonable price. The conversation extended to the topic of quality of the ones here or the ones there. Some preferred the ones left behind simply out of homesickness. Enjoying a family-size pie, fresh out of the oven, provided a good end to the match. Luck determined that Rafael would be the one to receive the delivery. With laughter and jokes he went to the door and suddenly warned: "Rocks find each other when rolling; I know the guy that will make the delivery."

They were face to face, trying not to look surprised. There were no greetings. Penetrating, unbelieving stares, then they parted. "I failed," was all Rafael could say as evenly as he could manage when he quickly placed the box on the table, his fingers burning from the heat.

That brief encounter affected him in the extreme. He didn't seem as hungry as he said he was a short time before. The pizzas were delicious and there was no reason for him to become apathetic so abruptly. To dispel the suspicion his friends were registering, he consumed a small portion, and unexpectedly, he was the first to leave. He didn't dare tell the truth, that the secretary of the syndicate in the last hospital where he worked in Cuba had made the delivery. An excellent doctor and superb human, but he wasn't considered worthy of a department vehicle nor could he participate in cutting sugar cane due to an allergy.

Rafael made all possible efforts to move forward, there was no lessening in his resolve. He bought newspapers, especially the Sunday issue in Miami-Dade County. He looked for information, he read the classifieds avidly, he was pressed to move out of a colleague's house who had offered him lodging and the possibility of a partnership some time before. One fateful night, he had reserved a great surprise for him. While they had dinner, with no qualms, he told him that there was no progress on the establishment of the partnership, he informed him of his irreparable losses, and said Rafael could not continue living under his roof. He knew all about good times and bad, and that when shit's gonna happen, no amount of greens can help, and that's what he thought the whole issue was about, "the greens" (American dollars).

He hadn't found anything of interest in the newspapers that Sunday midday. He reviewed the amount of money he carried and stopped on the first bill, the one with the image of George Washington. He surveyed the seal of the United States for a long time, he turned it, read the ribbons with writing in Latin: "Novus ordo seculorum", "E pluribus unum". He realized that his fate was set, and it would be for the best. To achieve it proved to be difficult, he would require spiritual support to give validity to his impetus. He would defend his future with sharp claws. He would make his way in what seemed a "complicated world", distant. He called upon La Esperanza.

Communication with Prieta, her intermediary with Aunt Iluminada, was not frequent. He would snatch the first opportunity to let her know of his situation:

Prieta:

I'm in trouble, I need your help. Do exactly as I tell you:

On the summit of La Esperanza, on the way to Antonio Cañon's house, you should still find the dirt path (the only way to get to the little blind well). Midway, between the hunchback mango and the avocado trees, barely ten meters away, look to the left and you will find a small rocky tract. Pay close attention from that moment. Most of the rocks you find will probably have white stripes. Find a dark gray one with no stripes, and no cracks either. Don't pick a real big one, it must fit comfortably in a medium dark pot. Find also a tobacco sheaf; tell Tomás to twist a few with rough and dark surface.

Once you have the rock and the tobacco in hand, find my godfather in Havana, you know his address. I've already spoken to him, but please tell him to act with urgency. I need to erase who I am from the inside out, to be myself again. You can imagine the condition I'm in. It's difficult to get rid of misery, but I will do it.

Please, rip this letter immediately after you read it, and don't talk about it. I'll write to Aunt Iluminada too so that she'll mobilize Gregorio without delay.

Damn, Prieta, don't dawdle, show me who you are one more time.

Rafael

As it was asked, so it was done, for Prieta was also one who believed that God helps those who help themselves. She was passionate about actions of significance to her. When the next day dawned, she was already at the place indicated with the instructions safe in her coin purse. She wouldn't use them until the last minute, when it became imperative.

The problem was finding the mango and avocado trees for reference to locate the small rocky tract. It wasn't working. The avocado tree was in a battle to the death with the marabú and couldn't breathe, and the mango tree no longer existed. Not far from there she should find the great mamoncillo tree, the place where little Rafael one morning, while collecting fresh grass for Rompetambor, was visited by a little virgin and spoke to her. He ran to the house eager to tell his tale. According to him, the little virgin was newer and prettier than the one on his grandmother's altar. He also shared the message she brought that his mother should bet on the number fifty, but she wouldn't gamble, she was a good Christian. Then, he ran a long way looking for his grandmother. She understood, it was true that the virgin of Las Mercedes had visited her little grandson. She played the number and the next day her happiness was complete when the lottery clerk gave her seven pesos.

Prieta remained in the refuge of her memories, she fixated on how the boy's apparition had become an event. Everyone wanted to go anxious to benefit from the virgin's blessing, to have her grant them some much needed luck. However, it was only he who could see her. The village priest rejoiced, he informed devout Paula that she would be able to show off her spirituality by praying a rosary nine mornings in a row. With blood, sweat, and tears, and the participation of the hopeful villagers, Paulita complied with the Padre's order.

Once again, Prieta would concentrate all efforts on the errand entrusted to her. Amid the brush and so many thoughts clustered together, a chill ran down her back. She began to break down, she needed to sit, but she didn't. She walked, breathed deeply, and remembered Catulo: "Sometimes the simplest things get complicated; perhaps the answer is that the closer you are to what you seek, the longer it takes to reveal itself." An iguana scurried between her feet. She was afraid of chameleons to an extreme, and at that precise moment, one was glaring at her. But she had no choice. She had to buck up, recover her breath, and leave that place.

A scratch on the ground reminds her of something important. The dirt, although dry, was sufficiently disturbed to call her attention. Undoubtedly, someone had been there before her recently, wanting gold, she thought, or maybe for the same reason she was there. She rubbed her eyes with her fingers. She needed rest. A section of root served her as a rake. The small rocky tract

266

dazzled her. Incredible things were said about that place and particularly those rocks.

It was time to summon help from the little paper she had in her coin purse. She read it over and over. Among so many, only two stones filled all the requirements. She thought of taking them both and keep one for herself. After all, she more than deserved a little luck in life. She didn't dare. She was convinced that such things arrived by mandate.   She picked one stone. She judged it her duty to visit the old mamoncillo tree where her brother had found the virgin of Las Mercedes. Could it be that the memory of that day had been complicit in her fortune? She was near the place where her brother had found the virgin. She would smear dirt from that place on the stone. Obatalá would be happy and help her resolve whatever situation, no matter how awkward.

Chapter 19

Rafael woke up more sedate than usual that morning yet especially alert. He looked at his watch and saw that it was early. He remained in meditation until light smiled faintly at his room, and suddenly the lamp behind him turned on: a good omen, he told himself. He remembered he must be punctual, the interview granted for that afternoon was not like any other.

For some time, Doctor Paz was in need of help from another doctor, preferably someone he knew, someone he could trust. Business in Washington demanded his personal attention.

Consequently, Rafael started working in the administration of clinics and from there, good winds began to blow. Painting also gave him another opportunity, a chance to become involved in Florida's canvas and brush art.

Eager to carefully study a painting before buying it or the exhibit ended, he would make repeated visits. He wouldn't abandon the idea of painting, he never thought of it as work. It would be spiritual recreation, a way to bring forth any long-standing repressions. To see his work in his friends' homes, perhaps in important rooms, would stimulate him.

He persisted in his attempts to communicate with Elizabeth. With Laura as intermediary, he obtained an acceptable lead. Beth would be in France dealing with formalities regarding the inheritance left to her by the elderly woman who had lived in Lyon. His information was insufficient, he needed more details to locate her.

He had no presumptions of success when he called Mrs. Durand's residence. There was no answer. Then, he called the hotel where they had stayed together during the controversial trip to Paris. The delay, the waiting for an answer, overwhelmed him with anxiety. He noted that the front desk clerk was bad-tempered when he hung up on him before he was done asking his second question in English. Had he known the cretin only spoke his native language, he would've asked in French. He was convinced that his reasoning was solid, she was there. He would repeat the call because he decided the sly deceiver was enjoying Paris with someone clearly quite special. She was in her favorite hotel and had requested not to be disturbed.

The French are fanatical about their language, they're proud of it, so this time he wouldn't miss the opportunity, the little bastard clerk would have no excuse to hide the truth.

"Do you speak English?"

"Sir, excuse me sir, the lady you wish to contact is not on the list of guests. Also, I am not authorized to offer information. There is nothing I can do for you, I'm sorry, sorry."

"Please, it's urgent, don't let me down."

"Nothing I can do, sir."

"Another try, another, one more. I would be very grateful. I will call again in five minutes."

"Pardon me, it is impossible."

In anguish, defeated once again, he thought so much, that he began to believe his own imaginations. He gathered the letters intending to burn them, but it wasn't worth wasting a match on them. Everything there was expensive. When he had some time, he would throw them in the trash. Life was shit. In primitive communities, men feel happier than in this uncivilized civilization where so many insults await, and in the end, everything turns to salty water.

A popular tale from his country helped him reflect.

"A man traveled down a path not frequented by many. A rear tire on his car went flat. Not far away lived someone that could help him. The miserable man was so used to obstacles and negatives, that he kept thinking of all the excuses the other man would give to refuse him help. "Fuck the times we live in. Solidarity has gone to hell, and no one helps anyone."

These and other things came to his mind. He became ever angrier, ever more convinced that his efforts would be useless, that he wouldn't solve anything, that humanity had become petty. He was aware of what the answer would be, but to turn back on his heels was ridiculous, someone could see him and think him crazy.

When he was face to face with the owner of the jack, he wasted no time and got ahead of him:

"Shove your jack up your ass, I don't need it!"

Rafael was still dissecting the moral of the story when he received a call from the hotel with apologies, a thousand apologies. Madame Elizabeth had left a note: "Please inform the gentleman that wishes to speak with me that I will be ready to receive his call at seven this evening."

Fire burned through his body, further assurance of his assumption: Beth was enjoying the company of some lover. Without a doubt, he was the actual intended recipient of the note, plus she was in her favorite hotel.

There was little else he could do. Sleep would do him good, or better yet, just sitting in the toilet as he had done during another painful night. But he didn't move from the chair. Even if uncomfortable, he wouldn't. He feared he would lose his concentration. From that position he would discover the truth.

Like Boccaccio's stable boy, he relied on his shrewdness. Aware of Beth's punctuality, he would call her five minutes before the appointed time; this early bird would catch that worm.

Startled, Beth lifted the receiver and heard soft instrumental music, "My Blue Unicorn" by the Cuban minstrel Silvio Rodriguez. She knew the piece. She didn't answer, her nerves wouldn't allow it.

His speculations were different now. She was waiting for a call from her attorney, or perhaps from her brother living in Switzerland to reestablish their relationship. Either would be reason enough to defuse her anxiety. It could also be a most incredible option, that her husband had arrived from Australia to spend a few days together, yet she was intelligent enough not to keep unnecessary company.

The greatest possibility escaped him when he so needed to find her. He thought there was always a second time, but he couldn't fail, third time's the charm. At the same time the next day he would repeat the action, he would play the same song perhaps louder than the day before.

The first ring put her on alert, she knew and she was willing to listen. Since Rafael's "disappearance", Beth had established the habit of leaving a message with the probable schedule for her return as she had no set time. It was just a premonition, but some day she would receive news.

Rafael tried to start a conversation with a witty monologue:

"I'm not looking for the unicorn misplaced by Silvio Rodriguez, my countryman. Mine is more evasive, even pretentious. I will pay well for any information."

No one answered. He would wait patiently.

Neither dared to hang up, but in the end, she did.

Three days passed. At the same time, Rafael charged again. There was no doubt she would be in the same room, sitting in her favorite armchair during those distant days, loaded with cushions piled around her. Beautiful, certainly. He couldn't allow himself to stop for fantasies, he needed to buy time. Without another introduction,

"What happened to the lemur? Did the hungry fossa devour him in time?"

"Please! I'm troubled, I could sound incoherent... Something strange is happening to me. I can't. I can't..."

"Now this is getting tricky!" Rafael said in a low voice while Beth remained glued to the receiver.

Rafael prospered in business, he found time for painting even if his ambitions were never great, they couldn't be. It was simply one of his dreams, a need for expression.

He participated in collective exhibits with flattering results, he sent paintings to institutions responsible for helping people in need, and he made gifts to dear friends. He would take his time until the right moment came to choose a provocative topic.

He began to penetrate the United States. Unexpectedly, he found himself in the Grand Canyon, Niagara Falls, even Oyotunji, home of Walter Eugene King, student of voodoo. After traveling through Europe, North Africa, and becoming Ifá of the Yoruba religion in Matanzas, Cuba, King returned to the United States and founded "Dambalah Hguedo" and later Babalao.

New Orleans was one of the first cities he wanted to visit. He found a thousand reasons to justify the

273

desired trip to the city flanked by the Mississippi. He felt nostalgic, as an immigrant after all, looking to take hold of anything that evoked kinship.

He went there with a sample of five paintings, each with a trumpet as focus. The choice wasn't random but the result of musical influences between Cuba and that southern city. He also went to enjoy the parties and parades on Fat Tuesday.

It was a rewarding and fun time, and he visited beautiful places, participated in art exhibits, and danced like he hadn't for a long time. The King Cotton float reminded him of his childhood. He would've liked to share the indescribable spectacle with everyone, even the disagreeable, argumentative, quarrelsome little fat boys. New Orleans is designed for just that, for delighting, for people to feel free, to abandon prudishness and affectations.

In the French Quarter, the historical museum of voodoo was the culmination of what he pursued. For some reason he always associated Marie Laveau with the stunning Cecilia Valdés of Havana, protagonist in the first Cuban novel of manners, with whom he fell in love from the delicious pages where Cirilo Villaverde describes her in impeccable form. He harbored envy of those who complimented and admired her on those afternoons when the pretty little mulatta came down La Loma del Ángel. She welcomed the flattery and sensed the desire they felt for her in her daring innocence at the mere age of fourteen.

Perhaps he had related the two women from his reading of Francine Prose where Laveau appears as a main character, and the song by Mary Gautier Wheel Inside the Wheel, that typifies the mambo.

When he saw the portrait by Frank Schneider, he realized that his imagination had played tricks on him and the two beauties were different and distant from each other. He was facing an adult woman of dark skin and penetrating gaze, certainly beautiful. Her black hair escaped to her forehead and temples from under an elegant bright yellow cap. Madame Laveau appeared gifted with a special authority. Her sorcery earned her the title of most powerful of all witches of color. She attracted many rich white women from New Orleans with her voodoo practice and all the ingredients only she knew how to use. Madame Laveau could solve anything. No question, she had skills. And if it had to do with love affairs, she could make them or break them with whatever speed was necessary, she was supreme. Traces left in diverse art manifestations are witnesses to her reach. It is not unreasonable to think that she received good lessons from her late husband of Haitian origin, who according to malicious rumors, died under unclear circumstances.

An invitation to participate in a ceremony officiated by a houngan gladdened him greatly yet didn't surprise him. He felt extremely well and at ease. He was also granted a meeting alone with him, quite agreeable with the future his godfather in Havana had anticipated for him. It was enough to continue feeling satisfied.

As he prepared to leave, he stopped to listen to the priest whose parting words a few seconds earlier had been, "You need to go There, go, jump to La Esperanza, catch it with your eyes from its summit; there, take in the air, breathe deeply three times, as deeply as possible, and then, when you return, I will be happy to see you again."

Those random words served him as motivation. He felt the need to speak with familiarity, but he didn't dare. No. Without a second goodbye, with a daring, audacious look, he pretended to leave, but the face of the man, who thought himself confronted, began to transform. The extreme slenderness and the ample separation between the head and the feet of that man brought light to an appearance of little elegance, quite disheveled, going within seconds from bad to worse. Some great concern disturbed the man who had seemed knowledgeable, and to an extent, polite. One careless look shouldn't have caused such an effect. There was no logical reason. The extremely visible change in him, made the great azogwe look frightening. He probably wasn't aware of the distress that enveloped him. He endeavored to hide his unease which grew rapidly. His forehead was covered with little drops of sweat that soon traveled his face and dripped down his terribly disjointed body.

The truth was that rage from his own spirits possessed him from the moment he felt judged with irreverence, and he became something different from what he had presented earlier. Perhaps he thought of taking a short rest, turn hoodoo, pay his petulant visitor for his intrusion and return to normalcy. He needed to recover, but the chilling tremors that began in his legs and ran up his body wouldn't allow it. Leaning on a table, he remained in the same position but increasingly slouched. In his failed attempt to recover, he opened his wild eyes and nailed them on what he saw as a minuscule human figure positioned comfortably. The episode proved to be a great drama with no alleged assassin.

"Leave, go to hell and don't return. You're an ignorant fool. Don't come back to this city. Go away before they kick your ass out or shred you to the bone. Go. Disappear immediately from my sight. I see your skin hanging from a nail in this room, and not even filthy dogs will bark for your death."

The news about the path and strength of hurricane Katrina were increasingly abundant and terrifying. It left no room for doubt; the southern United States would be affected. Louisiana would not escape its devastating consequences. Rafael still remembered New Orleans vividly. It had left a mark and more than enough reasons to never forget.

It was much worse than predicted. Those who managed to escape New Orleans were horrified. Nearly everyone lacked direction in looking for an open door as they tried to distance themselves as much as possible.

The best-chosen words to express what happened would always be out of context: chaos, disarray. The levies gave in against the onslaught of unstoppable hurricane force winds. The waters of the Pontchartrain river occupied the city, Katrina owned it and its people. The reality was unbelievable, the disaster moved the world. No one remained indifferent before the great misfortune.

Like many others, Rafael volunteered to help. His first image upon arrival, when the waters hadn't yet receded, was sadly moving. Near the disaster area, a black woman, barefoot and with barely any clothing to cover her, walked in fast circles. Her eyes wild, completely disengaged, played impossibly in their stretched orbits. At intervals, she would slow down; when she appeared to stop, she couldn't, a force bigger than her hindered her. She would glance around, presumably looking for something horrifying she didn't want to see. She guided her weak attempts in the direction where her family stood hours before, toward all that she once owned. She continued running as if sure that an enemy followed her, knife in hand. No one tried to stop her, nor could they avoid her tremendously shocked pupils. When she couldn't go any longer, when her pain was at its strongest, the knife took her life. She fell dead.

Regrettably, the warrior gods had conspired, but New Orleans would blossom again. Someday the houses would reappear with their beautiful gardens, the moving music, the nightclubs, the laughter… When time and man do their work, legend follows. The reward for the underserved curse that befell those people, noble fighters to the marrow, would one day come.

For Beth the experience in New Orleans would have been too much, unbearable, but what a pleasure to savor New York despite the winter. What better choice to brighten the sad image of that morning when he left her at the Seychelles international airport, in suspense over his silence, unable to understand what could be happening with that man, so simple and so complicated at the same time. He couldn't fathom how exceptional it would be to live the moment together.

On those nights, Rafael passed the time with visits to other galleries before he arrived at the place where his painting was on exhibit, afraid of disappointment, overcome by the idea that something could happen. It was the first landscape he had painted since his arrival in the United States with his mind still infused with the rural environment that saw him grow up. On the canvas he captured a section of La Esperanza, an abandoned cart in a pasture, a wheel on the ground, a few broken boards and others old and loose.

This time, attendance was less than on previous days, perhaps because of the cold and the snow. He didn't recognize any of the people present. He didn't notice anything extraordinary in the first room, so he moved to the smaller room where his painting was displayed. Totally disenchanted, he would later look for reasons. It seemed less attractive, the lighting inadequate, too small. He went to the restroom and when he returned, he ate a cheese hors d'oeuvre and a small glass of wine. He needed some time to shake off such a jolt. It was impossible that he could've played the fool by presenting an unworthy painting.

Could it be that my country crudeness turns off the people of New York? On second thought, I could've brought a better one. Certainly, it should've been more presentable, not so broken and battered, with that wheel strewn on the ground and partly hidden by the underbrush. I painted the little girl's shoe that hangs because of an unpleasant memory. Yes, I remember, that's how it ended up when we were playing. I threw it and Ñata quickly threw herself from the cart to rescue her little pink shoe, and sadly, her small right arm broke when she fell over the abandoned wheel.

He had to admit what his mother had foretold was true when he came to her loaded with dreams and fantasies, his heart bursting with wishes: "Son, keep your feet on the ground, misery drags on."

Searching for adequate reasoning, he reviewed all the paintings in the exhibit one by one. He found them so different, that he convinced himself his should not have made the trip from so far away. It would take him time to learn what those from the north could like, as he was certain they had not understood the message. No question, people want what they want. He could have avoided the unpleasant moment, not to mention what awaited when he faced the gallery director.

With nothing left to do, he decided, what's done is done. What's bred in the bone will out in the flesh!

By pure coincidence, the top administrator was before him.

"I was anxious to see you, sir."

"Forgive me, you need not make excuses. In any case, I will always be grateful. Perhaps another time."

"Are you unwell? I don't recognize you, sir. In the past, you haven't shown disappointment as you are now. Cheer up, my good man, our gallery is celebrating."

"Don't worry, even though in reality I had my hopes placed on the good fortune you would bring me. I'll recover quickly, I'm used to unexpected difficulties."

"Come, come! Let's go to my office. There's someone waiting."

"Someone's waiting for you?"

"No, for you, sir."

"Interesting," he answered now reticent to communicate further.

A fiftyish Jewish woman, with the appearance of having money to throw away, extended her hand to him wearing a wide smile.

"Sir, I like your painting very much. Yes, that one on the table is beautiful, fascinating."

"You really like it?"

"Most decidedly. You can do fantastic things. Here's my card. I'll have it picked up tomorrow and I will send you a check."

"Unbelievable!"

Cheered up by the results of the New York exhibit and the favorable reviews, he took bold action. He knew that an eminent professor of the Yoruba language at the university of Lagos traveled frequently to the United States to teach courses and speak in conferences about African religions in several southern universities. He was also passionate about visual arts.

Filomeno had been more powerful than history told in books and Africa's location in the Indian Ocean in opening Rafael's fantastic appetite for that continent. Other than for a marked economic interest, many prefer to ignore it, others to deny the blood that courses through their veins. Cuban dark skin also called. He urgently needed a different look at the black continent. The Nigerian, cultured and artistically sensitive, could show him the best way to achieve that happy merger.

Long hours of dialogue on the most varied topics made a friendship develop between the professor and the Cuban, who met for the first time in Atlanta while participating in an art exhibit. There were toasts with Havana Club and cigars almost always. Many reasons tethered them to the common branch that united their respective cultures. One day they centered on the names Cuba and Nigeria. Sifting through the various theories regarding the island's name took them some time before they arrived at the most plausible. Christopher Columbus initially thought he was near a peninsula he called Juana in honor of Prince Juan until finally, the Spanish learned that it was an island, Cuba.

It wasn't a Nigerian who named his country. Flora Shaw, an Englishwoman of the nineteenth century named the territory with one of the most ancient human populations Nigeria. It appeared for the first time on American newspapers in 1897.

Those talks enlivened Rafael's interest in making a trip to Africa. He would begin in the Seychelles, the islands that inspired such affection and unequaled moments. As if in great warlike conflict, the apparent cause was nothing more than a return to the place where he had worked the first time he left Cuba, yet the underlying interest was finding the woman whose memory he couldn't dismiss; he needed her presence.

Chapter 20

In Mahé, his memories unraveled, he was in constant anticipation, every new day could bring the opportunity he awaited. He chose the hotel Bou Vallon where he enjoyed the atmosphere. Tropical nights were brightened by the presence of a Cuban musical group on tour in the islands. It was a huge event, guests anxious to enjoy the good music. No one could remain dispirited in such a contagious setting.

Two charismatic siblings, a man and a woman from Madagascar, were the happiest and most fun. They were there to participate in the All-Africa Games and were favored to win. Mandrika, the boy whose life Rafael saved in Mahajanga, was the man. Rafael was moved as they rejoiced in the reunion and the legend of Manhakanony's son who incredibly came back to life, and now was an athletic favorite. The animated Malagasies surprised everyone with "La Guantanamera" in Spanish, and later, guitar in hand, reminded Rafael of Compay Segundo: "From the high cedar I leave for Markané, I arrive at Cueto on the way to Mayarí...."

The joy multiplied when two days later the skilled siblings won first place in their competition and gave Rafael the gold medals. Visibly stirred, he returned them. The much-deserved trophy belonged to their country.

The city of Victoria was one huge party in those days. However, news about Elizabeth brought Rafael little hope. She had abandoned her business in the Seychelles years before and only returned for brief periods to keep her summer residence. Rafael perceived that her spirit was still there. He felt it in the people he spoke to, in so many places and moments they had shared. They deserved an encounter even if just for a few days.

Unexpectedly, he was informed that Laura had just arrived in Praslin. There was no time to lose, he would see her. Certainly, Beth was in her favorite hotel. The music scheme hadn't worked, nor did the lemur and the fossa, so he would have to be more creative, backwoods Cuban style. He would appeal to Cirilo, the storyteller of his childhood.

A man from the Canary Islands living in Cuba received insistent letters from a brother asking for news about him on behalf of his family. His mother was consumed with sadness and nothing they did cheered her. The Canarian, slow to speak and even slower to write, answered:

My beloved family:

It is my greatest wish that you're all well. I'm well, thank God. With this letter I hope to satisfy our mother and you who love me so.

About this place, I will say that island after island, they're just islands, so don't worry, I feel well. Along with the letter, I'm sending an animal that after a time will speak of the island charm. You will be awed. But, you must have patience.

I can also tell you that I hooked up with a country girl that seems unbeatable. She's still skinny and somewhat gawky, but she's got good bones. I caught her a short while ago, but she's already showing signs of having fat calves, which is rare around these parts, and her ears are already big. So, I've told you everything: "Good leg, good ear, signs of a good beast."

With the help of Catalino, Ramón's son, Papa's nephew, who is my scribe, I've been careful to send two letters in case one gets lost on the way, the other might be luckier, though they're both in the same envelope. As you see, everything here, even envelopes, is not as abundant as you think.

With love,

Juan.

Note: Ah, Diantre, I forgot the most important thing. If you see a blue trunk arrive, the one behind is Juan, and I am Juan.

Cirilo clarified the message that the parrot Juan's family received was a male.

With nothing to add or delete, that letter went to France to none other than Cirilo.

Three days later, in the first hours of the morning, Beth received the letter. She didn't need Aspasia's intelligence. Tremendously surprised, she returned to her room and in bed she read the message several times fully convinced of who the real sender was.

Being someone of open feelings and sincere heart, the letter produced a loud and honest laugh in her. It wasn't simply a funny moment as the pleasant surprise filled the room, her man was alive. She began to tremble, and a shower of tears covered her face.

Once calm, she wanted to know where to find Rafael, and surveyed the Seychelles stamp on the envelope. The immediate intention was to take a flight with that destination, she would go, but it was too late. When she communicated with her friend Laura, he had already left.

A week before the exhibit opened, Rafael arrived at the Nnamdi Azikiwe international airport near Abuya, the best planned city in Africa. It had been sufficiently long, the letter should be in Beth's hands.

At 6:55 in the evening, nighttime in France, he made a phone call. Busy. Good sign. Now the pigeon would capture the little dove. She must be resting, or why not,
having sweet nothings whispered in her ear. Five minutes later, he made the call again. On the other side, a familiar voice asked if it was Cirilo on the phone. The laughter was prolonged, they couldn't contain themselves.

The plane that carried Beth landed with some delay, as is common with planes arriving or leaving from many places in the world. The elegance of her clothes and her deportment as she descended the plane stairs distinguished her. She was now a mature woman, attractive, more confident than in those faraway days when he left her in the Seychelles. He had arrived in a taxi. He wanted nothing to interrupt that moment. He waited with a yellow rose in his hand. Without display, a kiss on each cheek and another on the forehead, he welcomed her. They went to the exhibit holding hands as if they had seen each other just a few hours before. They were in no hurry to review the details of their lives. What was truly important was the happiness they felt once again.

They joined as one into the preparations for the exhibit with the support of friends and assistants. For many reasons, they believed it would be a success. Unfortunately, some obstacle always appears when in the course of great achievements. The selected gallery was extremely small and wouldn't allow such a large gathering, but then, the largest in the city agreed to host.

From early in the day, guests waited for the opening with anticipation. The Nigerian professor, the exhibit coordinator, cut the ribbon and declared the event officially open while Cuban music played in the background. The artist was satisfied, expectations had been surpassed, and success was guaranteed.

Elizabeth seemed moved, convinced she had traveled to support the man with whom she had enjoyed perhaps the happiest time of her life. She owed him that encounter. By sheer courage he made his way to painting while she hadn't even the fiber to disengage from Frederick. The moment and circumstances didn't justify dwelling on such considerations when she needed to radiate joy, but her face reflected the conflict within her, until she took a deep breath to fill her lungs for relief. In the meantime, Rafael watched over every detail and found answers for the most varied questions from those around him who were interested in his art.

Free from the initial tension and now convinced of the positive results of the exhibit, Rafael's attention was captured by an extremely heavy black man intent on making his way to him. He thought it impossible to recognize anyone there as it was his first visit to Nigeria. The gushing greeting from the man who treated him as a friend startled him, and his surprise grew when he called him Doctor Rafael.

Manhakanony had learned from his children, Mandrika and Pacalhita, that Doctor Rafael was in Africa and about his art exhibit in Nigeria. He felt obligated to travel to the Continent. For a long time, it bothered him not hearing from the person to whom he owed immense gratitude. He confessed he thought it unusual that a doctor so skilled in healing extremely ill people would now appear as a painter. But after inspecting the exhibit and remembering the moments they lived together, he understood.

During a farewell lunch, they enjoyed a few anecdotes about the circumstances of their first meeting. Beth felt proud as she remembered Rafael's trip to Madagascar to help the merchant of whom she was a good customer. She took the opportunity to give him credit for the experiences retold upon his return to the big island. At the time, she had believed them excessive, sometimes incredible, perhaps because she had become used to the idea of having a man with a great sense of humor at her side, fond of exaggerating stories to make them fun, or because he came from a place where the uncommon was simple and real.

They had limited time to visit the city. Zuma Rock, formed by water erosion, and the impressive National Mosque suggested intimacy and peace. They wanted these outings to replicate as much as possible the vacation they enjoyed in Paris. The present would always be important, and neither was willing to let it slip away.

They intended to reach Porto Novo in the Republic of Benin, Kenya, to participate in a safari, but sadly, they had already exceeded their available time. Two countries would be left for the next time, but Nigeria still held some new thrills for them and they wouldn't waste the chance. The Nigerian friend would not continue with them for work reasons. Certainly, they would meet again.

Beth's exaggerated insistence in not visiting Oyo's marginal neighborhoods, bothered him. It wasn't that he was being obstinate or had extreme zeal, he simply felt the need to see something perhaps unique.

Days full of activity followed, especially in the most impoverished sectors of the city. After intermittent periods of walking and rest to undertake new adventures, one memorable morning, at a market entrance, Rafael came face to face with an illusory figure with a strange and penetrating gaze. It could've been something or someone he had never seen, but he thought her familiar. She matched the description her son gave on the day they plowed the land and ate baked sweet potatoes. Also, blue-black, of somewhat distorted speech, Petrona came into view among the multitude in a worn yellow gingham dress. Her damaged hand was held by a red kerchief made into a sling. Her twin sister was with her, the young woman who jumped overboard on her way to slavery in America and threw herself into the ocean to return to where they had taken her, so she could reunite with her nationals.

He saw them both, and to be sure they were real, he tried to call their attention by saying the name Filomeno. He felt Petrona's burning glare, and just as she had been painted with words, she stood before him as if wanting to know something about the part of her flesh she had left behind in the greatest of the Antilles.

It was possible that African spirits traveled to any place in the Continent. Another possibility was that the

291

beverage he prepared and offered his friend Simón when they finished plowing the land didn't agree with the elderly man. That day, while sitting on the root of a cedar tree, when he said his mother was Congolese, his spirit was in Oyo.

Rafael couldn't shake his surprise. He made no remarks. Dreams surpassed reality. He had acquired new strength from complete satisfaction with the success of the exhibit, and he felt the urgent need to stay in Africa to visit Equatorial Guinea, the only African country where Spanish is spoken. He would be careful not to tell Beth what he had just witnessed. He knew her well enough to know what her reaction would be.

They went on an excursion she wasn't on willingly, she wasn't interested. She said she hadn't learned how to engage with that strange world. She preferred not to see the natural beauty of the island and missed the opportunity to observe gorillas in the plain, elephants, the variety of squirrels. She decided to stay in the hotel fearing that so much social unsightliness could affect her. Nothing could stop Rafael, forced onward by his persistent premonition that his curious eyes would behold something new. He began to enjoy long trips, primarily on foot, around Malabo, the capital and oldest city in the country, located on Bioko island. Every detail attracted him, the back of a door, a rock, or simply whatever was in front of him, invisible to others.

On their last day, he became disconcerted while making attempts to have Beth accompany him on his travels around the city, but she remained as apathetic as ever wanting urgently to leave. No matter how much he tried to ignore it, a certain distancing began to affect them. She didn't agree to go with him to the port either, where he longed to look out into the far horizon, breathe deeply, bid farewell to those waters, that sun, to that which he never found.

Rafael didn't cease in his determination, he had a goal. A few minutes before arriving at the pier, he could already smell the sea, his ambition simply to reach that goal, when he saw an old man, no more than skin and bones, returning with a string of fish in his right hand, in no other clothing but white pants folded to mid-calf. In the middle of his chest, between the nipples, a small cross marked his dark skin. It was the mark of Cuban slavery. Herrera had ordered them branded immediately after buying them. They faced each other. Without breaking the stares that connected them, like a goat playing the flute, Rafael exclaimed, "Guacamaya!" But the surprised man introduced himself as Munga, the name he answered to before they took him to Cuba.

Munga was Matungo, one of the four slaves that Rafael's great-grandmother Micaela bought from Herrera, a man of little ingenuity.

"We'll walk to the entrance of the bay. In Puerto Viejo there is a tally that indicates the place where 260 of us entered. There was no one here to work, so the queen of Spain sent us. We were nearly dead, but I don't remember losing anyone during the voyage," he said naturally, as if he'd always known him.

From a young age, Rafael had heard about the complex African slave, famous for changing names easily, for being sickly, and for other deficiencies not outwardly shown. Herrera sold Matungo cheap, he didn't produce, he was always weak, and the more the foreman punished him, the less he did. He seemed to live in another world. He was no good for trapiche, it would make him cough, and the heat from the boilers choked him. He was even more worthless for field work; the itching from the cane gave him hives and he bled from scratching. Worst of all, his hands and feet were always cracked.

What almost no one knew was that Guacamaya had lived as a fugitive in the hills of Guayabo for a long time before the dogs got him at his weakest: He had cholera. A black witch in the infirmary they put up near the barracks healed him to some extent with wood herbs. The master decided to sell him. He wouldn't comply, had too many defects. Even worse, when he had high fevers, he spoke of Africa and the voyage he would make to never return to the damn hell in which he had fallen. Matungo did everything he could to get his wish.

They said Gener, Matungo, Guacamaya, whatever his name, was the one who taught Gregorio what little Spanish he learned, although to tell the truth, after his death, Gregorio always spoke Kikongo.

The two Africans got along. Once a year, on holy week, they would go to the door of La Guacamaya to collect a fistful of dirt and deposit it in the trunk of the ceiba to revive spirits. They said it was a way to see their loved ones, the ones left Over Yonder. They called them because they never knew whether the beasts had killed them in the jungle or if they were alive.

Every Sunday, Matungo went with Gregorio dressed in pure white. They took their habitual walk around the woods, collected carefully selected dry leaves to feed a flame signifying strength and purification. They ignited a sacred fire, sang prayers and songs while the fire remained ablaze. Sometimes they invited other slaves to share their beliefs, fantasies, and stories. They were still visible under the ceiba after dark.

Some things are a cluster fuck. Life is shit! How far can human selfishness go! Not even Mrs. Micaela, who was considered a sensible woman, understood the suffering of those wretches, because, in truth, and according to rumors, Micaela freed the slave for being useless, incapable, responsible for any evil that happened. One fine day, Matungo Gener disappeared. No one listened to the Mrs., afraid by his vanishing. They didn't look for him, they didn't want him. Not even the vultures, which never fail, found a trace.
No one ever found out that the useless slave had been received by the Royal Order from Queen Isabel authorizing the transfer of all black slaves and free

mulattos from Cuba who would willingly go to Spanish Guinea. No one wanted to go, perhaps out of fear, conscious of the possibility of worse things to come. They forced 259, but Matungo Gener went delighted hidden from those who knew him and with a new name. Quite readily he rounded off the 260 that arrived in Bioko, a section of the kingdom of Oyo, where he always wanted to be. The cross on his chest was the visible trace that still identified him.

While they walked, Munga spoke about his worst times in Cuba, his arrival on the San Juan river, which according to him, is at the very end of the island. He lived in one of the ravines that slide into a deep precipice.

He also spoke of his tears from all the abuse, and the sweat from building Herrera's homestead, of how he worked on the train tracks for moving sugar cane to the plant. He didn't see in Cuba any rivers that resembled those in Africa; only when it rained hard did water run with vigor.

"No one can imagine the suffering and misery they piled on us blacks when they took us out of our nations to enrich themselves, but the black gods are stronger and many, more than theirs, one by one they will pay."

Listening to those words, Rafael had a sudden urge to embrace Matungo, pay the debt he was owed, even if he hadn't been complicit. But Matungo didn't hold feelings of vengeance toward those who hurt him even if justified. There was no choice but to accept that

Africa is full of spirits that left their hopes, bones, and descendants in other lands. In Cuba, they remain in its beliefs and culture to enhance it and give it a distinctive luster.

Strangely, he found no trace of Gregorio. Maybe everything had been said, his power transcendent. He can speak any language, take any name he pleases: Francisco, José, Juanillo de la Luz, Tomasito… In the gray stone and the twisted tobacco, in the round pumpkin, in the call of the horn, in the red ribbon, in the American penny, in the brown hen, in black, crimson, green, yellow… In the woods, in the bell flower, in Africa, in all of Juana, Gregorio lives.

Chapter 21

I will go to La Esperanza. I had found opportunities for everything, but that was the account to settle, the promise to keep, the silent truth, the necessary trip I always delayed. I will go. It's true that I didn't ask to be born, they made me, and one cold morning, I showed up. And as they do with everyone before they have form and body, they gave me a horrible name (begging the pardon of those most illustrious lords that have had it as well). It should've gone to my older brother to please my grandfather, but my parents didn't consider that.

I began to grow, then I shrunk, and there is no way that with the passage of time I will stop being me, the guajiro, the doctor, the painter. And each tries to squash the other to defeat him. But the first to appear, the guajiro, has incredible power. He was born with me Over There, that's why I'm going.

The entanglements and rumors from the moment I came into the light are clear in my memory, the immediate complications and misfortunes. Nevertheless, none of it can compare with my great wish, to return to the place where I was born and raised. That is the dilemma. What matters are experiences and memories. I'm afraid to damage them, to let them get twisted, to be unable to rebuild them because it's too late.

Perhaps I can't call my first years my golden era, but that doesn't preclude them from being my strongest bond on my path toward a future that doesn't exist, and if it does, I never see it; it's always today, not tomorrow.

Those years of growing up, or when my grandmother pushed me to grow up, I remember them as the best. And they were. I told the truth as I saw it. Every day adults need to have things explained to us in detail, almost always we misinterpret them, we complicate them, we distort them. We welcome each new day with lies on our lips, in or words, in our gestures, in our smiles, our laughter, our tears, in sex, in faith, we lie.

My son will go with me, kicking and screaming, unwillingly he will go with me. I am convinced that when he is face to face with that landscape, he will put his head between his legs and no god will get him to speak.

Thinking about the arrival at José Martí airport makes my hair stand on end and my skin crawl. That day when they turned me into someone else still makes me shake. It was the prelude to unhappiness. Now I've come to the conclusion that the damned arrival is primarily responsible for so much absence. I will go soon, very soon.

Who will be waiting for me? Where will I stay? I cannot imagine that moment. I must react in a civilized way toward so many people that perhaps won't recognize me. Surely some will call me by those old nicknames that sound so horrible to me now, they'll remind me of all my mischief, or that of my siblings, or my cousins, and they'll credit me with it to ingratiate themselves, or to confirm that they haven't forgotten me.

I won't be surprised when they reprimand me even before the greeting, as they have done to the majority of those who left their country, for drinking the "Kool-Aid of oblivion". Seldom do those who remain understand the friend or brother who left toward the unknown. They stayed in the nest, fledglings, but in their element. Besides, the reasons for the long absences are all different, and regrettably, the ostentatious insist on portraying an image of abundance at all costs. Even if they owe a peso to every virgin and saint in heaven, not a dollar goes to the mother that birthed them. Hah! If they don't have enough money to hire a "turitaxi," they won't go, lest their ego doesn't appear at its highest. And what shall I say of the luminous chains hanging from their necks, excessively thick and allegedly made of gold. That damned obsession with not showing what they lack on the outside won't allow them to think about what's lacking on the inside, what's important. Humans are becoming nothing more than peacocks.

Once my feet are on La Esperanza, I must not forget to find my stool, the one we covered with Rompetambor's leather. I'll take a picture of it as a keepsake. I hope I don't see León. I can't forget how he arranged a fight with a guy older than him without Tata's approval. Not even knowing León, and much less wanting to fight him, he was forced into a mutual beating in León's courtyard. The women and children screamed when they saw them almost dead, bleeding profusely for no reason. I don't want to see him.

We will have a feast with aromatic spices recently pulled from the herb patch, like we used to do on Christmas Eve. It'll be outdoors, under the tamarind tree, near the well, where birds and all kinds of animals take care of the music, although it wouldn't be a bad idea to invite Pichy and his band Los Paraítos. I'll bring some guitar strings for him; he only has three, three strings on his guitar, that's why they call it Pichy's Three String. They say Pichy has talent. He took the strands from an old tire on a Karpaty motorcycle. Those are the strings on Pichy's Three String. I like the idea of Los Paraítos playing during our meal.

After all, it'll be a fun holiday, but probably more complicated than anyone can predict. I must give the impression of serenity yet be always alert so I won't commit indiscretions or get in trouble. I won't tell anybody, but if I get a good-looking mature female, I won't think twice about finding a way to lasso her. She'll fall easily. No farm hen can resist when there's corn in the pockets.

What are some things I shouldn't mention? So it all runs smoothly, I should only preach half the sermon. I will say little about my life and how I've lived it. If I speak of the hard years when I had no one coming to my rescue, they won't believe me, they'll say to go elsewhere with my story, that I'm in an earthly paradise and have all the best of this world.

I hope Prieta doesn't share my troubles, if she hasn't spilled them already. For plenty of reasons, I shouldn't talk to excess when I tell them about my periods of abundance. They would think it wrong, so I won't overdo it. I don't know if I can help myself, though, not out of vanity, but out of a need to provide a way for them to feel represented. We'll see what happens when they give me a few shots of the Guarfarina they prepare; it could make me spill it all. Under no circumstances must I express my opinions on certain issues, since complications are always a threat, and God knows what price would be paid.

Come to think of it, I'll only speak of trivialities. Those who never leave their country like to hear stories, they want to know. Some learn new things and others are entertained.

I will tell them about my visits to the best beaches in the world, about the nudist beaches, the famous hotels in Saudi Arabia, about Qatar. And about the funniest things, like how much I lived it up with a curvy mulatta during my vacation in Acapulco. I came back loaded with big sombreros and speaking with a Mexican accent. But I won't say anything about business, or painting classes, dancing classes, language classes. Nothing about the taxes I fork out every year or the trouble I got myself into once for not paying them on time. Or about the car that was stolen with a wallet containing all my documents. Or about the house and yacht, I can't do that to them.

I'm sure they want to know about the cruises from Miami and other places, because they believe themselves so informed about such things, that they don't find credibility in anyone who hasn't vacationed around the Mediterranean at least once. But I will pretend not to know, and I will give little importance to the topic. I won't speak of how from one of those cruises I saw Pan de Matanzas, and had to harden my heart, like the romantic Cuban poet José María Heredia who, while in exile, traveled to Mexico and when he caught sight of the place where his mother and sisters still lived, his tears overflowed. It's a darn shame to be so close and unable to visit!

I won't open my mouth to comment on how because of exhibits, or work problems, or because I damn well pleased, I've traced and retraced the four corners of the world. To be honest, I haven't been to the Macedonia of Aristotle and Alexander the Great. Africa fills me with passion. I'll speak of the buffalo I caught in Tanzania. Its head presides over the living room in my house. Also, I will tell how it was possible that in just one shot, the animal fell dead, like that time when I killed the woodpecker with the first shot I ever fired in my life. I was in anguish when I approached the buffalo, as its cloudy eyes watched me with great sadness. I felt sorry for it as I did for the poor bird on the banks of the river in Guayabo.

I will take some paintings as gifts, but I won't say how many I've painted because they won't believe me, or the galleries where I've had exhibits. Nor will I tell them that I collect hats and have a room just for them. Hats make me somewhat nostalgic. Since I was a boy, I yearned for one that wasn't made of straw, a good one for important outings.

I'm an amateur photographer, close friends with my camera, but I won't take any of my photographs. If they see me on an elephant in Kenya, they'll think it's a trick, that it's not me, that it's the last thing I would ever do. I will take the camera, though. I'll take pictures and depending on how things go, I'll keep them. I can almost hear them saying I'm taking pictures willy-nilly, but the landscape from the summit of La Esperanza must be with me forever, it will never leave me. Also, as I was instructed, I will take three slow and deep breaths.

It'll be prudent not to speak about politics, to remain silent if any controversial or suggestive challenge is presented by anyone. Every Cuban is a potential leader, knows better than anybody else the right way to do things, but then gets his roles mixed up, acts as he pleases, and no god matters, even if the path is evil. Likewise, many are dying to come here, because their belt prongs are on the last hole, but no crying or fits will move me, I'm bringing no one back. Out of sight, out of mind. Others are like Cubano, Manuel's son, may they both rest in peace and may I remember to take some flowers to the cemetery, happy with the life they live.

Perhaps they're desperate on the inside, looking at my pocket and waiting for something.

It's a proven fact that Cubans are experts at everything, and if it relates to baseball, we're the best. I include myself. I will talk up a storm and debate one on one about the sport, about the indignation I feel for the shit from managers, players, and all of them together. I have my reasons for the whys and the wherefores. Daaamn! I get pissed off just thinking about it. Over there, from under any yucca plant, comes out a baseball player, and now it turns out, any little bird-witted team from any nameless island can beat our teams, and they have no other choice but to return with their tails between their legs. I know the arguments will be long, it's an important, beloved topic. Win or lose, the Pativerdes are still my team. Little is left to say about other sports. They've all gone by the wayside, although boxing comes up, not without great disagreements.

I'll make an effort to make the conversation as enjoyable as possible, it would be impolite to displease; besides, damned the bird that shits in its nest. It's not a new discovery that giving people free rein is healthy. Each person should be able to express himself as he pleases, no more, no less. I'll avoid hassles and awkward moments.

I'll have lots of fun, I know I will. Although it is written that I'm not one with great patience. If they screw around with me too much, I'll tell them to go fuck themselves no matter how much I love them, even if I later regret it.

It's urgent that I go as soon as possible, for a nightmare torments me and won't let me live. What to take? Who are the truly needy? Fuck! Giving them money is probably best, but in the airport, they confiscate everything, they eat you alive. I'll arrive loaded like the Moors that rode on mules as traveling salesmen around the fields. I barely remember the size and shape of each person, knowing that they want to squeeze large Havana into small Guanabacoa with little success. Those that come from over there and know the issue say that the women like sequined blouses, and for both men and women, tee-shirts and jeans should have plenty of embellishments. And I'll be the useless arbiter between them when the distribution gets going. I can already see Rafaelito looking up to the ceiling, desperate for those moments to end.

But no doubt about it! The "bundles" must go! Our evaluation relies on how many bundles we take. They don't realize how much more they can do with cash! Still it is well-known that carrying money into the airport is playing with fire; they'll seize it. I won't even take razor blades. And men long for lighters and Gillette blades! Neither will go. Nothing that can complicate my life. The women request Goya spices, mosquito netting, and some house coats to have on hand in case of an emergency. I won't forget the fishing hooks and line for Tomás, who tells me that if it wasn't for how wildly the catfish behave, you could catch them with your hands from any creek. If Uncle Florentino wasn't so deaf, I could take a little bell for him to ring and entertain his old age. For Aunt Iluminada, hidden in the double lining, I must take the medication they requested to keep her calm.

Based on the news I get, communications by telephone have improved greatly. Even in houses where there's nary a place to sit, a telephone exists, always waiting for that opportune call, even if just to say that chicken has arrived at the butcher shop in place of fish, or dietary meat for the ill. A long time ago, when Prieta went to find the "saving" stone at La Esperanza, she told me of her trouble finding it. The marabú had swallowed up all the useful vegetation. My soul turned gray.

Nostalgia for those no longer there is the hardest to take. It pounds on my bones, it pushes me in that direction, then it pulls me until my heart is a dry fig. The longing for those who had the sad need to abandon this world brings me sorrow. I've decided not to ask as they, the living, will tell me who's absent and will give me the reasons for their absence.

Did the royal ipecac survive, the one Mamma used to water because the resin from its little flowers could heal our eyes? And the hummingbirds! The couple that was there every day eating together, making their nest in the garden. Will I find the yellow lily and the aromatic gardenias that She always preferred? I wasn't as concerned about flowers and little birds as I was about

Them, my departed family and where they are. The young ones, always willing to go with me, will know nothing. It could get serious, but I've come out of worse situations. Perhaps I'll find them where they liked to go or where they stayed the longest out of necessity. I'm sure of their presence, I can almost see them, and to describe them as the humblest of beings is not enough. I'll speak to each one, or I will stay silent. I don't know. I'll meditate on their sweat, the sweat they left in La Esperanza and its surroundings, sweat that won't escape but will expand and strengthen the land.

I won't list the places I'll visit one by one, I may change my mind on one or another, but I will go to the ceiba where the slaves had their rituals. For one reason or another, all of us would bring them at least one rusty cent. I will make offerings to the ceiba, I will go to the American church too. It may sound strange, but there I learned to dream.

Once I've worked through all my emotions, I will make a jump to Havana. I'll go alone, and I'll see it on foot. I want to smell it, its moist fragrance so different from all the cities in the world. Havana attracts with the force of a magnet. Those who visit her for the first time won't be able to break free of its charm. I won't rent a car. I'll travel in a shared classic "almendrón," squeezed until I can't breathe, but I want no worries. I'll visit my godfather and throw a little dirt on his grave. In truth, when things got ugly, it was he who lit my path and gradually, I came to the surface. Certainly, when he

308

speaks to me, he nails it. If I go where he warns me not to, I get slammed. I know what to expect.

I'll make a trip to Santiago de Cuba to visit the sanctuary of Virgen del Cobre, the one Juan Odio, Juan Indio, and Juan Esclavo saw appear over the waves. I'll go with Rafaelito; he's a good driver, and he'll get to know the island from end to end. Some relatives and friends will come along for a nice jaunt. I will also go to El Rincón to see San Lázaro, the old man with the crutches and the dogs. I can do that any day, early in the morning, before the sun lights up the road.

Memories come mostly at night. I think a lot about the trip, the arrival, La Esperanza.

I'm finally at the Miami airport! I must ask no questions, all the "gusano" duffels are big and black, their real contents always overweight by about fifteen kilograms. How can anyone recognize their own amid so much blackness? Passenger planes don't move such an overabundance of luggage to any other destination. The line is long, and I have to drag the packages to the check, counter-check, and weighing zone.

Rafaelito was "so excited" about the trip that he forgot the documents. I have no choice. As they say in Cuba, you must resist. He sleeps like a neutered dog even if he's traveling to China the next day, and then, it is what it is. I can't. I have to take care of the fucking task of keeping my heart from coming out of my mouth while I

309

wait for him to show up with all his blessed patience. When my nerves are shot, he'll show up with some excuse.

The PA system repeats ad nauseam the maximum amount of money allowed when traveling Over There due to embargo problems. A pittance, almost nothing. I'll bet this all goes to hell!

Look at the time and this kid isn't here! Dante comes to interrupt, to ingratiate himself, rubbing in the trouble he went through on his way to his Inferno. He did have obstacles, but it wasn't that bad, he had Virgil for a guide, but I, wretched sinner, I've had to do everything on my own, because that's the way it had to be. That's why I'm going to where I belong. This trip is not a whim, it's my duty. My people call out to me.

I can almost see my son always in the background, surely recoiling because he doesn't understand what's happening. Damn, I shouldn't have glanced at my face when I went to the bathroom! Who told me to lift my head while I was washing my hands? The problem was not the mirror. No question, my face is the problem. Who the fuck is going to recognize me the way I look now? I don't look at all like I did. I hadn't thought about that. I'm not as I was when I left.

I have to push these bags even if with my feet. It's almost my turn to present documents and I need to pee again urgently. I'm in a cold sweat, I have a splitting headache. Fuck, I knew it, this kid is a fucking problem! They're starting to call us, and I'm stuck here by myself.

Thousands live like Carmelina and don't even remember being born Over There, or they pretend well. And here I am, damn obsessed with not betraying my memories. I don't know how to live without them.

It can't be true that the marabú destroyed everything. I see the fields of corn, tobacco, yucca, the orchards ready for the harvest, and the grass knitting an extensive green carpet to the edges of the dirt paths. The tree groves are pregnant with fruit clusters, and the palms, the royal palms welcome me with the waving of their fronds. The children will climb on horses to follow me as I round the curve where the creek lets loose on the pasture. That's probably where I lost the two pesetas. The excited animals will fight to free themselves from the ropes so they can run when I whistle. I'm convinced that they will recognize me by my whistle, they will rejoice in my arrival.

It's not the season for lilies to bloom, but the one with the yellow flower, the one forever on the cows' plain, will be waiting for me with open petals.

And the house, at night filled with people and their fears and fantasies, waiting for the colada because they want to drink that little shot of hot coffee, and because they know that La Esperanza is enveloped in quiet mystery. It will be a celebration, joy from the moment I arrive.

"Buddy, fuck! You're too much! I was desperate. I can't handle all this. And if you hadn't come, son, I wouldn't go. I'm not going without you. You may not understand, but I need the color of your eyes to paint the guayaba singing, the smell of the mockingbird, and the neighing of the wind on the summit of La Esperanza."

Pastor Castillo
Miami 2020

Author

Pastor Castillo Díaz (Pinar del Río, Cuba 1945) - He studied up to the fourth grade of Primary Education. He needs to work and is dedicated to growing tobacco in Pinar del Rio. From a young age he joined the guerrilla movement in the hills of Pinar del Río, serving as a messenger in the Rebel Army led by Fidel Castro. As a teenager, he reached the 6th grade and continued his studies until he graduated as a doctor from the University of Havana. He practices his profession in Cuba and in the Seychelles. He comes to the United States as a political prisoner. He resides in the United States.

See Pastor Castillos's work in pastorcastilloart.com.

www.ingramcontent.com/pod-product-compliance
Lightning Source LLC
Chambersburg PA
CBHW071108250626
47159CB00002B/650